A Dangerous Hand

"Are you going to Janet McGreevey's house to play on Wednesday?" I asked.

"I should have known," Marylou said, rolling her eyes. "Janet doesn't waste any time." She nodded. "Yes, I'll be there."

"Good," I said. "With both you and Sophie there, I won't be so nervous about going."

"I'm sure you'll enjoy it," Marylou said, "no matter what Janet does."

"What do you mean?"

Marylou waved a hand nonchalantly. "Oh, it's just that Janet is a very competitive player, and she can be a bit rude to her partners if she thinks they're not playing as well as they should."

I groaned. "Then I hope I don't have to play with her. I'm liable to bash her over the head if she gets nasty with me."

Marylou threw back her head and laughed. "I wish you would, Emma. It would save one of the rest of us from putting poison in her coffee."

She laughed even more heartily at that, and I couldn't help but join in, though I felt more than a little uneasy. I wasn't sure I would enjoy this bridge party, after all. . . .

ON THE SLAM

♠ ♥ ♦ ♣

A BRIDGE CLUB MYSTERY

Honor Hartman

A SIGNET BOOK

SIGNET
Published by New American Library, a division of
Penguin Group (USA) Inc., 375 Hudson Street,
New York, New York 10014, USA
Penguin Group (Canada), 90 Eglinton Avenue East, Suite 700, Toronto,
Ontario M4P 2Y3, Canada (a division of Pearson Penguin Canada Inc.)
Penguin Books Ltd., 80 Strand, London WC2R 0RL, England
Penguin Ireland, 25 St. Stephen's Green, Dublin 2,
Ireland (a division of Penguin Books Ltd.)
Penguin Group (Australia), 250 Camberwell Road, Camberwell, Victoria 3124,
Australia (a division of Pearson Australia Group Pty. Ltd.)
Penguin Books India Pvt. Ltd., 11 Community Centre, Panchsheel Park,
New Delhi - 110 017, India
Penguin Group (NZ), 67 Apollo Drive, Mairangi Bay,
Auckland 1311, New Zealand (a division of Pearson New Zealand Ltd.)
Penguin Books (South Africa) (Pty.) Ltd., 24 Sturdee Avenue,
Rosebank, Johannesburg 2196, South Africa

Penguin Books Ltd., Registered Offices:
80 Strand, London WC2R 0RL, England

First published by Signet, an imprint of New American Library,
a division of Penguin Group (USA) Inc.

First Printing, May 2007
10 9 8 7 6 5 4 3 2 1

For my regular bridge partners, Sandra Wallesch, Angela Miller, and Edith Brown, for many fun hours spent at the bridge table.

Acknowledgments

Thanks, as always, to my agent Nancy Yost, for everything she does. Martha Bushko expressed interest in the series and offered advice and very helpful criticism before acquiring it, and Kerry Donovan has very gracefully and graciously taken over the reins, and I appreciate her interest and enthusiasm very much indeed. Julie Wray Herman and Patricia Orr continue to offer support and constructive criticism, without which the writing process would be much more difficult. And finally, Tejas Englesmith continues to offer the support that only he can give. My heartfelt thanks to them all!

Chapter 1

I stared down at what remained of the corpse. Then I looked at Hilda.

Hilda yawned.

"I wish you'd stop doing this," I said severely, but Hilda gazed blandly back at me. "I'm tired of cleaning up after you."

"That's what you get for having them in the house," Sophie Parker said from behind me. "They're insensitive most of the time. Just plain brutal, if you ask me."

"I've certainly had enough evidence of that where Hilda is concerned." I sighed heavily as I reached for a couple of paper towels.

Bending down, I scooped up the still-twitching remains of the large cockroach, scrunched them up inside the paper towels, then strode over to drop it all into the garbage can.

Hilda, disgusted by yet another instance of my lack of appreciation of her feline prowess, stalked away, her tail standing up with a little curl at the tip.

"See?" Sophie said. "See what a little diva she is? Mariah Carey only wishes *she* could strut like that." She let out a peal of laughter, at which Hilda paused in midstalk. She turned her head in Sophie's direction, and I would almost swear she curled her lip. Then, head forward again, she disappeared down the hall.

Sophie laughed all the harder after that. "I've been snubbed by a cat."

I felt a deep pang of loss at the sound of her merriment. Baxter always found Sophie immensely entertaining, though I wasn't sure he would have wanted to live next door to her, as I did now. But thoughts of Baxter threatened to bring the tears back. I had had enough of crying the past few months.

Olaf, Hilda's brother, blinked at me from his vantage point in one of the chairs next to the kitchen table. Olaf occasionally chased bugs, but he preferred to eat them himself rather than offer them to me. I wished he'd do neither, but at least he cleaned up the evidence himself.

I washed my hands at the sink, even though I hadn't actually touched the bug. I hated the darned things, but thanks to the lovely tropical climate of Houston, Texas, they never went away.

"More coffee?" I brandished the pot in Sophie's direction, and she grimaced.

"I really shouldn't, because the caffeine will wind me up like you wouldn't believe, but why the heck not?" she said.

I filled her cup, and she added several spoons of sugar and a dollop of cream. How she managed that and still kept her trim figure, I didn't know. She claimed she had a treadmill she used, but I had never seen it.

I refilled my own cup, set the coffeepot back in its place on the counter, then resumed my seat at the table across from my best friend.

"Pets can be a comfort," Sophie said after a sip of her coffee. "At least, if they're dogs. Dogs love you and lavish you with affection. Cats treat you like servants."

Sophie had two dogs, Boston terriers named Martha and Mavis, and they were adorable, I had to admit. Hilda and Olaf hadn't been all that impressed with them, though, which is why Sophie had left them at home this morning. The dogs were too lively and inquisitive for my cats, who much preferred quiet indolence most of the time.

"Your dogs are as cute as they can be, and so affectionate," I said, "just like their mommy."

Sophie rewarded me for my sarcasm with a glance that might strike an ordinary human dead. But I've known her since she was a baby, and I've built up a considerable amount of immunity over the years.

"How are you settling in?" Sophie asked. "Anything you need me to do?"

I almost laughed. By "me," Sophie meant her long-suffering housekeeper, Esperanza, and some of Esperanza's many family members. Sophie never lifted a finger unnecessarily, particularly when she could pay someone else to do it.

"Oh, I'm doing just fine," I said, waving a hand vaguely. "Still a few boxes to unpack, that sort of thing, but nothing terribly urgent. Thank you, though."

I had been in the new house for only a week, and Sophie had kept a close eye on me. She was, after all, the one who had talked me into buying the house next door to hers when it came on the market, and I knew, in her way, she was trying to look out for me. Though we occasionally drove each other completely nuts, we were like sisters, and I figured the advantages of being right next door to my best friend probably outweighed any of the disadvantages.

"You needed a change," Sophie said bluntly. "I couldn't stand the sight of you another minute, moping around that huge house, wearing nothing but those disgusting clothes." She glared pointedly at my warm-up pants and T-shirt. "You've got to get on with your life. And the first chance I get, I'm going through your closet, and I'm going to burn those things."

I wished Sophie wouldn't keep harping on the subject. I had a hard enough time on my own, trying not to think about it. Yesterday marked six months since my husband, Baxter Diamond, had been killed in an accident on the Gulf Freeway. I still woke at odd moments during the night, thinking I could feel him lying beside me in bed.

Sophie's glance softened as she read my thoughts in my face. "It takes time, Emma. Just give it time."

I smiled. Sophie had always been able to read me, certainly more easily than I could read her. She understood what I was going through. For eight years, Baxter had given me a stability and a confidence that I desperately needed. Now that was gone, and I had to start over.

"It's a quiet neighborhood," she said, "and the other neighbors will be dropping by to meet you."

"I've met a few of them already," I said. "One of them wanted to assure me that he could help me with any insurance needs I might have. He was pretty slick about it, too. First he asked me if I needed any help unloading the car, and when he was helping me carry in a heavy box, he just happened to mention he sold insurance."

Sophie laughed. "I should have known," she said. "Bert Sylvester never wastes a minute trying to sell somebody insurance. That man is always on the make." She paused. "If he bothers you, let me know. I know how to make him back off."

And no doubt she did. People rarely made the mistake of annoying Sophie more than once.

"He seemed pleasant enough," I said, "and when I told him I was very happy with my current agent, he took it well."

"Don't let that fool you," Sophie said. "He won't give up that easily. At some point you'll get another pitch." She snorted. "A lot of people just give in. But you don't have to. I certainly didn't."

"I can be pretty stubborn when I need to be," I reminded her. I'd had to be, growing up with parents who cared more for their wardrobes and the state of their liquor cabinet than they had for either of their children.

Sophie didn't respond to that. Instead, she said, "So, who else have you met?"

I laughed. "The only other person was some harpy who came marching up to me two days ago while I was taking Olaf and Hilda out of the car—in their portable kennels, mind you— and started lecturing me about letting animals run loose in the neighborhood." I shook my head. "And if that wasn't enough, she tried to hand me a bunch of papers. Bylaws of the homeowners' association, she said, and some sort of application form. Then, before I could think of anything to say to her, she told me that I couldn't have my porch swing out at the front of the house."

Sophie rolled her eyes. "I should have known she would strike right away." She took a sip of coffee. "I should have been here with you that morning, but I had that meeting with John's lawyers." John was her soon-to-be ex-husband (number two). "I couldn't put it off any longer."

From the grim set of her lips, I knew she didn't want to discuss it at the moment. She would tell me all about it when she was ready, and not before.

"I was about to put Olaf and Hilda back in the car and head for San Antonio, after that woman got through preaching at me," I said. "Who died and made her queen?"

Sophie's face darkened. "Janet McGreevey is a gigantic pain in the posterior most of the time. Unfortunately she's also impossible to ignore. She's quite a power in the neighborhood, ever since she got herself elected president of the homeowners' association six years ago. Knows everybody's business better than they do. Or at least she thinks she does."

"If any other neighbors were watching, they certainly got an eyeful and an earful," I said. "I have a slow fuse, but when I get angry, I get really angry.

I'm afraid I told Mrs. McGreevey what I thought about her lack of manners, and she didn't seem to like my talking back to her."

"Most people just try to steer clear of her," Sophie said, "though it's not that easy to avoid her. Plus she's got the board of the homeowners' association in her back pocket. Nobody wants to cross them."

I grinned. "And here you were, telling me this is such a nice neighborhood I've moved into. You're supposed to be my best friend."

For a moment she looked guilty, and then she giggled like a teenager. "Touché. It really *is* a nice neighborhood, Emma, but we do have a few crosses to bear. Fortunately you've met the two worst ones. Your other neighbors are mostly a very nice bunch."

"If not, then I'm going to hold you personally responsible for this," I said, mock-severely. "After all, making me buy this house was your *scathingly brilliant* idea."

Sophie laughed at my use of the catchphrase from our favorite Hayley Mills movie. Whenever one of us was in need of comfort, we got together and watched *The Trouble with Angels* and *The Parent Trap* over and over all night. Consumption of massive amounts of ice cream and chocolate was another key ingredient to our tradition.

Olaf leaped onto the table and walked over to rub his head against my hand. "Olaf! You know you're not supposed to be on the table." The cat paid no attention to my scolding. He purred as he rubbed on me. I picked him up off the table and settled him into my lap. He made himself comfortable, and I glanced over at Sophie.

"He's a lover, at least," Sophie said, rolling her eyes. "Unlike that little witch, Hilda."

"Oh yes," I said, stroking Olaf's long silver-gray hair. He really was a pretty kitty. "I probably should change his name to Velcro. He wants to be in my lap like a dog, most of the time." I rubbed Olaf's head, and his purring grew louder.

Then the doorbell rang.

Olaf dug his claws into my legs. The old jogging pants I was wearing weren't much protection against talons. I uttered an obscenity, and Olaf jumped down from my lap to hide as I stood up. Both the cats hated the doorbell.

Sophie smiled, as if to say I got what I deserved for having cats. I ignored that. "You're going to hang around, aren't you?"

"I'm all yours, darling," Sophie drawled. "Esperanza is doing her cleaning-frenzy thing, and I'm much more comfortable here."

I grinned at her. Sophie's presence was reassuring, and as long as she was around, I wouldn't be inclined to mope, as she called it.

I strode down the hall toward the front door as the doorbell rang again.

"Hold on, I'm coming," I muttered. I put an eye to the peephole. Then I groaned.

What on earth was the blasted McGreevey woman doing at my front door?

Maybe I could just pretend I wasn't at home, and she'd go away. Then I remembered my car was parked in the driveway, not the garage, so she would know I was home. She probably would have looked in the garage anyway.

As I dithered, the doorbell rang again. She held her finger on the bell, and the buzzing sound irritated the heck out of me. I could just imagine how happy Olaf and Hilda were about now.

I snatched open the door. "Would you please not ring the doorbell that way? It frightens my cats."

Janet McGreevey drew back as if I'd thrown hot water on her. "Well, really, Mrs. Diamond. No need to take that tone with me, I'm sure."

Get a grip, Emma! Don't antagonize the woman any

more than you have to, I fussed at myself. Sighing, I said, "I'm sorry, Mrs. McGreevey, I shouldn't have spoken so sharply."

She sniffed, her face pinched up into a disapproving glare. "Perhaps you are rather tired from all the work of moving into a new house, Mrs. Diamond. That I can understand."

"Yes, exactly," I said, smiling in what I hoped was a conciliatory fashion. "Was there something you wanted?"

She thrust a decorative tin into my hands. "I felt we got off on the wrong foot the other day," she said, not meeting my eyes, "and I thought you might like a batch of my special brownies."

Taken aback, I stared at her, the tin almost slipping from my hands. "Thank you," I finally managed to say. I was about to invite her in, though I didn't really want her in the house, when she stepped past me into the hall.

"I see you've had some painting done," she said, her head popping back and forth as she tried to take in everything she could. "Much better than the previous owners managed to do."

"Thank you," I said. "I'm afraid I found the colors they used a bit too harsh. I prefer lighter, warmer tones myself."

She walked down the hall toward the kitchen. "I do hope you manage to do something with the kitchen. The Latimers made rather a mess of it."

I trailed along behind her. "Sophie Parker is here. Why don't you have a cup of coffee with us, now that you're here?"

If she detected any irony in my invitation, she didn't acknowledge it. "Thank you, that sounds nice." She strode into the kitchen. "Sophie. I was coming to see you this afternoon. This saves me a trip."

"Hello, Janet, how are you?" Sophie did nothing to hide the expression of boredom on her face.

"I'm doing quite well, thank you, Sophie," Janet

said, plopping herself down in the chair I had recently vacated. She shoved my coffee cup out of the way and placed her hands, palms down, on the table. "Now, we've got to do something about Mrs. Anderson over on Elm Lake Crescent. She's eight months—no, now it's nine—months behind on her association dues, and she can't keep putting us off, Sophie. Someone's going to have to talk to her, and you seem to be the only one she'll listen to." Her nostrils flared. "She tried to get her dog to attack me."

I hoped the dog hadn't bitten her. The poor thing might have died from it.

Stop it, Emma, I told myself.

I had set a coffee cup down in front of Janet McGreevey, and she picked it up and sipped from it without ever acknowledging my presence. She stared fixedly at Sophie.

"Janet, I don't know that talking to her will do any good," Sophie said, ignoring the comment about the dog. She picked up her coffee cup and stared into it, as if seeking answers there. "I don't think she has the money. Why don't you just go ahead and have her evicted? That's what you want to do anyway."

"It doesn't have to come to that," Janet McGreevey snapped. "If the woman can't afford to live here and keep her house up properly, then she needs to sell the house and go live with one of her children. We want to maintain our standards in this neighborhood, along with our property values."

My eyes widened at the tone of triumphant malice in Janet McGreevey's voice. What kind of shark-infested waters had I jumped into?

"Then why don't you just call her daughter and dump the problem in her lap?" Sophie stared straight at Janet McGreevey. "Stop all this passive-aggressive bullshit, and just do it."

I sat down in the chair nearest Sophie and glanced back and forth between the two women. Janet McGreevey appeared dumbstruck at Sophie's last comment.

"How about some brownies?" I said, opening the tin and shoving it into the center of the table.

"Oh, no, thank you," Janet McGreevey said, diverted. "I never eat them myself. Too many calories, and I have to watch what I eat. Can't let myself go, you know. Other people don't have to worry about it like I do." She was looking straight at me when she said it.

Now I was dumbstruck. The woman was colossally rude, no doubt about it. I struggled for a suitable rejoinder.

Sophie took a brownie from the tin. She bit off half of it. "A little on the dry side, Janet," she said, after chewing for a moment. "I think you left this batch in the oven a little too long." She got up from her chair and pointedly dropped the rest of the brownie into the garbage can under the sink.

I struggled not to laugh. The expression on Janet McGreevey's face was priceless. Sophie gazed blandly back at her as she resumed her seat.

Her face slightly flushed, Mrs. McGreevey turned to me.

"Do you play bridge, Mrs. Diamond?" She smiled. "Surely, with a name like that, you must."

"I do," I said, before I thought about it. "But I'm not very good," I added hastily. "I just started playing about four months ago, not long after my husband died."

Which was the truth. I had never really wanted to learn to play bridge. It was a game my parents played, and anything my parents did, I wanted no part of. But after Baxter died, my brother Jake tried to get me interested in different things. I had drawn the line at rollerblading and rock-climbing, and bridge seemed like the safest alternative. Jake and his partner, Luke, were bridge fanatics, and they kept inviting me to their place to play. Giving in to the younger brother I adored was easier than continually saying no.

Janet McGreevey laughed, not a particularly pleasant sound. "I'm sure you're much better than you're willing to let on, Mrs. Diamond. But it doesn't matter. We can use all the bridge players we can get." She leered at me. "Though some of the wives in the neighborhood might not like having such an attractive young widow sniffing around their husbands."

The woman was crass beyond belief, and I had to hold hard to my temper to keep from telling her how tasteless her remark was. Something of my feelings must have registered on my face, however, because Janet McGreevey drew back slightly.

"We have a very active bridge group in the neighborhood, Emma," Sophie explained. "What Janet's trying to tell you is that we're always looking for players, since a few of the husbands travel frequently on business. We almost always need someone to round out a table."

"I see," I said, my heart sinking. I had found, greatly to my surprise, that I really enjoyed bridge. I wanted to play more often and develop my skills, but I wasn't sure that playing with the likes of Janet McGreevey would be all that much fun. "Well, as I said, I'm not very good, but I'd be willing to play occasionally."

"Then it's settled." Janet McGreevey slapped a hand on the table as she stood up. "We're playing at my house on Wednesday night. Seven o'clock. No need to bring anything, unless you like wine or something like that. No dinner, just some healthy snacks while we play."

I racked my brain, trying to think of some excuse, but I doubted anything less than a scheduled kidney transplant would do any good.

"I'll be there, too, Emma," Sophie said reassuringly. "We have a good time on these bridge nights. You'll enjoy yourself, and don't worry about how well you play. It's all just for fun. No one takes it too seriously."

I shot her a look of gratitude. "Okay, then. I could certainly use the practice."

"See you on Wednesday," Janet McGreevey said. "I'll see myself out, Mrs. Diamond."

I nodded, but she had already turned and headed out the door and down the hall. Moments later, the front door opened and closed. I swear the house itself breathed a sigh of relief with that poisonous woman gone.

I turned to look at Sophie. "Why hasn't someone murdered that woman by now?"

Chapter 2

Hardly were the words out of my mouth when the doorbell rang. I grimaced at Sophie. "Do you suppose she heard me?" Reluctantly I got up from the table.

"I wouldn't put it past her to have bugged your house before you moved in," Sophie said. "She's incredibly nosy, besides being the world's biggest buttinsky."

For a moment I thought she was serious about the bugging. She caught my expression and said, *"Kidding."*

"Don't go anywhere, just in case," I said as she cast longing looks at the back door.

She glowered. "Okay."

The doorbell rang again before I reached the front door. At least this time she wasn't leaning on it. I was prepared for the worst as I peered through the peephole, but fortunately for my blood pressure, it wasn't Janet McGreevey at the door again. The plump, older woman on the stoop did look familiar, though.

I swung open the door. "Good morning."

Now that I had a better look at her, I recognized her as my next-door neighbor on the other side. Sophie hadn't told me much about her, but I dimly seemed to remember that she was a widow, like me. She was several inches shorter than my own five seven, and her gray hair was neatly coiffed. She had a pleasant face and sparkling blue eyes. Her slacks and blouse were deceptively simple, but, thanks to years of tutelage from Sophie, I recognized that they were expensive.

"Good morning," she said, her hands nervously clutching a cookie tin. "I'm your neighbor right next door, Marylou Lockridge. I hope this is a good time, but I just wanted to stop by for a moment and give you an official welcome to the neighborhood."

"How kind of you," I said, stepping back and waving a hand. "Do come in."

She took a step forward, then hesitated. "If you're sure you don't mind."

I laughed. "No, this is my morning for meeting the neighbors, I think."

Unexpectedly, her face split into a broad grin. "I know. I was watching out my window. I waited until I was sure Her Miserable Highness was gone before I came over."

"Mrs. Lockridge," I said, trying not to laugh again, "I do think we're going to be good friends. Now come on in, and let's have a look inside that tin of yours. Suddenly, I'm very hungry."

Smiling, she followed me back to the kitchen where Sophie stood at the back door, her hand on the knob.

"Sophie," I said, "you get right back here and sit down. The coast is clear."

She rolled her eyes at me, but she came back to the table. "Good morning, Marylou. How are you?"

"I'm fine, Sophie," Mrs. Lockridge said. I pulled out a chair for her. "Thank you, Mrs. Diamond." She sat down.

"Please, call me Emma," I said.

"And I'm Marylou." She crossed her plump hands over the tin, which she had set on the table in front of her. A large diamond ring sparkled on her left hand, and on her right she wore a large emerald.

"Would you like some coffee, Marylou? I think

there's enough for a cup, or I could make some more."

"One cup will be fine, thank you, Emma," Marylou said. "And milk or cream, if you have it, and three sugars."

"Certainly," I said. "Coming right up."

"You barely missed the Wicked Witch, Marylou," Sophie said. "She's already been over here this morning, trying to stir up trouble."

"Oh dear, what is it this time? Thank you, Emma," she said to me as she accepted the mug of coffee.

I sat down at the table and picked up my own cup. The liquid inside was stone cold now, but I didn't feel like getting up to microwave it.

"Oh, she was going on about poor old Mrs. Anderson," Sophie said, "talking about how she was behind in her association dues, and how the board was going to have to take action."

Marylou glared at Sophie for a moment. "Mrs. Anderson isn't that old, Sophie. She's only about five years older than I am."

Sophie bared her teeth in a grin. Her father had spent a lot of money for that beautiful orthodontia when she was a teenager. "I never think of *you* as old. Not like that poor old thing. You're just one of the girls."

Sophie was teasing, but I knew her well enough to understand the affection behind it. Marylou wasn't so certain. She stared at Sophie for a moment, but Sophie was at her most seraphic.

"Thank you, dear," Marylou said before turning to me. "I just turned sixty-five a few weeks ago."

I was surprised, and I told her so. "You surely don't look it. I would have said you were in your early fifties, at the most."

She threw back her head and laughed at that. "You are now my new best friend, Emma."

"Seriously," I said, "you look great."

"I pamper myself," Marylou said. "Now that I'm on my own again, I spoil myself."

"It works," Sophie said. "I'm certainly going to follow your example. Now that John is gone, more or less, there's only me." She made a stab at looking wistful, but I wasn't buying it. She was as happy to be rid of John as he was of her.

"Don't fret, dear," Marylou said. "You're such a beautiful girl. When you're ready, you'll find the right man. Don't let one bad apple spoil it for you."

I started to laugh, then quickly converted it into a cough. Sophie's judgment where men were concerned was—well, the kindest thing I could say was "deficient."

Sophie ignored me.

"Back to the matter at hand," she said. "I think someone needs to talk to Mrs. Anderson before the barracuda gets on to her again. You've known her longer than I have, Marylou. Can't you talk to her?"

"I can talk to her," Marylou said, frowning. "But she just doesn't have the money. She really can't afford to stay in that house without financial help from her children, but she's too proud to tell them. They think their father left her a lot better off than he really did."

"Could someone talk to one of her children?" I asked. "I don't know her, of course, but that seems like the sensible thing to do."

"She's very proud," Marylou said, sighing. "And I can understand that. It's a hard thing for a parent to ask for help from a child."

Sophie and I exchanged glances. Neither her parents nor mine would ever have asked one of their children for help. That would have meant actually talking to one of them.

"If it's a choice between talking to one of her children," I said, "and letting the Janet McGreeveys of the world harass her, well . . ."

"I see your point," Marylou said, sighing again. "I

suppose I'd better try to talk to her daughter." She looked down at the table and noticed the tin she had brought.

"Oh my goodness," she said, blushing slightly. "Where are my manners? Here I brought you something, and I didn't even have the grace to give it to you."

"We've been sidetracked," I said, smiling at her. I accepted the tin from her and opened it carefully. After the disaster of Janet McGreevey's brownies, I was prepared for the worst.

The aroma was heavenly. Fresh oatmeal raisin cookies. "My favorite!" I took a cookie out, then proffered the tin to Sophie. She didn't hesitate.

"Marylou makes the best cookies in the world," Sophie said happily. "This will be worth the extra minutes on the treadmill." She took a hearty bite of her cookie.

I was too busy savoring mine to pay much attention to her, though I almost laughed at her reference to that semimythical treadmill. The cookie was absolute bliss on the tongue, and I chewed slowly to make it last, forgetting everything else for the moment.

"Oh, that was wonderful," I said, turning to Marylou. "Thank you. You can make cookies for me anytime." Then I grinned ruefully. "But I'd have to rent time on Sophie's legendary treadmill, I'm afraid." I cut a sideways glance at Sophie, but she gazed blandly back at me.

Marylou laughed. "I'm glad you like them, Emma. I love to bake, but I can't bake just for myself. Heaven knows I don't need any extra temptation in the house." She looked down ruefully at her plump body.

"Maybe," I said, taking another cookie, "but I tell you, this is comfort food at its best. Aren't you going to have one?" I pushed the tin toward Marylou.

She stared down at it, her lower lip caught in her teeth. "Well, maybe just one." She laughed and took a cookie.

I offered the tin to Sophie again, but she shook her head. She stood up. "Ladies, I hate to, but I really have to get going. I'm going shopping." She smiled suddenly. "I saw this totally amazing dress at Etui, and I just have to have it."

Sophie had enough clothes to outfit half the women in a small country, but she bought clothes the way I tended to buy books. I had to admit that she wore them well. She'd had a flair for clothes since she was three, and by the time she was six, she was giving me advice. Considering I was fourteen at the time, it was pretty funny, but she was right, though it had pained me to admit it. Why she hadn't become a world-famous designer, I didn't know. Except that Sophie much preferred buying and wearing clothes to doing the actual work of designing them.

"Have fun," I said. "Give me a call later on, okay?"

Sophie nodded. "Bye, Emma. Bye, Marylou, and thanks for the delicious cookie."

As the kitchen door closed behind her, Marylou said to me, "That poor child."

"What do you mean?" I asked, a bit startled.

"That divorce," Marylou said. "What she must be going through."

"Yes," I said, "it has been a bit rough, but, frankly, she's well rid of him. He really is an awful jerk."

Marylou nodded. "I know. But how someone that angelic looking could be such a shit, I just don't understand."

I coughed to smother a laugh. Marylou had such a wholesome look to her, I was a bit amused to hear her utter a vulgarity. She smiled impishly at me.

"Sophie has never had much luck with men," I said. "And that's putting it mildly. She's very shrewd, most of the time, but when testosterone is involved, she's about as dumb as they come."

"You've known her a long time, haven't you, Emma?"

I nodded. "Since she was a baby. Her family lived next door to mine, and I used to babysit her from the time she was about four. I'm eight years older than she is, and we've always been very close. She's the little sister I never had."

"Then it's good that you're living next door to her," Marylou said. "It's good to have friends close by when you're going through a difficult time."

I glanced at her, and she nodded reassuringly. She reached out to pat my hand. "It's okay, Emma," she said softly. "Sophie told me about your loss."

Unexpectedly, I had a huge lump in my throat. At that moment Marylou was so warm and comforting, I wanted to lay my head on her shoulder and bawl. She nodded in sympathy, apparently reading my thoughts with ease.

My own mother would have sniffed and turned away, despising any sign of weakness. Emotion of any kind, with her, equated to weakness.

"I know all about that kind of loss," Marylou said, her voice becoming brisk and bracing. "I've lost three dear husbands, Emma, and if ever you need a shoulder to cry on, you just give me a call. You'll get through this, I promise you. You never forget them, not for one day of your life, but it does get easier, I promise you."

Sniffling, I patted her hand in return. I got up to retrieve a paper towel, and I wiped my eyes and blew my nose. Crumpling the paper towel, I clutched it in my hand as I sat down again. Just in case.

"Do you play bridge, Emma?" Marylou asked. The abrupt change of subject took me aback.

"Yes," I said, "though I haven't been playing for long. I'm not that good, but I do enjoy playing."

Marylou beamed. "Then we'll keep you busy, as long as you don't mind playing with a bunch of old hens like me."

I had to laugh at that. "Old hen" was the last thing I would have thought to call her.

"Are you going to Janet McGreevey's house to play on Wednesday?" I asked.

"I should have known," Marylou said, rolling her eyes. "Janet doesn't waste any time." She nodded. "Yes, I'll be there."

"Good," I said. "With both you and Sophie there, I won't be so nervous about going."

"I'm sure you'll enjoy it," Marylou said. "No matter what Janet does."

"What do you mean?"

Marylou waved a hand nonchalantly. "Oh, it's just that Janet is a very competitive player, and she can be a bit rude to her partners if she thinks they're not playing as well as they should."

I groaned. "Then I hope I don't have to play with her. I'm liable to bash her over the head if she gets nasty with me."

Marylou threw back her head and laughed. "I wish you would, Emma. It would save one of the rest of us from putting poison in her coffee."

She laughed even more heartily at that, and I couldn't help but join in, though I felt more than a little uneasy. I wasn't sure I would enjoy this bridge party, after all.

Chapter 3

By the time Wednesday evening rolled around, I had come up with seven different excuses for ducking out of Janet McGreevey's bridge party. I even practiced them, using Hilda and Olaf as my audience, but the cats weren't any more convinced by the excuses than I was. Short of claiming I was in an ambulance on the way to the hospital to have an emergency appendectomy, I doubted I could wriggle out of playing bridge. Sophie had been no help, either.

Finally, beyond exasperated with me, she said, "Oh, just suck it up, Emma. You are totally paranoid about this. As smart as you are, you're being ridiculous. I play bridge over there all the time. It's not going to be as bad as you think. Trust me."

That shut me up.

In between making up excuses and continuing to unpack boxes, I spent some time at the computer playing bridge. My brother Jake had given me the software not long after Baxter died, and I did enjoy playing bridge on the computer. The computer didn't criticize my mistakes, nor was it as competitive as my beloved younger brother.

I finally decided that if Janet McGreevey wanted a green player like me at her party, well, it was her lookout. Marylou had also told me to relax and not worry about a thing, but despite the best efforts of both my neighbors, I remained apprehensive.

Marylou repeated her assurances about ten minutes before seven on Wednesday evening when I opened the front door to admit her.

"I hope you're right, Marylou," I said.

"Nonsense," she said briskly as she stepped inside. "I'll be there, and so will Sophie. Then there's a young couple who'll probably be there, and they're still new at the game. Neither of them has played very long, and I'm sure you're a much better player than either of them, Emma."

I pointed at a large plastic container she was carrying. "What's that? Am I supposed to bring something?"

"Oh, this is just some of my spinach dip," Marylou said. "Janet loves it, so I always bring a batch when we play bridge." She sighed. "It seems silly, I suppose, but it's just one small thing I do to try to keep on Janet's good side."

"Sounds delicious," I said, forbearing to express my doubts that Janet McGreevey actually had a good side.

Sophie spoke from behind me, startling me. "We'd better go."

"Where did you come from?" I asked.

"You left the back door unlocked, and when I knocked and no one answered, I just came in," she said. "What else was I supposed to do?"

"Sorry," I muttered. I had left the back door unlocked for her; I had simply forgotten about it.

"Shall we go?" Sophie asked, giving me a gentle push toward the open front door.

"Yes," Marylou said, "Janet's a stickler for time, as you can imagine." She laughed.

"Did you lock the back door?" I asked Sophie. She nodded.

We went out the front door, and I checked to make sure it was locked. Hilda and Olaf would be annoyed with me for leaving them alone for several hours, but

I had left the television set in the living room on to keep them company. They really loved cartoons.

I followed Marylou and Sophie down the driveway to the sidewalk and across the street. Janet McGreevey lived two houses down. As we approached, a car pulled up and parked along the curb in front of the McGreevey house.

"Evening, Paul, Shannon," Marylou called. The young couple who had emerged from the car looked in our direction and waved.

"Good evening, Marylou, Sophie," the young woman said. "How are y'all doing?" She had short blond hair, a pert nose, and friendly blue eyes. About ten years younger than her husband, I figured, who looked about my age, fortyish. He had a craggy face, sunburned and attractive, and close-cropped black hair.

"Let me introduce our new neighbor," Marylou said as we drew closer to them. "Emma Diamond, this is Shannon Hardy and her husband, Paul. Shannon, Paul, this is Emma Diamond. She's just moved in to the house between Sophie and me, where the Latimers used to live."

We exchanged pleasantries, shaking hands, and so on, and then we all followed Marylou up the walk. Shannon went ahead with Marylou and Sophie, and Paul took the opportunity to quiz me about what I did.

I explained that I was a high school history teacher, but I was currently taking a leave of absence, and that seemed to satisfy him for the moment. He was more interested in telling me what he did. He provided financial counseling and investment services and made sure I tucked one of his cards in a pocket of my skirt. I thanked him, and by that time, we were at the front door. Janet McGreevey waved us in, ignoring Shannon, cooing over Sophie and admiring her dress, then cooing even more over Paul, telling him how handsome he looked. Her greeting to me was polite, but cool. I was equally polite in return, thanking her for inviting me to join the party tonight.

"And you didn't let me down, Marylou," Janet McGreevey said, turning away from me and reaching out to pull the plastic container from Marylou's hands. "Our bridge games just wouldn't be the same without some of your wonderful spinach dip."

Janet led the way into her living room. I glanced about, trying to get a sense of the place. I wasn't surprised to see that the room was ultramodern, cool and antiseptic. White walls, chrome and black leather furniture, sharp lines, only a few knickknacks and photographs in a large room. Pretty much what I had expected, given my experience of Janet McGreevey so far. The room felt chilly and not particularly welcoming.

Sophie stepped closer to me and whispered, almost loud enough for Janet to hear, "Doesn't it make you want to spill something somewhere? Anything, for a bit of color."

I cast a sideways glance at her. Tonight she was wearing enough vivid color to counterbalance even this sterile room. I was getting dizzy just looking at her. The dress she wore could have been designed by Jackson Pollock—on speed, that is. I turned my eyes away from her, and the white almost seemed restful.

"I wouldn't put it past you to do that," I hissed back at her. "Behave."

"Yes, ma'am," she said, daring me to laugh at the penitent expression she had put on. I rolled my eyes at her and advanced farther into the room.

At the other end of the large space, three tables were set up for bridge, and there were five people seated on two couches in the space between the tables and where we stood. Janet marched over and set the spinach dip down on the long bar counter that separated this area from the kitchen. On the counter were more food, plates, and napkins, and an array of soft drink and liquor bottles.

"Everyone, let me introduce our new neighbor, Emma Diamond," Janet said. "We're so delighted Emma could join us tonight. Aren't we lucky to have another bridge player move in next door to Marylou and Sophie?"

Without waiting for a response, she continued her introductions. "Emma, this handsome scamp is my husband, Gerald. Try to remember that he's a happily married man." Rolling his eyes slightly, a portly, white-headed man of about sixty stood up from the left-hand couch and stepped forward to proffer his hand.

"Glad to meet you," he said, his voice gruff. "Welcome to the neighborhood."

"Thanks," I said. He was holding my hand a shade too long, and I smiled as I firmly withdrew it from his grasp. He was attractive, in a conventional sort of way, but not nearly as attractive as he thought he was.

"This is Amanda Graham," Janet said, "and her husband, Eric." A couple in their fifties smiled and nodded in my direction from their perch on the couch Gerald McGreevey had shared. They looked very much alike. Same hair color—gray— and same basic shape—pudgy. They were even wearing matching outfits. I tried not to shudder as I nodded and smiled back at them.

Janet waved next at the two persons on the right-hand couch. "And this is Bootsie Flannigan and her friend Dan Connor." Was it my imagination, or had Janet's voice taken on the slightest touch of frost? Particularly on the word "friend."

Speaking softly, so that only I could hear, Janet said, "I don't know *where* Bootsie's getting the money to pay for all the gifts she gives that young man. Isn't it sad to see a woman her age behaving like that?"

I made no reply to those indiscreet remarks, but I must admit, I surveyed Bootsie Flannigan with considerable interest now. Her hair, upswept in a high bouffant, was a shade of red I had never seen before on a human being, and she had on enough makeup to be on stage under bright lights. The makeup didn't disguise the fact that she was fifty desperately trying to hang on to thirty. She flourished her ample bosom in my direction and hit me with a thousand-watt smile. I couldn't help grinning back. If Janet made catty remarks about her, she was probably okay.

Her "friend," Dan, was about twenty years younger than Bootsie. He had "boy toy" written all over him, with his slightly pouty face and his painted-on jeans and muscle shirt. He grinned in my direction, in what he mistakenly must have thought was a seductive manner, and I inclined my head politely. I decided if he could play bridge, I sure the heck could.

"Wanna guess what *his* long suit is?" Sophie muttered in my ear.

I almost lost it right then and there. She was completely incorrigible. I did my best to maintain my composure, but I knew every time I looked at the man tonight I would hear Sophie's voice in my ear.

"Now," Janet said, clapping her hands, "Carlene should be here any minute. She's always a few minutes late, but I'm sure she'll make a special effort tonight." Janet laughed. "Especially when I told her there was another attractive young woman who could give her some competition in the neighborhood. But of course dear Sophie's almost back on the market, too, aren't you?"

I gritted my teeth to keep from saying something I shouldn't, at least not in front of all these people I'd just met. I wanted to bash Janet McGreevey over the head. How insensitive could one person be? She knew that I was only recently widowed and Sophie was going through a nasty divorce.

I caught Marylou Lockridge's eye. She winked. I expelled a breath slowly and tried to calm down. Janet McGreevey had already turned her attention elsewhere. I was surprised Sophie hadn't said something, but she was probably biding her time to strike when

Janet least expected it. She drifted over to speak to the Grahams.

Gerald McGreevey approached me and said, his voice low, "Pay no attention to my wife, Emma. I don't." He grinned. I smiled back, but I didn't let him edge any closer to me. Then, in more audible tones, he said, "Don't know if anyone's explained how this party bridge works. Have you played much?"

"Just a bit with my brother and his friends," I said. "But I've never played with a group like this."

Gerald McGreevey nodded. "It's a bit different with party bridge. We'll all have a sheet with number combinations on them, and each of us has a different number. Each round, you'll be matched with a different partner at a particular table. You play four hands of bridge, add up the scores, and take that score with you to the next round. You might be at the same table, but with a different partner. Or you might be at a different table. That way you have the chance to play with quite a few different partners. Got that?"

"I guess so," I said. I was hoping fervently that I wouldn't end up at the same table with Janet, at least for a while.

Gerald laughed. "Don't worry, you'll soon get the hang of it."

The doorbell rang. Janet turned. "Gerry, darling, will you get that?"

Winking at me, Gerald ambled off in the direction of the front door. Bootsie Flannigan shimmied up to me, her considerable cleavage even more impressive on closer inspection. I tried not to notice, but she made me feel downright underdeveloped. I couldn't help glancing down at my own chest.

"They're something, aren't they, honey?" she drawled in an imitation of Dolly Parton. "But I'll have you know they're one hundred percent all me. No surgeon's had his hands on me." She paused. "At least not to operate."

"How lucky for you," I said, not knowing what else to say and feeling a bit of an idiot.

I glanced over her shoulder to find Dan giving me the glad eye again. Mr. Boy Toy was being a little too obvious for my comfort level. What would Bootsie do if she saw him making eyes at me? And why would he even notice *me*, with Sophie in the room? I did my best to ignore him.

Bootsie had launched into some anecdote, the subject of which I couldn't quite fathom, when a voice called out, "Hello, everyone."

I turned to see Gerald McGreevey and a newcomer advancing upon Bootsie and me. Gerald was grinning down at his companion like Olaf about to pounce on a particularly juicy bug.

I could see why. She had a gamine look, with auburn hair cut short, framing her head like a cap, and sparkling green eyes. Her mouth curved in a warm smile, and she extended a hand.

"Hi, you must be Emma Diamond," she said. "I'm Carlene Newberry. Welcome to the neighborhood."

"Thank you," I said. "It's a pleasure to meet you."

Gerald reluctantly turned away at a call from his wife. Carlene grinned at me, then leaned close enough to whisper. "And whatever Janet McGreevey told you about me, don't believe a word of it. She thinks every woman *has* to be after Gerald."

I tried not to laugh. "She's certainly something, isn't she?"

Carlene surveyed the rest of the company. "All of the usual suspects," she murmured. "I'm sure you've met Bootsie and her plaything." She leaned a little closer. "Watch out for him. He's always on the make. I don't how on earth Bootsie can afford him."

Frankly, by now I'd heard enough about Bootsie and her gigolo. Janet McGreevey came bustling up to us, sparing me from having to reply to Carlene. "Carlene, darling, I can't believe it, but you're practically early! At least for you." She laughed.

"Don't get used to it, Janet," Carlene responded, her voice slightly tart.

"Oh, I'm certain I wouldn't expect it again any time soon," Janet said, her eyes narrowing slightly. "I'm sure you made an effort for Gerald's sake."

"Of course, Janet," Carlene cooed back at her. "Who else?"

Without waiting for any kind of response, Carlene moved on to greet the rest of the assembled party. Janet glowered after her for a moment, then turned to me, a fake smile plastered on her face.

"Just Carlene's little joke, of course," she said, forcing a laugh. "She and Gerald work together. They're both lawyers." She named one of the city's largest and most prestigious law firms. I tried to appear suitably impressed.

A young man, tall and thin, about Sophie's age, appeared from the kitchen and approached Janet and me. His eyes were busily scanning the room beyond us, and a faint smile curved his mouth when he spotted someone. "Ah, Nate, come over and let me introduce you to our new neighbor. Why you persist in lurking in the den when you know I was counting on you to help with the refreshments . . ." Her voice trailed off. Nate's glance at her could have cut through granite.

"Well, here I am, Janet," he said, his voice cool. "And who's this?"

"This is Marylou Lockridge's new neighbor, Emma Diamond," Janet said. "She and Sophie Parker are friends, and it was Sophie who talked her into moving to our little neighborhood." Turning to me, she continued, "Emma, this is our son, Nathaniel, or, as he prefers to be called, Nate."

I offered my hand, and Nate took it. He held it as if he couldn't bear to touch me, then quickly let go. "Actually, Emma," he drawled, "Janet is only my stepmother. My mother died when I was ten."

Well, no love lost there, I figured. Somehow I couldn't blame Nate McGreevey. Janet didn't seem terribly maternal to me, unless she were one of those species that devoured their own young.

Flushing, Janet turned away and started clapping her hands to get everyone's attention. "Are we ready to play? Gerald, will you do the numbers?" Nate disappeared into the room off the kitchen. He was evidently not interested in bridge.

Gerald did the numbers. We all stood round, and Gerald went from one person to the next, handing us each a slip of paper. I was number nine, I read, when Gerald reached me. The nine was written at the top of the page. Below it was a numerical table, with the numbers of my partner for each round.

Janet pointed out the tables, numbering them in succession. "This is table one, that's two, and the one by the fireplace is three."

I glanced at my paper again. I was at table two this round, and my partner was number twelve. I walked over to table two and waited. Sophie and Marylou had ended up at table three, evidently partners. I wished one of them were at my table for the first round.

Carlene Newberry turned out to be number twelve. Our opponents for this round were Bootsie and the male half of the Graham couple, whose given name escaped me at the moment. The four of us sat down at the table, and Graham—Eric, wasn't it?—drew a deck of cards toward him and fanned them out on the table.

"Draw a card," he told me. I did, and he and the others did the same.

Eric turned his over. The two of clubs. I had the ace of hearts. Carlene and Bootsie had chosen cards of lesser value than mine.

"You get to deal first," Carlene told me. "I'll be scorekeeper, if no one objects."

No one did. Bootsie sat to my right. I offered her the other deck of cards to cut, and she did so, pushing the cards back to me. I took them and began dealing, while Carlene shuffled the deck we had used to decide the deal.

The deal finished, I began assembling my hand. My eyes widened as I examined my cards. I had certainly done well by myself.

♠ K Q J 3
♥ A 7 4
♦ 10 8 5
♣ A Q 6

Sixteen high-card points and a balanced hand. A nice way to begin the evening. I hoped my luck would continue like this. I frowned. What should I bid? I wished I had a cheat sheet with me, like the one Jake and Luke let me use when I played with them and their friends.

I glanced around the table. Three faces gazed expectantly at me.

"One no trump," I said.

Eric Graham, sitting to my left, said, "Pass."

Carlene smiled at me. "Two clubs."

Bootsie sighed, folded her cards, and said, "Pass."

They all watched me. I looked at my cards. What did Carlene's two-club bid mean? Wasn't there some convention that called for a two-club response to one no trump? I thought furiously back over the reading I had done yesterday and today.

"Stayman," I said, not realizing at first that I had actually spoken.

Carlene nodded approvingly.

"You're new at this, aren't you?" Eric said politely.

"Yes, sorry," I said. "Didn't mean to blurt that out, but I'm still learning."

"That's okay, honey," Bootsie assured me. "It's not like we're playing for money." She giggled. "Or even strip bridge."

I decided to ignore that and concentrated instead

on my hand. How was I supposed to answer Carlene? I think her bid meant I was supposed to tell her whether I had a four-card major suit. *Well, here goes nothing.* "Two spades."

Eric passed.

Carlene looked at her cards. "Four no trump."

Bootsie sighed again, even more loudly. "Honey," she told Eric, "you and I are out of this one."

Feeling panicky, I struggled to interpret Carlene's bid. I knew I knew the answer, but I wasn't prepared for something like this. She was telling me she thought we had a slam, and I had never played a slam hand before. Her four no trump meant that spades were the suit to play, but now I had to tell her how many aces I had. How did it go?

"Five clubs for none or all four aces," Bootsie recited, taking pity on me. "Five diamonds for one, five hearts for two, and five spades for three."

"Thanks," I muttered gratefully. "Five hearts."

"Pass," Eric said, sounding extremely bored.

Carlene examined her hand for a moment. Then she looked up and smiled at me. "Let's go for it, Emma. Seven spades."

Bootsie shook her head.

I drew a deep breath. "I just hope I don't let you down."

"Don't worry," Carlene said. "You'll do fine."

Eric pulled a card from his hand and dropped it on the table in front of me. The nine of clubs.

Carlene put her hand down on the table in the dummy position and arranged it for me.

♠ A 10 6 4 2
♥ K Q J 6
♦ A K 7
♣ J

"Holy moly," I said. I began counting. Eighteen high-card points. How did I count the singleton jack of clubs in this case? As one high-card point, or as two points for the singleton? At this point, I decided, it really didn't matter. Time to focus and figure out how to play this hand without screwing it up.

The only real danger, it seemed to me, was one diamond trick. If I could discard one of my loser diamonds, then we'd be home free. I could trump the dummy's loser diamond. I breathed a sigh of relief. I could do this. With all four aces, we had first-round control, unless Bootsie was void in clubs.

I played dummy's jack of clubs, and Bootsie played the two. I played my six, and dummy took the trick. Did Bootsie dodge the finesse, such as it was, or did Eric have the king of clubs?

No matter, I decided. I led dummy's two of spades to begin pulling trumps, and I used my three high spades to do it. Next I led my ace of clubs, discarding dummy's seven of diamonds.

All during the hand, as I took my time to be sure I was playing it properly, Bootsie kept distracting me with her fidgeting. She shifted around in her chair, shut and fanned her cards in her hand, and sighed a couple of times. I was sure she was bored with her hand and my slow pace, but I had to force myself to concentrate on what I was doing so as not to let her rattle me.

Eyes on my cards and the board again, I played my ace of hearts, and after that my four of hearts to run the dummy's three good heart tricks.

And that was it. Grand slam bid and made. Carlene clapped as I scooped up the final trick. "Well done, Emma. You don't look like a beginner to me."

I grinned. "I don't think even I could have screwed that one up."

Carlene began jotting on the score pad. "That's two ten for the seven spades, and a thousand for the grand slam, not vulnerable. One thousand two hundred and ten points, Emma. Not bad for a first hand."

"No, and I bet I'll get lousy cards the rest of the night after that," I said, smiling ruefully.

"Just cut the cards," Eric Graham said, almost growling at me as he shoved the other deck at me.

"Sorry," I said, as I cut the cards for him. Bootsie was shuffling the deck we'd just played.

We were all startled by a shout of rage from one of the other tables. I turned to look.

"You stupid, stupid woman," Janet McGreevey said, standing and shaking her finger across the table at her partner, Shannon Hardy. "I can't believe you screwed up like that. I refuse to play any further with you." She stalked off into kitchen, and we all sat there, stunned.

Chapter 4

For a moment, all I could do was look down at the table. I've always hated situations like this, and not really knowing any of the people around me made it much worse. I wished I was at home with Olaf and Hilda right this minute.

"Don't pay any attention to Janet," Carlene advised me in a low voice, reaching a hand across the table to me. "She usually blows up like that at least once every time we play, and then she settles down again."

To my right Bootsie muttered something under her breath, and the few words I managed to catch were far less polite than what Carlene had just said. Bootsie was still fidgeting in her chair, and I wanted to snap at her and ask her to stop. I held my tongue, though, not wanting to add further to the strained atmosphere.

"Why do you all put up with this?" I asked, keeping my voice down. I stared straight at Carlene, who shrugged.

"Mostly for Gerald's sake," she said.

"Never should have married her," Eric Graham said. "I'd sooner get in bed with a chain saw."

Bootsie guffawed loudly at that. I couldn't help grinning myself. I wasn't the only one who disliked Janet McGreevey intensely.

At the table where the disruption had occurred, Shannon Hardy was indignantly explaining why she had played the card she did. "Her first slough was a spade, and all I did was lead a spade when I had a chance. Isn't that what I was supposed to do? It's not my fault her ace was trumped."

The others at her table made suitably soothing noises, and I noticed that Gerald McGreevey had evidently followed his wife. He was nowhere to be seen.

I glanced over at the table where Sophie and Marylou were playing, and Sophie was staring at the cards in her hand. She had always been indifferent to outbursts like that, having become inured to them, thanks to her mother. I don't think Sophie even hears them. I wished I could be that way.

"Go on and deal the cards," Bootsie was urging her partner. "Just play, and forget about Janet." She poked at my arm to claim my attention. "Cut the cards."

I cut the cards, and Eric Graham began dealing them. As I waited for him to finish, I glanced around. The McGreeveys hadn't returned, and I was beginning to wonder if the party was going to end abruptly.

I had picked up my cards and was arranging them when the host and hostess reappeared. Janet's face was set in stone, and walking behind her, Gerald shrugged and waved his hands in the air. We all became absorbed in our cards.

I tried to focus on my hand, but I was listening for more eruptions from Janet's table. As far as I could tell, she offered no apology, but play did resume at her table. The others were obviously used to her behavior and ignored it.

A quick glance at my hand affirmed that I wouldn't have much to contribute this round. I had the ace of diamonds and the jack of clubs. Five high-card points this time, in marked contrast to my first hand. Not even any points from distribution, because I was 4-3-3-3. Oh well, I knew it was too good to last.

To my left Eric Graham opened with one no trump, Carlene passed, and Bootsie responded with three no trump. I passed, and Carlene wrote down the bid. Then she looked at her hand, debated a moment, and finally led with the seven of hearts.

Bootsie laid down her hand on the table, and I frowned, wondering why she had responded with three no trump to her partner's opening bid. She had only eight high-card points, and she also had a singleton heart.

Surprised, I glanced up at Carlene, who offered me a slight shrug. Then I snuck a quick look at Bootsie, and she was pushing back from the table.

"You'll be just fine, Eric," Bootsie said. Then she simpered. "I've just *got* to go to the little girls' room."

Eric scowled at her, obviously unhappy with her bid. I thought a moment about how I would have responded in her situation, and I didn't think I'd jump to game with her hand. She did have five clubs, including the ace and the queen. She also held the queen of diamonds. It wasn't much of a hand for someone playing no trump. Watching how Eric played this hand would be interesting.

After studying the board and his hand in turn for nearly two minutes, Eric finally pulled Bootsie's lone heart, the ten, from the board. I covered it with my jack, and Eric played the two.

Carlene pulled the cards from the board and arranged them in front of her, while I contemplated my lead. Obviously I should return my partner's lead. I had two hearts left, the three and the four. Shrugging, I pulled the four and dropped it on the table.

Carlene took the next two heart tricks, but after that Eric took control with the ace. He had three club tricks and five spades, plus the ace of hearts. He made three no trump with no problem. I estimated that he'd had twenty high-card points in his own hand, and with Bootsie's eight, they easily had game.

Bootsie wandered back to the table as Eric was cutting the cards for Carlene. With a plate in one hand and a glass in the other, Bootsie stood over us for a minute. She peered over at the score pad, then beamed at Eric. "See, I told you you wouldn't have any problems. You never bid one no unless you have at least twenty points, anyway."

Eric glowered at her for a moment, but Bootsie paid him no attention. Instead, she set her plate and glass on the table at her place. "Anybody want anything to drink while I'm up? Or something to nibble on?"

"No, thanks," we responded, almost in unison. Shrugging, Bootsie sat down and munched on Goldfish crackers while Carlene finished the deal.

Bootsie was the only person at my table who seemed inclined to chat. More relaxed now, she made numerous remarks during the remaining two hands we played, but neither Eric nor Carlene responded to her. Carlene rolled her eyes at me twice when she thought Bootsie wouldn't notice, and I gave only the barest acknowledgment by shifting my head a bit. These people were all obviously well attuned to one another's idiosyncracies, and I was a stranger. That was one of the reasons I always hated being pulled into a group where I hardly knew anyone.

Carlene was dummy again, during the third hand, when I was playing a four-spade contract. I watched her enviously as she excused herself from the table. I wished she were playing this hand. Bootsie's chatter was getting on my nerves.

By the time Carlene returned to the table, I had made the contract. I also had to play the next hand, the fourth and final one, but this time Carlene stayed to watch.

When we had finished, Carlene added up our scores, and we duly noted them on our cards. Carlene and I had won a rubber, and we got a part score for a game in the second rubber, which was incomplete.

"I enjoyed that very much, Emma," Carlene said as we got up from the table. "You play well, and you keep your head."

"Thank you," I said, pleased. "I just about panicked that first hand. I've never played a slam hand before."

Carlene laughed. "Well, you played it like a veteran."

"I probably will never have another hand that good," I said, "at least not tonight."

"You never know," Carlene said as she consulted her card. "That's part of the fun of bridge. Every hand is different, and when you and your partner do have slam, it's exciting."

I nodded, looking at my card. According to it, I was to move to another table. I walked over to where Sophie was sitting. Her table had just finished, but while Marylou and Dan got up to move, she didn't.

"What number are you?"

She showed me her card, suppressing a yawn as she did so.

"Are you bored?" I asked teasingly. I leaned down closer to her ear. "Especially with Mr. Long Suit at your table."

She giggled. "He looks good, but he can't play worth a damn." At least she had kept her voice low. "Watch out when you play with him. He doesn't know how to bid."

"Thanks for the tip," I said. I tapped my card. "Looks like you and I are partners this round."

"Good," Sophie said. "I know you won't do anything stupid."

I just shook my head at her. She was extremely competitive. We all liked to win, but when Sophie played bridge—any kind of game, really—she was a barracuda.

"I'll try not to," I said. "Do you want something to drink? I'm going to have a glass of wine, I think." I put my card down in my spot.

"Sure, a glass of wine for me, too," Sophie said.

Janet McGreevey and Paul Hardy came up to our table just then, and inwardly I cursed. I'd have to spend the next round with our hateful hostess. I hoped I'd be spared after that. Unless, of course, these bridge parties went on till late.

I might have to plead a headache at some point, and it probably wouldn't be a lie. It wouldn't take much of Janet McGreevey to give me one.

I walked over to the island between the living room and the kitchen and found two clean wineglasses. Pouring a very nice white wine into them, I glanced over the array of snacks. Plenty of Goldfish crackers, a platter of crudités, Marylou's spinach dip and some wheat crackers, and even a plate of petit fours. I'd have to try some of Marylou's spinach dip before the night was over, and I hoped it would be as good as her oatmeal cookies.

I glanced over at the doorway, and Nate McGreevey stood watching, again looking past me at someone else in the room. I started to speak to him, but Janet came up just then and picked up a small paper plate. She spooned a large amount of the spinach dip onto it, then added a handful of wheat crackers on the side. At this rate, there might not be spinach dip left for much longer.

Janet caught my expression, and her gaze hardened. "There's plenty of food for everyone," she said.

"Yes, of course," I murmured politely and started to turn away.

She wasn't paying any attention to me. She scooped up a large dollop of spinach dip with a cracker and popped it into her mouth. She smiled as she chewed.

I heard her murmur "yummy" as I headed back to my table.

Then, suddenly, I heard gasping, choking sounds from behind me.

I turned back, and to my horror, Janet was clutching her throat with both hands. Her plate had dropped to the floor in front of her. She reached out a hand toward me, but I was rooted to the spot.

A split second later, I recovered my voice. I yelled out, "Gerald! Something's wrong with Janet."

The room went completely still behind me, and for a long moment, no one moved. No one except Janet, that is. She collapsed against the island, hands still clawing at her throat. The platter of crudités went flying as she elbowed it on her way down.

Chapter 5

"Somebody call nine-one-one," Gerald McGreevey ordered as he brushed past me.

Rooted to the spot, unable for the moment to move away, I watched Gerald tend to his wife. With deft hands he shifted her away from the island and began probing the pockets of the skirt she wore. What was he looking for? My brain seemed as frozen as my feet, and for a moment I couldn't imagine why he was wasting time sticking his hands in her pockets.

"Damn it," Gerald said, "where the hell is it?"

By this point Janet was limp and unresponsive in his arms. He stuck his hand inside the neck of her blouse and felt around. He pulled the necklace she wore from beneath her blouse, then let it go. He stood up quickly, letting Janet slide to the floor none too gently. Striding over to the sink, he began rummaging through one of the cabinets over it. All the while he kept muttering, "Where the hell is it?"

"Can't we do something for her?" I asked. I became dimly aware that the others had crowded around me, and we all stared down at Janet, dying right in front of us. At least two people were crying. I could hear sobbing in two different pitches.

"Gerald, where's her epinephrine?" Carlene said, stepping past me.

"If I knew where it was," Gerald said savagely, "don't you think I'd be giving her some?"

"Here it is," Nate McGreevey said, bursting into the kitchen from the opposite side. He thrust something that looked like a pen toward his father. Gerald, startled by Nate's sudden appearance, didn't move for a moment. Then he grabbed the medicine from Nate's hand and dropped down on the floor by his suffering wife.

Gerald's back was to me, blocking my view of what he was doing. I could see his arms moving, but that was it. After a moment he sat back on his heels. Slowly he stood and turned to face us. His visage was grim.

"I'm afraid it was too late," he said, his voice dull. "Janet is gone."

Before any of us could comment or even check to see if he was right, the paramedics arrived. We all got out of their way and let them do their work. I went back to my table, accompanied by Sophie and Marylou. We all sat and stared blankly at one another. What did one say or do at a time like this?

It didn't take the paramedics long to get Janet on a stretcher and out to the waiting ambulance. We all watched from our chairs as they carried her away. Gerald went with them. A visibly shaken Nate accompanied his father to the front door. Father and son stared at each other a moment, and then Nate closed the door after his father followed the paramedics.

Nate leaned against the door for a moment before slowly returning to where we all were sitting. The color was slowly returning to his face, but he stared blindly into the room as he approached us.

"What happened to her?" Shannon Hardy was shivering, and her husband slung an arm around her shoulders, pulling her close to him. She buried her head in his neck and started sobbing.

Nate McGreevey stared at us almost hostilely, I thought. "Janet was deathly allergic to peanuts," he said, his words coming out in a rush, "and she had a severe allergic reaction just now. That doesn't make any sense. How did she come into contact with peanuts?"

There was complete silence for a moment. "She was eating some of the spinach dip with a cracker just before she collapsed," I said.

Someone gasped, and then I figured it must have been Marylou. "I don't put peanuts in my spinach dip. There must be some mistake." Her voice trembled. "I know Janet is allergic to peanuts, and I would never put anything like that in my spinach dip."

"What about the cracker?" Sophie asked. "What kind of cracker was it?"

"They're just plain wheat crackers," Nate said. "I don't think it has anything to do with the crackers." He looked away.

Sophie and I exchanged glances. I could see her mind was racing along the same lines that mine was. Someone had put peanuts into the spinach dip deliberately. But who? And why?

Sophie shrugged as if to say, "I don't know."

"What should we do now?" Amanda Graham spoke up.

"Go home," her husband said. He pushed himself up from his chair. "Come on, Amanda. There's nothing we can do here."

Amanda had a slightly mulish look on her face, and I figured she wanted to hang around so she wouldn't miss anything. But she didn't argue with her husband, following him docilely to the front door.

No one made a move to stop them, though Nate frowned at them severely as they walked by him.

As the Grahams reached the front door, Paul Hardy stood up, Shannon still clasped in his arms. "I'm going to take Shannon home," he announced to the rest of us. "This has been a terrible shock to her, and I need to get her home."

"Make sure you give her something warm and sweet to drink," Marylou said. Paul nodded.

"Come on, Bootsie, let's get out of here," Dan the boy toy said. "This is giving me the serious creeps."

Bootsie tried in vain to shush him, but he kept grumbling. Casting a helpless glance at the rest of us, Bootsie allowed Dan to tug her to the front door.

"Nate, call me if there's anything I can do," Bootsie said. Then she was out the door, and Dan pulled it closed behind him.

Five of us remained, and I wasn't sure what to do. I hated to go off and leave Nate alone, even though it seemed he had cared very little for Janet. When tragedies like this occurred, someone should offer comfort.

"Nate, will you be okay?" Carlene asked. She approached him and rubbed his right arm.

Nate offered a brief, strained smile. "I'll be okay," he said, but to me, at least, he didn't sound very convincing. "I'm not going to start pretending that I cared for Janet very much. Even so, it was a shock to see her . . . like that."

Marylou wrapped a motherly arm around his shoulders and gave him an affectionate squeeze. Nate looked almost pathetic in his gratitude for the comfort.

In my brief acquaintance with Janet McGreevey, I had found nothing in particular to like about her, but, like Nate, I was still shocked by her death. Despite the fact that the paramedics had taken her to the hospital, I knew it was no use. She was beyond reviving. I think she was dead even before Gerald had tried to save her by injecting her with her allergy medication.

"We all know Janet was a gigantic pain in the ass," Nate said. "There's no point in pretending otherwise, like I said." He frowned. "But there's something really odd about her having an allergic reaction to that spinach dip of yours, Marylou. Are you sure you couldn't have put peanuts in there by accident? Or maybe used some peanut oil by mistake?"

"No, I did not," Marylou said. She puffed up like an angry hen. "I don't like peanut oil, and I don't even have it in my kitchen, I'll have you know. And I wouldn't put peanuts in my spinach dip either." She paused for a deep breath. "Are you accusing me of deliberately trying to poison Janet?"

Nate regarded her silently for a moment. "Not you, in particular," he said, his voice soft. "But someone did, didn't they?"

"It's probably just some kind of freak accident," Carlene said, her impatience obvious. "I can't believe someone did it deliberately. It's just ludicrous to think that."

Sophie made a loud—and rude—sound of disgust. "Come off it, Carlene. If you really believe that, then you need to hand in your law school diploma and enter a convent. You can't be *that* naive."

Carlene flushed unbecomingly. "I'm not naive, Sophie. But I'm having a hard time imagining that someone here tonight could have hated Janet enough to want to poison her deliberately."

"It could be one of us," Sophie said, her tone deceptively mild. She stared at Carlene.

I stared at her. What little game was she playing? Was she deliberately trying to bait Carlene?

Carlene flushed again. "Don't be ridiculous, Sophie."

She was clearly uneasy. What nerve had Sophie struck?

"Oh, I don't know," Sophie said airily. "There's just been some talk going around the neighborhood that Gerald is having an affair with some attractive younger woman." She flashed an apologetic glance at Nate. "I'm sorry to talk about your dad like this, Nate."

Nate McGreevey sighed. "It's okay, Sophie. It isn't that much of a secret. Even Janet, as stupid as she was about a lot of things, had begun to catch on that Dad was running around on her."

Carlene stood mute before us. She had that deer-in-the-headlights look. After a moment, she spoke. "I really don't think we should be discussing such things at a time like this. It's highly inappropriate."

She was the very picture of outraged propriety now.

No one knew quite what to say, because it had become perfectly obvious to the rest of us that Carlene was very much on the defensive.

She stared at us all a moment longer. Then she whirled away from us, located her purse, and stormed out of the house.

And then there were four.

"That was interesting," Sophie said, her voice cool. She and Nate exchanged glances. He shrugged.

"Actually, I like Carlene a lot," he said. "And if I'm going to have another stepmother in my future, she's certainly a big improvement over Janet." He paused. "But even Janet didn't deserve what happened to her."

Sophie left her chair and headed for the kitchen. "Come on, y'all. Let's look around. See if we can figure out how it happened."

"Shouldn't we be calling the police?" I asked. "I mean, if Nate thinks this was deliberate, then the police need to know about it." I felt extremely uncomfortable about poking my nose into this. Surely this was a job for the police.

"All in good time," Sophie said. "Don't be such a wet blanket, Emma. You're the one who read me all those Nancy Drew books when you used to babysit me. Back then, you wanted to be Nancy. Here's your chance." She got up from her chair and moved toward the kitchen.

"It's not quite the same thing," I protested. "We're not looking for hidden staircases or secrets in an old attic. Someone died." I crossed my arms across my chest and stayed in my chair. "I still think Nate ought to call the police if he thinks there was foul play."

"I guess you're right, Emma," Nate said, looking at

me with an unreadable expression on his face. "I'll do it right now." He turned away from me and went to the phone in the kitchen.

"Come on, Emma, Marylou," Sophie said, hands on hips. "Now's our chance, and you're just sitting there like two bumps on a log. I thought you both had more gumption than that. Come help me look."

Marylou, who hadn't had much to say for a while, cast me a funny look as she got up from her chair. I stared at her for a moment, realizing how little I really knew about her. What if she really had put peanuts in the spinach dip? Maybe Janet had finally driven her over the edge.

"I didn't do it, Emma," Marylou said, her voice low.

I was embarrassed that she had read my thoughts so easily.

"Of course you didn't, Marylou," Sophie said. "Why do you think I want to poke around, Emma? Marylou is going to be a suspect, and it's up to us to help her. Now get off your derrière and help us."

Except for her notable failures in the romance department, Sophie was generally a decent judge of character. If she was sure Marylou hadn't poisoned Janet, then I supposed I had better help prove she hadn't.

I joined Sophie at the island where all the food still sat, except the crudités on the floor. "Watch out for those," I said, pointing at our feet. Sophie glanced down and frowned.

"There's Janet's plate, too," she said. "Someone has already stepped on it."

"We'd better leave everything as it is for the police," Marylou advised.

"Yes," Nate said. He had hung up the phone and stood staring at us. "They said to leave everything alone, and someone would be here very soon."

"Then we don't have much time," Sophie said. She didn't touch anything, but she examined everything atop the island as carefully as she could.

I couldn't imagine that she would find anything

helpful there. What was she expecting? An open jar of peanuts just sitting there?

Marylou was bent over at one end of the island, looking at something. As I watched, her back stiffened, and then slowly she stood. "Nate, do you have tongs somewhere?"

"Probably," Nate said. "What on earth do you want them for?"

"Could you just get them for me?" Marylou said, her voice sharp.

"Yes, ma'am," Nate said, saluting. He moved over to one of the drawers beneath the kitchen counter and rummaged around. "Here you go." He stepped over to Marylou.

Marylou took the tongs and bent down again. Sophie and I both moved closer. She was poking into a garbage can.

As we looked on, Marylou grasped something with the tongs. Straightening up, she held out the utensil, a small plastic bag in its claws. "Look at this," she said triumphantly. "What do you think is in here?"

Nate, Sophie, and I all moved even closer, peering at the bag. There didn't seem to be much of anything in it except a few crumbs.

Sophie took the tongs from Marylou and held the bag up closer to her eyes. She stared for a moment, then handed the tongs to me.

I examined the contents of the bag as closely as I could. Nate watched me, and I could feel the tension mounting as I offered him the tongs.

I looked at Sophie, and Sophie looked back at me. Slowly, we both nodded.

"Ground peanuts," we said in unison.

Chapter 6

I awoke with a start as something landed heavily on my stomach and didn't move. Groaning, I lifted my head and opened one eye.

"Olaf," I said in a tone heavy with resignation. "Why do you insist on doing this?" He stretched forward on my stomach to nestle his head and front paws between my breasts. He blinked sleepily at me before he yawned.

From her favorite spot beside my pillow, Hilda also began stretching and yawning. She would have been perfectly happy to stay right where she was, but once Olaf started his wake-up-Emma routine, she knew as well as I did that resistance was futile. Unless I forcibly removed Olaf from the room and shut the door, he would continue to shower me with attention. If I ignored the tummy pounce, he would proceed to licking my hands. If they were hidden beneath the covers, he would head straight for the kill. He would find one of my earlobes and start licking it. Since I made this easier for him by keeping my hair cut very short, I couldn't blame him completely. Frankly I would rather have him lick an earlobe than keep jumping on my stomach. He felt like a small buffalo landing on me, though he weighed only about ten pounds.

With my right hand rubbing Hilda's head and my left rubbing Olaf's, I peered across the room at the cable box atop my television set. "You bad cat," I said to Olaf. "It's barely six o'clock. Why couldn't you let me sleep late this morning?"

Olaf meowed at me. In that one plaintive cry he managed to make me aware that: (a) he was hungry to the point of starvation (despite the fact that I knew he probably had more than enough food in his bowl downstairs); and (b) he was desperately lonely and needed some attention.

I rubbed heads for a few moments longer, then shifted Olaf onto the bed beside me. He leapt to the floor in anticipation. I threw back the covers and got out of bed. Both cats accompanied me to the bathroom.

My head aching from lack of sleep, I found some aspirin in the cabinet over the sink. After swallowing two pills with a cup of water from the tap, I brushed my hair, trying to tame the inevitable goofy cowlick I got every night. Baxter always gently teased me about it, calling me "Alfalfa," and now when I saw it in the mirror in the mornings, I had to struggle not to cry.

Downstairs I peered at the coffeemaker. I couldn't remember whether I had set it yesterday. By the time I came home from the McGreeveys' house it was past one in the morning, and I was so tired I didn't think about morning coffee.

The coffeemaker went to work while I was staring at it. The digital clock on it read 6:15. While I waited for the pot to fill, I checked the cats' food bowls and water dish. Then I went to the laundry room off the back of the kitchen to clean out their litter box. My cats were inside cats. There were too many dogs in the neighborhood and too many cars, so I didn't let them outside. There was a screened-in porch across the back of the house, though, and they did enjoy it and the view of the backyard it offered them.

I retrieved the paper from the front stoop, and by the time I returned to the kitchen there was enough coffee in the pot for a decent-sized cup. I poured myself some, adding some sugar-free cream and sugar substitute for sweetening, then sat down to begin perusing the paper.

Rather quickly I discovered that I couldn't focus on the paper. The newsprint swam before my tired eyes. The combination of aspirin and caffeine had dulled my headache to a very mild ache, but trying to read threatened to bring back the throbbing.

As I sat with my eyes closed, sipping coffee, listening to Hilda and Olaf at their morning repast, I replayed the events of last night in my head. This morning it all seemed more than a bit surreal, but the awful truth of it was that Janet McGreevey had died, probably after eating ground peanuts mixed into the spinach dip. I shuddered. What an unpleasant way to die, too. Selfishly I wished I hadn't seen her dying. I was spared that with Baxter, though my imagination sometimes taunted me with visions of his body mangled by the wreck.

The scene that ensued when Gerald McGreevey returned from the hospital to find the police in his house had been hugely uncomfortable. Poor Nate McGreevey had tried to explain to his father why he had called the police, but Gerald was livid, berating his son harshly in front of all of us. At that point one of the police officers had stepped in to defuse the situation. Gerald eventually apologized, but Sophie, Marylou, and I could hardly look him in the face after that. He was certainly due some leeway because of the stress of the situation, but we all felt he had overreacted.

We three women had huddled in the corner for what seemed like hours while the police investigated. Patrol officers had responded first, and when they heard Nate's story, they quickly called in for a detective. After that the events began to blur in my memory.

Sophie, Marylou, and I each had a turn with the detective, who was kind but firm. His name was

Burnes, and his face was a polite mask as he took me through the story at least three times. Because I had actually seen the beginning of Janet's allergic reaction, he seemed to focus on me. I found his unwavering scrutiny more than a bit unnerving, and before it was over I began to think maybe I had put the peanuts in the spinach dip myself. Silly, I know, but I had never had that kind of intense interview with a homicide detective before.

When Nate showed Burnes the plastic bag containing what we all believed was ground peanuts, the detective's expression turned grave. I think at first he had been inclined to the idea that we were all over-reacting. That little plastic bag changed his mind, though. There was enough residue in it, with a few bits of peanut large enough to identify, so that none of us doubted what had happened.

After that we all had to answer more questions, and, no, we assured Lieutenant Burnes, none of us had seen anyone with a plastic bag that evening. Even Gerald McGreevey was silenced by this evidence of probable foul play. He went practically mute, staring at the floor. I wondered what was going through his mind. Had he done it? Somehow I thought if he had, he wouldn't have been so cavalier with the evidence. The killer had been careless, and perhaps that was a mark in Gerald's favor. He seemed to me a careful, deliberate sort who would make few, if any, mistakes.

Around 1:00 A.M. Burnes released Sophie, Marylou, and me, and one of the patrol officers escorted us home. We were all too exhausted to talk, and anyway, none of us wanted to talk in front of the patrolman.

In the morning light I couldn't honestly say that anyone at the bridge party had struck me as a potential murderer. Most of the guests, me included, didn't care much for Janet McGreevey, but which of them had hated her enough to kill her?

A rap at the back door interrupted my reverie, and

reluctantly I got up to open the door. I had been expecting this, and I was thankful that I'd at least had time for one cup of coffee before the onslaught.

"Good morning, Sophie," I said, standing back to let her in. She swept past me, radiating energy and determination. I was not a morning person under the best of circumstances, but Sophie was. Sometimes I hated her, and I could cheerfully have told her so. Part of her charm, however, was that she ignored my bouts of ill-humor and didn't begrudge me them.

"Morning, Emma," she said. She placed a foil-covered plate on the table before going in search of a mug for coffee.

I sat down at the table and poked a finger at the foil. "What's this?"

"Breakfast," Sophie said. Her cup full of coffee, black, no sugar, she sat down at the table across from me. She plucked the foil off the plate to reveal a pile of kolaches. "I picked them up from the bakery this morning."

"Don't you ever sleep late?" I asked.

Sophie smiled at me. "Don't be grumpy, Emma. Have a kolache, and you'll feel better."

I glared at her a moment before complying. I bit into the warm crust and tasted the ham and cheese inside. Delicious.

"Comfort food," I said between bites.

"Yes," Sophie said. She took one from the plate and bit into it with gusto. We ate in companionable silence for a minute or two.

"So, who do you think did it?"

I ignored her question for the moment while I got up from the table for some paper towels. I tore a couple off the roll over the sink and handed her one before sitting down again.

"How should I know?" I said. "I don't know any of these people. You do. What do you think?"

"It could be just about any one of them," Sophie said, reaching for another kolache. "Everyone there last night, including the not-so-grief-stricken widower, detested Janet. She did her best to make things unpleasant for just about everybody." She chewed for a moment. "There'll be a lot of dancing on that grave, let me tell you."

"That's sad," I said. I actually felt sorry for Janet McGreevey. What an epitaph.

Sophie shrugged. "Just consider it karma. If you spend most of your life being deliberately unpleasant to people, you should pay for it somehow."

"I suppose," I said. "I hope the police will get it sorted out quickly. The sooner the killer is identified, the easier I'll sleep at night."

Sophie set her half-eaten kolache down on her paper towel. "The police are all well and good," she said. "And that Lieutenant Burnes is certainly attractive, in a drill-sergeant kind of way, and bright enough. But I think he's going to find this a difficult case to solve."

"Why so?" I asked, startled.

Sophie shrugged. "Look at the evidence. A plastic bag with some ground peanuts in it. And I'll bet you there aren't any fingerprints on it." She paused. "Can you even get fingerprints off a plastic bag? I don't know. Anyway, any one of us could have brought it and then dumped it in the spinach dip. People were busy playing bridge, and no one would have noticed. How is the lieutenant going to prove anything?"

"I don't know," I said, thinking over what she had said. It would have been very easy for someone to add the peanuts to the spinach dip without worrying too much about being caught in the act. I had been so worried about playing well that I hadn't paid attention to much else.

Sophie leaned toward me. "That's why I think we ought to lend a hand."

"What? What do you mean?"

"Oh, come on," Sophie said, her impatience obvious. "Remember Nancy Drew and Judy Bolton? Who

was it who wanted to own her own detective agency
when she grew up, like Trixie Belden and Honey
Wheeler?"

I had to laugh at that. When I was a gawky teenager, I thought that being a detective like all those
girl sleuths seemed incredibly glamorous and exciting.
"Don't be ridiculous, Sophie," I said. "I was just a
girl, and I've certainly gotten over any such notion
long since."

Sophie stared at me, one eyebrow cocked to demon-
strate her skepticism. "And who, may I ask, is always
poring over the murder cases in the newspaper, offering opinions and trying to beat the police to the
punch?"

Sighing, I held up both hands. "All right, I surren-
der. Guilty as charged." I put my hands down on the
table. "But that's all a game, more or less, a puzzle I
can play with because I don't know any of the people
involved. This is different. I actually witnessed the
murder."

She made a face at me. "That's the point. Aren't
you the least bit curious about it? Don't you want to
find out who did it?" She paused for a moment. "Can
you honestly tell me that you don't want to try to
figure it out yourself?"

She had me there. Sophie knew me too well. Of
course I was curious. I had a nosy streak a mile wide
and ten times as long. It was one reason I found history so fascinating. What was it that made famous
historical figures like Elizabeth I or Napoleon do what
they did?

But this was different, and I stubbornly tried to
argue that point with Sophie.

She simply sat there, staring at me, arms crossed
over her breasts, and let me ramble through all the
reasons why it wasn't a good idea for the two of us
to play detective.

I was already running out of steam when the doorbell rang at the front door. Sighing, I pushed back

from the table. "I'll be back in a minute. Don't you dare go anywhere."

Despite my protests to Sophie, I had to admit to myself that I was very curious about Janet McGreevey's death. Maybe Sophie was right. Maybe between the two of us, we could figure this out before the police did.

I peered through the peephole. Marylou Lockridge stood on the stoop. Quickly opening the door, I stepped aside and invited her in.

"Emma, have you heard?" Marylou said. She was puffing with exertion. She must have run over here.

"No, what?" I said. "Come on in the kitchen, Sophie's here." I started to walk away after closing the door.

Marylou stood rooted to the spot, and I turned back to her when she began to speak. "Emma, you won't believe it. I just heard it myself. The police found an opened jar of peanuts in Nate McGreevey's room last night, and they've arrested him."

Chapter 7

Marylou didn't wait for a response from me after announcing her news. She was so wound up she just kept talking. My head started aching again.

"Come on into the kitchen," I said, breaking into the flow. "You don't want to have to repeat all this for Sophie."

Marylou paused for a breath, and I moved toward the kitchen. She came behind me, continuing to puff a little.

"Marylou has news," I announced to Sophie when we were within earshot. I shepherded Marylou to a seat, then went to the cupboard to get her a mug.

"What news?" Sophie asked.

Repeating what she had told me, Marylou reached for the coffee I handed her. She set the mug down on the table, then went back to gesturing with her hands as she talked.

"I just can't imagine that Nate did it," she said. "He's really a nice boy. I know he disliked Janet intensely, but I don't think he's a killer. I don't know why the police would arrest him just because he had some peanuts in his bedroom." Her hands finally settled on her mug, and she took a sip.

From my seat I regarded Sophie, waiting for her response. I wanted to hear her take on Nate McGreevey.

"You're right, Marylou," she said. "I don't think

Nate did it either. He *is* a nice guy, but he's also pretty spineless. I don't think he'd have the gumption to do anything like that. He'd rather complain and ask for sympathy than take action."

"Well, I suppose you're right," Marylou said.

Sophie rarely doubted she was, and I almost laughed at the expression of smug satisfaction on her face as she fixed her gaze on Marylou. "Of course I'm right. If Nate had any backbone he wouldn't be living at home at thirty-three. He needs to get a job. He's actually quite bright, and he's certainly attractive. If his father would push him out of the nest, he'd do just fine."

Something in her tone made me suspicious. I tried not to be obvious as I examined a startling new thought. Nate McGreevey, as Sophie described him, was just the kind of man she usually fell for. Surely she hadn't set her sights on him, with her divorce not even final yet? This would bear some further thinking about.

"Marylou," I said, "how did you hear about this? And are you sure that Nate was really arrested?" I shoved the box of kolaches toward her.

Marylou shifted in her chair. She reached for one of the kolaches and took a bite before answering. When she did, her tone was sheepish. "Well, I heard it from Amanda Graham. She said Bootsie had called her this morning, and Bootsie had talked to Gerald. Bootsie and Gerald have known each other for donkey's years, and of course she couldn't stand not knowing what was going on."

"Doesn't anybody in this neighborhood sleep past six a.m.?" I asked.

"Who could sleep this morning?" Marylou asked before gulping down the rest of her kolache. "We haven't had this kind of excitement in the neighborhood since Lily Steinbrenner sued Marjorie Lewis because Marjorie's randy little Pekinese got Lily's prize-winning poodle pregnant."

It was all I could do to keep from spewing a mouthful of coffee all over the table. I swallowed hastily, hoping I wouldn't choke. Then I couldn't help myself. I laughed.

"You can laugh all you want, Emma," Sophie said. "And I suppose it was funny, in a way. But Lily and Marjorie had a couple of knock-down, drag-out catfights before it was all over." She giggled. "Or maybe I should say Pekidoodle fights."

That did it. We were all guffawing like crazy women.

When we finally settled down again, I said, "We probably shouldn't be laughing like this. A pregnant poodle is one thing, but a cold-blooded murder is completely different."

Marylou nodded. "Yes indeed. This is much more serious. And that's why we can't sit by and let poor Nate take the blame for something someone else did. Unlike Marjorie's Pekingese."

"That's just what I was telling Emma before you got here," Sophie said, beaming at Marylou. "She's always loved mysteries anyway, and I don't see any reason we can't try to figure this out ourselves. After all, we're the ones who were playing bridge with a murderer last night."

"Now, hang on a minute," I said, but they both ignored me.

"I've been thinking about that," Marylou said, leaning over the table and fixing her eyes on Sophie. "You know how we can get the suspects talking, don't you?" She paused briefly but didn't really give Sophie any time to respond. "We play bridge with them, that's how."

"What good will that do?" I asked, taken aback.

Sophie rolled her eyes at me. "Come on, Emma, you know how it is when people get together for a friendly game of bridge. Think about the times you and I play with Jake and Luke. We spend about as much time gossiping as we do actually playing bridge."

"Jake and Luke?" Marylou asked, momentarily diverted. "Who are they?"

"My brother and his partner," I said briefly. "Jake, my brother, is a doctor, and Luke is a lawyer. They live in the Heights." I wondered how she would respond to that. It couldn't be more obvious that my brother was gay.

"They play bridge?" Marylou asked, her eyes gleaming. "That's great. You'll have to invite them over, Emma. I'd love to meet them."

Evidently all that mattered was that they played bridge. I stifled a laugh. "Oh, they play bridge, all right," I said dryly. "They're both absolutely nuts for it. In fact, that's how they met, fifteen years ago when they were both seniors in college. They play duplicate, too, and they're a formidable team."

"Even better," Marylou said. She frowned. "I wonder if I've ever seen them at the bridge studio."

"It's very likely," I said. "I know they play pretty often at the one off the Southwest Freeway. They've been trying to get me to go with them, but I'm not sure that I'm ready for duplicate just yet."

"Then I probably have seen them, and of course I didn't know them," Marylou said. "I'll have to keep an eye out for them."

"Trust me," I said, "you can't miss them. They're both over six feet tall, and Luke is absolutely dropdead gorgeous. My brother is attractive, but Luke could give Brad Pitt or George Clooney a run for their money any day."

"Amen to that," Sophie said. Whenever Sophie and I played bridge with "the boys," she had a hard time keeping her eyes on her cards. Luke was a much more attractive prospect.

"I *have* seen them, but I've never really talked to them," Marylou said. "I know exactly who you mean. They are a very handsome couple."

"I'll invite them over soon so you can meet them properly," I said. "They're both extremely busy with their jobs, but maybe the next weekend or two they can come over."

"A doctor and a lawyer, no wonder," Marylou said.

"Speaking of doctors," Sophie said, "why don't you call Jake before he leaves home this morning and ask him about peanut allergies?"

I glanced at the clock. "It's a little early to call them right now. It's only ten to seven. They're usually doing their workouts about now. I can call in about twenty minutes." Jake and Luke had an exercise regimen they followed resolutely, and I didn't like to interrupt them.

Marylou and Sophie nodded with enthusiasm, and I knew they wouldn't leave the house until I had talked to my brother. I also knew they were bound and determined to stick their noses into this murder, and I had to admit my own growing curiosity about the case. I've read thousands of mystery novels over the years, but this was the first time I had ever had one happen right in front of me.

"I like your idea of playing bridge with the suspects, Marylou," Sophie said. "And we can use the fact that Emma is new to the neighborhood to our advantage. I know Amanda Graham will be champing at the bit to get inside Emma's house." Sophie turned to me. "Amanda watches all those decorating shows on TV, and she's always saying how she could do a better job. She loves poking around in other people's houses, so you'll have to watch her when she comes over here."

"When?" I said. "How about if? From the way you talk, I'm not sure I want the woman in my house."

Sophie brushed that aside as irrelevant. "Of course you don't, Emma, but that's not the point. We need to get Amanda to talking. She and Eric hated Janet, I know that much, but she's been pretty tight-lipped about the whole thing."

"And that's not natural for Amanda," Marylou said. "Janet did something to them, and if we can find out exactly what it was, that might help us figure out if they could have done it."

"Same thing with Shannon and Paul Hardy," Sophie said. "Janet really had it in for Shannon, though I'm not sure why."

"Probably because Shannon is such a lovely girl, and Gerald was always flirting with her," Marylou said wryly. "Janet never could get used to the way Gerald behaves around other women. He doesn't really mean anything by it, he's just a natural-born flirt."

I held back my retort that Gerald was a dirty old man. Marylou was from a different generation, and she was inclined to be indulgent where men like Gerald McGreevey were concerned. I was not, however, and neither was Sophie. I saw her lips tighten, but she didn't say anything either. I had no doubt that Gerald had made advances toward her, but he had probably drawn back a nub when he did.

I glanced at the clock again and decided that it would be okay now to call my brother. I got up from my chair and went to the phone mounted on the wall near the refrigerator. After punching the speed dial, I leaned against the fridge and waited for an answer.

After three rings my brother picked up. "Jake Brett speaking."

"Jake, it's me, Emma," I said. "I hope I'm not interrupting your workout."

"No, we're all done and I'm just about to hop in the shower," Jake said. "How are you? Is anything wrong?" I didn't usually call him this early in the morning.

"I'm fine, Jake, honestly. Nothing's wrong with me, but I did want to ask Dr. Brett a question or two about food allergies."

Jake was an internist, and a very good one, and I knew he would be able to answer my questions. "Sure, what do you need to know?"

"It's about peanut allergy, to be specific," I said. I quickly filled him in on the details of what had happened last night.

"Poor woman," Jake said. "When someone has an

allergy like that, it doesn't take long for the reaction to set in, once they've ingested the substance, in this case, peanuts. Usually, the worst can be averted with a quick shot of epinephrine. I would have thought she'd have some on her. People with that kind of severe allergy usually have it with them at all times."

I frowned, remembering Gerald's frantic search last night. "I think she usually did," I said slowly. "The first thing her husband did was search her clothing, and evidently he didn't find what he was looking for. He got up and started looking through the drawers in the kitchen. Then his son came into the room with some kind of penlike thing. By then it was too late, evidently."

"That's a bit odd," Jake said. "I wonder why she didn't have the device with her."

"Maybe she didn't think she'd need it in her own home," I said.

"Maybe," Jake said. "But usually people with allergies like that are in the habit of having the device with them wherever they go."

"Can people really die so quickly from an allergy, if they don't get treatment in time?"

"Yes, they can," Jake said. "Of course, some of it can depend on other factors. She might have had a weak heart, for example. There are severe respiratory problems, too. They can't breathe properly because the throat closes up, and that could exacerbate any problem with the heart."

"It sounds just dreadful," I said softly.

"It is a dreadful way to die," Jake said. "I'm sorry you had to see that. Are you sure you're okay?" The love and concern in his voice warmed me.

"I'm okay," I told him in a stronger voice. "Sophie is here, and she sends her love, especially to Luke." I heard an outraged squawk from Sophie's direction. She hated it when I teased her about Luke. "Give him my love, too. I want you both to come over soon and meet my new neighbor, Marylou Lockridge. She's as bridge-mad as you and Luke are." This time I heard a deep chuckle from Marylou.

We chatted for another moment or two, and then I said good-bye.

Seated at the table again, I repeated what Jake had told me. "Pretty wretched," Sophie commented. "Thank goodness I'm not allergic to any food that I know of."

"What shall we do now?" Marylou said.

"I don't know about you two," I said, "but I'm going back to bed. I didn't sleep well, and I'm not going to function too well today without a little more sleep." I smiled to remove any sting from my next statement. "So if you don't mind, I'm going to shoo you both out. We can talk in a few hours, if that's okay."

"Of course, Emma," Marylou said, contrition in her voice. "I know just how you feel. You get some rest, and Sophie and I will talk with you later." She stood up from the table, and Sophie did too. "Come on, Sophie, over to my house, and we can start planning."

"Get some sleep," Sophie said, pausing to give me a quick hug. "I'll make sure the door is locked behind us."

"Thanks for understanding, you two," I said. They were already busily plotting something as they left the kitchen, and I don't even think they heard me.

Sighing with relief, I contemplated the quiet of my kitchen. It was pleasant to have it to myself again. I sat that way for a few minutes, drinking in the silence. Then I went back upstairs to my bedroom and climbed into bed.

Sometime later I awoke to the ringing of the front doorbell. Peering at the clock as I hurriedly threw on my robe, I saw that it was nearly eleven o'clock. I really had zonked out.

"I'm coming," I called down the stairs as the doorbell rang yet again. I ought to give Sophie a key to the house so she could let herself in and out. I knew it would save time in the long run. I figured she and Marylou had come back to wake me up and fill me in on their plans.

Except that it wasn't Sophie or Marylou on my front doorstep. It was the police, in the form of Lieutenant Burnes.

Chapter 8

I had been so certain that I would find Sophie or Marylou at the front door I hadn't stopped to consider what I must look like. My hand went automatically to the cowlick on the back of my head, and, sure enough, I could feel the hair sticking up.

Lieutenant Burnes cleared his throat. The corners of his mouth twitched as he tried, not too successfully, to keep his eyes from following my hand in its compulsive stroking of my head.

"Good morning, Mrs. Diamond," he said, his voice brisk but friendly. "I hope I haven't come at a bad time, but I'd really like to talk to you some more about last night."

"Certainly, Lieutenant," I said, "please come in." I waved him inside, clutching my robe tightly against me with one hand and shutting the door with the other. "Why don't we go into the kitchen? Perhaps I can offer you something to drink."

"Thank you," the lieutenant said. He stood waiting for me to lead the way.

"I tell you what," I said, the words tumbling out, "why don't you go on into the kitchen, and I'll just dash upstairs for a moment? I was napping, and I really should change clothes."

"That's fine," Burnes said. "I'm sorry I disturbed your rest."

"Oh, I needed to be up anyway," I said, one hand on the newel post at the bottom of the stairs. I pointed the way to the kitchen for him. He nodded and turned away.

I scampered up the stairs and into my bedroom. Hilda and Olaf regarded me sleepily from the bed. Hilda yawned and stretched, while Olaf blinked. I told them to stay where they were, as if they would really pay any attention to what I said. I hoped the lieutenant didn't mind cat hair, because one or the other of them would be sure to test him.

I washed my face quickly and brushed my hair back, praying that the cowlick would behave. I didn't want to take the time to gel it into place. I applied some light makeup, then slipped into a dress and some flats. Checking myself in the mirror one last time, I decided I looked far more presentable now. And all in only seven minutes.

The detective was seated at the kitchen table with Olaf in his lap when I entered the room. Olaf was purring loudly and rubbing his head against Burnes's hand. "I'm sorry if he's being a pest," I said, dismayed and resigned at the same time. "He thinks everyone is going to adore him, and he's shameless about demanding attention." I shook my finger at Olaf, but he was blissfully ignoring me. "His name is Olaf. His sister, Hilda, is still upstairs, I think."

"Not a problem," Burnes assured me. "I've got two of my own, plus two dogs." His dark green eyes glinted with suppressed humor as they strayed to the top of my head. I resisted the impulse to stick a hand up to smooth down my hair.

"Would you like some coffee?" I asked. "Or maybe a soft drink? It wouldn't take long to make some coffee."

"Actually, I'd love just a glass of water if you don't mind," Burnes said. "I'm trying to keep off the caffeine. If I don't, my doctor's going to lynch me."

He smiled companionably at me, one hand still

scratching Olaf's head. He was a few years older than I was, about forty-five, and he had an assurance about him that I found attractive. I had always been drawn to self-confident men, and this man exuded a quiet authority that suited him well. His demeanor was professional, but amiable, and he was easy to talk to, at least so far.

I went to the cabinet for a couple of glasses, then filled them from the pitcher of filtered water I kept in the fridge. I set his glass before him before taking a seat across from him.

"Thanks," he said, lifting the glass. He drank about half of it down in one go.

"Would you like some more?"

He smiled. "Maybe in a moment. I'm afraid I need to move on with things, if you don't mind. I'd like to take you through your story again."

Olaf looked like becoming a permanent fixture in the man's lap, but Burnes didn't seem to mind. He sat relaxed in the chair with the cat in his lap, regarding me in friendly fashion.

"Where should I start?" I asked, a little uncertain.

"Start with your arrival at the McGreeveys' home last night, and tell me anything you can think of. Anything you saw or heard. You never know what might have some bearing on the case."

"Do you really think it's a case?" I asked. "I mean, I suppose you wouldn't be here if you didn't, but it still seems like some kind of nightmare. Maybe it was just a freak accident."

"That's a possibility," Burnes said. "And I have to consider all the possibilities. If you would go on with your observations?" He was polite, but firm.

I nodded. As he had suggested, I started with our arrival at the McGreeveys' house last night, telling him everything I could remember about what people said or did. It took me about fifteen minutes, and I had drunk most of my glass of water by the time I finished.

"That's very organized and concise," Burnes said when I had finished.

"I need more water," I said, getting up from the table. I brought the pitcher of water back to the table and refilled both our glasses.

"Thanks," Burnes said as I sat down again. "Now let's go back a little further in time. I believe you said you only recently moved to this neighborhood. Is that correct?"

"Yes, just a week ago." I paused, counting back. "Today is the tenth day I've been in this house."

"Did you know anyone in the neighborhood before you moved here?"

"Just my neighbor on that side," I said, gesturing toward Sophie's house. "I've known Sophie Parker since we were both children. Her family lived next door to mine, and I used to babysit her when she was little. We've been friends for thirty years or so."

"What about the other neighbors? When did you meet them?"

"I met Marylou Lockridge, the neighbor on the other side, yesterday. She came over and introduced herself after . . ." I faltered for a moment. "After Janet McGreevey had been here."

"Was that the first time you had met Mrs. McGreevey?"

I shook my head. "No, I first met her a couple of days before that, when she came over to hector me about my cats. I'm afraid we didn't hit it off, and I let her know I didn't appreciate her manner."

"And yesterday?" Burnes asked, prompting me.

"Ostensibly she came over with a peace offering," I said. "Some brownies. Sophie happened to be here, and they started to talk about some elderly woman in the neighborhood who's behind in her homeowners' association dues. Mrs. McGreevey was evidently a force to be reckoned with in the homeowners' association."

Burnes nodded. "Did you talk about anything else?

Did Mrs. McGreevey express concern over any worries, anything like that?"

"No, she didn't, other than the elderly woman I mentioned. She seemed quite indignant, and insistent, over the poor woman. She certainly didn't act like she was worried about anything."

"What was your impression of Mrs. McGreevey?" Burnes regarded me casually as he waited for my response.

"I didn't like her," I said, not mincing words. "She was a nasty, interfering busybody, and I don't think anybody in the neighborhood cared much for her."

Burnes drank some water, and I waited for another question. When he didn't say anything right away, I decided to ask him one.

"Is it true that you arrested Nate McGreevey?"

"Who told you we arrested him?" The amusement in his voice was plain.

I felt flustered. "Well, this morning, my neighbor, Mrs. Lockridge, came over and told us she'd heard Nate had been arrested. She said she had heard it from another neighbor, Bootsie Flannigan, who had heard it from Gerald McGreevey."

"The neighborhood grapevine was at work pretty early this morning," Burnes said, still amused. "No, we haven't arrested anyone. Nathaniel McGreevey did come downtown to make a statement, but he has not been arrested. Before we can arrest someone, we actually have to determine that a crime has been committed."

"That's what I would have thought," I said, relieved.

"What do you think really happened?" Burnes asked.

"Do you mean, do I think it was an accident, or deliberate?"

He nodded.

Why was he asking me? I wondered. He was the expert here. Was he trying to get me to confide neighborhood gossip in him? I decided I had better choose my words with care.

"It's hard to see how it could be an accident," I said slowly. "I mean, evidently they all knew that Janet McGreevey was allergic to peanuts. And if that's what really caused her death, well, it would have to be a bizarre accident, wouldn't it?"

"That's my job, to figure it all out. Thank you for talking with me," Burnes said. He put Olaf gently down on the floor and stood up. Gray hair clung to his dark trousers, and he glanced down at the mess Olaf had made of his lap. He flashed me a smile. "One of the costs of being an animal lover."

"Here, let me get you something to take care of that," I said, hopping up from my chair. I went to one of the drawers and started rummaging. "I still don't have everything unpacked, but I usually keep a lint-removal roller in the kitchen. Olaf is always doing this to people." Surely I had seen one of those rolls of sticky paper somewhere in the last day or two.

Ah, there it was, pushed to the back of the drawer. I handed it to Burnes, and he thanked me. He pulled the cover sheet off, then rolled the sticky paper up and down his legs. It took two sheets to do the job, and I took the hair-covered sheets and put them in the garbage.

"Thank you, Mrs. Diamond," Burnes said.

"I'm just sorry Olaf made such a mess," I said, but he waved away my apology, insisting he hadn't minded at all.

I escorted him to the front door. On the stoop he turned to me and said, "Thank you again for your time. I might need to talk to you again at some point, if you don't mind."

"Not at all, Lieutenant," I said. "If there's anything I can do to help, I certainly want to do that."

"I appreciate your cooperation," he said. "I'll be speaking to the rest of your neighbors who were at the bridge party last night." He pulled a wallet out of his inner jacket pocket and extracted a card. Handing it to me, he said, "In the meantime, if you should think of anything else that might possibly be relevant, please let me know. You can reach me through that number." Then, sketching a quick salute, he was gone.

I watched for a moment, long enough to see that he was heading next door to talk to Marylou Lockridge. When he happened to glance back in my direction, I hastily shut the door, feeling a little flustered.

I headed back toward the kitchen, and before I was halfway there, I heard knocking at the back door. I hurried to answer it, knowing that it was probably Sophie.

It was, of course. I let her in, and she immediately sat down at the table.

"How about some hot tea?" I said. "I think I need a little boost, and then maybe we can scrounge up something for lunch. I'm getting hungry." I filled the kettle with water and set it on the stove to heat.

"Sure, sounds good," Sophie said. "Or we can go out for something, once Detective Delicious is through with Marylou."

"Really, Sophie," I said. "You're incorrigible."

"You have to admit he's attractive, Emma," she said. "I didn't mind being interrogated at all, let me tell you. He has a nice voice, and he's got that dark hair with a few streaks of gray in just the right places. And those big blue eyes of his. Oh my." She sighed heavily.

"They're not blue, they're green," I said, and as soon as I said the words, I knew I had walked right into her trap. "You rat."

Sophie giggled merrily. "You're no more immune to him than I am, Emma. Admit it. You think he's attractive too, don't you?"

"What if I do?" I retorted. "That doesn't mean anything. There are lots of men I find attractive."

Sophie eyed me shrewdly. "That's good. It means you're coming back to life."

I shifted uncomfortably in my chair. "Can we talk about something else?"

She knew when to back off the attack. "Sure. I think we ought to go out to lunch," she said. "We need to do a little shopping this afternoon."

"What for?" I asked. The kettle whistled, and I got up to prepare the tea.

"Food and everything," Sophie said innocently. "For the bridge game tonight."

"What bridge game?" I asked, not sure if I really wanted to know the answer.

"The one we're having here, with you, me, Marylou, and Amanda Graham. Just an innocent little hen party." Sophie gave me one of her most seraphic smiles.

"And if I say I don't want to have any bridge party here tonight?" I picked up the cups of tea and brought them to the table.

Sophie just laughed, and I sighed in resignation. If I killed her now, where could I hide the body?

Chapter 9

"Everything looks fine, Emma," Marylou said as she surveyed the kitchen. "Besides, it's much more comfortable playing in here, anyway. It's just us girls."

"If you're sure," I said, not quite convinced. My mother would never have played bridge in the kitchen. With her crowd, the kitchen was the domain of servants. In fact, I'm not sure my mother even knew how to open the refrigerator door on her own, provided she could remember where the kitchen actually was.

"Chill, Emma," Sophie said. "Amanda Graham is an ordinary woman. She's not going to report you to Emily Post because you made her play bridge in your kitchen."

At my age I supposed it was ridiculous for me to feel this kind of anxiety over a mere bridge game, but I could just hear my mother's voice in my head. "Really, Emma, how very lowbrow of you to entertain in a kitchen, of all places."

"Oh, shut up," I muttered, and I noticed Marylou looking at me with a slightly raised eyebrow. I smiled but didn't explain.

"All we have to do now is wait for Amanda to show up," Sophie said. She and Marylou exchanged glances.

"What time did you tell her?" I asked.

"Six thirty," Sophie said.

"And that means she ought to be here about seven or seven fifteen," Marylou added with a grimace.

I checked the clock. It was nearly seven now.

"Amanda runs on her own clock, which isn't quite in sync with the clock the rest of us use," Sophie said.

"That's just plain rude," I said, frowning. "Not to mention thoughtless." I considered myself late if I didn't arrive somewhere I was expected at least five minutes early.

Marylou shrugged. "It doesn't do any good to say anything to her. Believe me, we've tried, and basically we all decided that it was easier in the long run just to tell her half an hour earlier for everything."

The doorbell rang, and Marylou and Sophie laughed. "She's actually a little bit early, for her," Sophie said.

I headed for the front door.

"Good evening, Emma," Amanda Graham said, offering me a gay smile when I opened the door. "It's nice to see you again, and under nicer circumstances."

"Please come in, Amanda," I said, stepping back and waving a hand. "Yes, it is nice, isn't it?" I shut the door behind her.

She held out a covered dish. "Just a little something I whipped up." She laughed. "And not a peanut anywhere in it, I promise."

I gave her a weak smile for that thoroughly tasteless remark. I accepted the dish before turning to lead her to the kitchen. "Come on back to the kitchen. Marylou and Sophie are here."

"I'm always the last to arrive," Amanda said, sounding quite complacent about it. "I don't know how everyone else always gets places before Eric and I do."

"Here's Amanda," I said brightly as we stepped into the kitchen. "And she's brought something for us." I brandished the dish.

"And not a peanut in it," Amanda said, giggling.

Marylou smiled, and Sophie twitched her lips.

"What is it?" Marylou asked. "Is it some of your fudge, by any chance?" Her eyes sparkled at the thought.

"Yes, it is," Amanda said, "and there are plenty of pecans in it. Not peanuts."

"Yes, we got that," Sophie said tartly. "Now, what would you like to drink?" She waved a hand at the counter where she was standing. "We've got some white wine, or there are soft drinks, and I believe Emma even made some tea."

"Oh, white wine," Amanda said. "Since I'm not driving anywhere tonight, I can have wine. Eric always makes me be the designated driver whenever we go somewhere together, and I never get to have more than one glass."

"Wine it is," Sophie said. She poured a glass for Amanda and one for herself. Marylou and I had already fixed ourselves glasses of iced tea.

"Would anybody like anything to eat before we start?" I asked. "In addition to Amanda's fudge, I have some sandwiches, ham or turkey, with some chips, and I have a salad and three kinds of dressing."

"I'm fine right now," Amanda said. "Let's play." She drained her wine and poured herself more before she came to the table.

Marylou cast a longing look at the plate of fudge that Sophie had unwrapped and set on the counter with the drinks and sandwiches. She sighed. "Yes, let's play." She turned her back on the food.

I sat down, and Sophie quickly chose the seat opposite me. Marylou sat to my right and Amanda to my left. Sophie was going to be scorekeeper tonight, and that meant she would remain in the same chair while we played. At the end of each rubber, Marylou, Amanda, and I would shift seats so that, by the third rubber, each of us would have played once with everyone else.

Amanda cut the cards, and Sophie dealt. When the deal was finished, my hand looked like this:

♠ Q 6 3
♥ A Q J 10 9 4
♦ 3
♣ Q 6 2

I counted it as eleven high-card points, an extra
point for having six hearts, and two distribution points
for the singleton diamond. Grand total of fourteen
points, good for an opening of one heart.

Sophie passed after a quick glance at her cards.
Marylou sighed and did the same.

"One heart," I said.

Amanda passed with a scowl.

Sophie examined her cards. "One no trump."

Marylou passed again.

I stared at my cards and tried to interpret Sophie's
bid. There were aspects of bidding that gave me a
headache every time I played. Did Sophie truly have
a weak hand? At least six, but no more than ten,
points and even distribution, that's what she was probably telling me. But did she have six points? Seven?
Or the maximum, ten?

I didn't favor no trump, though three no trump is
the shortest way to game. With only one diamond,
and only a queen in both spades and clubs, I didn't
fancy our chances in no trump.

"Two hearts," I said.

Looking bored, Amanda passed. She folded her
cards, placed them on the table in front of her, and
sipped at her wine.

Sophie took one more look at her cards. "Pass."
She recorded the bid on the score pad as soon as
Marylou had passed.

"Your lead, Amanda," Marylou said.

"Yes, I know," Amanda said, her tone mild as she
picked up her cards again. She contemplated her hand.
Finally she pulled a card and laid it on the table—the
seven of diamonds.

Sophie laid down her hand. I examined my dummy with interest. Sophie held:

♠ K 7 4
♥ 8 6
♦ K J 9 8
♣ K 8 5 4

She had ten high card points and pretty even distribution. I was hopeful of making the two-heart bid without much effort on my part.

I played the king of diamonds from Sophie's hand, and Marylou dropped the ace. I played my singleton three. Amanda claimed the trick and placed it in front of her.

Marylou played the queen of diamonds. I trumped it with the four of hearts. Amanda played the two, and I pulled the eight from dummy and collected the trick.

What next? I should start pulling trumps. But was that the best strategy with this hand? I made a quick count. There were five out against me, including the king. Unless Amanda or Marylou held it as a singleton, I needed to try a finesse to determine who held it. In order to do that I had to get to dummy's hand and lead from there, hoping that it was in Marylou's hand and not Amanda's. If Amanda held it, a finesse wouldn't do any good.

Eyeing the dummy hand, I calculated my chances. I would need to use either the king of spades or the king of clubs to win a trick in dummy.

I played the queen of spades from my hand. Amanda dropped her ace on it. I smiled. Now if I could just get the lead again, I could lead to the king in dummy.

Amanda frowned as she looked at her hand. When she played the five of diamonds, I tried to hide my complete astonishment.

I heard Marylou's sudden intake of breath. She was not pleased with Amanda's choice of leads.

I took that trick with dummy's jack, and I sloughed a spade on it.

I pulled the eight of hearts from dummy, and Marylou played the three. I played the nine from my hand, knowing that only the king would be higher. Amanda played the two.

I got back to dummy's hand with a spade to its king. I played dummy's remaining heart, Marylou played the seven, and I took the trick with the ten, because Amanda had only a low heart.

Breathing more easily now, I played the ace of hearts from my hand and Marylou was forced to play her king. I was home free now.

We ended up making three hearts. I didn't think four was there, and I was pleased with my play. Of course, it helped that Amanda had made a bad choice for her second chance at a lead, though I'm not sure the outcome would have been any different. Sophie recorded the score, then cut the cards for Marylou while Amanda shuffled the deck we had just played.

With the first hand over I felt more relaxed. My mother had tried to teach me bridge when I was about fourteen, but she was so critical that I refused to play any more after a few lessons. I hadn't even thought of playing the game again until a few months ago, when my brother gently insisted I learn so that I could play with him and Luke. Under Jake's patient tutelage I found that I enjoyed the game, but playing with people I didn't know well brought back the insecurities fostered by my mother.

With these three women I figured I didn't have to worry too much about someone criticizing my play. I could relax and enjoy the game.

When Marylou finished the deal I picked up my cards and arranged them. I counted twenty high-card points, including a six-card spade suit to the ace-king. Marylou passed, and I opened one spade. Amanda passed, and Sophie bid two spades. That would give us the first game if we made it. Marylou passed, and once again I waited for Amanda to lead.

Once Sophie laid out the dummy, she stood up and said, "Would anybody like anything? I think I'm going to have a sandwich."

Amanda perked up. "Oh yes, I'll take some more wine, please. And maybe a ham sandwich."

"I'm fine, thanks," Marylou said.

"Me too," I said. I was too busy concentrating on the game to think about eating.

While the rest of us played out the hand, Sophie filled Amanda's wineglass and brought her the requested sandwich. Sophie sat down in her chair with her own sandwich. Catching my eye, she winked.

"Isn't it terrible about poor Janet?" Sophie asked. "I just couldn't believe something like that happened with all of us right there."

"I know," Marylou said. "I can't stop thinking about it."

Amanda hiccuped. "Excuse me." She giggled. "I did feel kinda sorry for Janet, but you know how she was. I'm just surprised somebody didn't do it long ago."

"Exactly," Sophie said. "She was always sticking her nose into everybody else's business. And this time, somebody cut it off, I guess you could say." She paused for a bite of her sandwich.

"Yeah, but who?" Amanda said. "Who do you think did it?"

Sophie shrugged. "I don't know. I mean, we all know how irritating she was, but who could have hated her enough to kill her?"

"Hated her, or feared her?" Marylou said.

I didn't contribute to the conversation, paying more attention to the game than to what they were saying. Marylou and Amanda continued to play as they talked, but I could see that Amanda's attention wasn't focused on what she was doing. Marylou wasn't much better. I ended up making five spades, but if Marylou and Amanda had been paying attention, I would have made only two.

"I know somebody who was afraid of her," Amanda said as Sophie gathered the cards for shuffling. Marylou cut the other deck, and I dealt.

"Who?" Sophie asked.

"I don't know if I should really say anything," Amanda said.

"Oh, come on, Amanda," Sophie said in an offhand tone. "What's it going to hurt? You can tell us."

"Yes, Amanda, do," Marylou urged. "After teasing us like that, you can't stop now. And you know you want to." She reached for Amanda's wineglass. "How about some more wine?"

"Sure," Amanda said. She giggled again. I suppressed a wince. Much more of her giggling, and I would have to throw something at her.

Marylou refilled the wineglass and gave it back to Amanda. "Okay, now," she said. "Spill the beans. Or the dirt, as the case may be." She laughed.

"Well," Amanda said, leaning forward, casting conspiratorial glances at us, "I know I shouldn't be telling tales out of school. But since it's just you girls, I'll tell you." She paused. "Janet was going around saying some really nasty things about someone. And if Janet was right, she could have ruined someone's career completely."

"Who?" Sophie said. "Who was she talking about?"

"Paul Hardy," Amanda said. "Janet was going around telling everyone that he must not be a very good financial planner, because he had lost some of his clients a lot of money. A *lot* of money."

"I hadn't heard that," Marylou said with a frown.

"Oh yes," Amanda said. "I heard Janet myself. And I also happened to know that Paul threatened her." She giggled. "He was certainly mad enough to kill her."

Chapter 10

Marylou said, "Well, I'm really surprised to hear that about Paul. What Janet said, I mean. He's always seemed like a pretty sharp cookie to me."

Amanda giggled again, and I gritted my teeth.

"Oh, I expect he is," Amanda said. "But you know how Janet was. You make one little mistake, and she never let you hear the end of it."

The bitterness in her tone made me suspect that Amanda had personal experience of Janet's carping on mistakes. Sophie, Marylou, and I exchanged swift glances.

"Surely Paul must have done *something*," Sophie said in a drawl. She yawned. "Janet didn't have enough imagination to just make things up."

"That's true," Marylou said, nodding.

"What was Janet going around saying?" I asked. I tried to keep my tone matter-of-fact. I had to admit, though, I was becoming increasingly fascinated by this whole situation. Janet McGreevey had apparently stirred up strong feelings in a lot of people.

Amanda was beginning to seem restive, now that playing had stopped and we were focusing more on her. She was acting like she hadn't heard my question. Maybe she would be more inclined to gossip if we started playing again.

"Who dealt?" I said.

"You did," Sophie told me.

"Oh," I said. I looked at my hand. Only eleven high-card points and even distribution. "Pass."

Amanda stared at her hand for a moment before repeating "Pass."

"Not me," Sophie said. Her eyes sparkled, and that meant she was very pleased with her hand. "One no trump."

Marylou folded her cards and laid them on the table in front of her. "Pass."

I checked my cards again. I had three queens, two jacks, and a king. "Two no trump." I didn't feel like my hand was strong enough for me to take us to game. Sophie would have to do that, depending on the strength of her hand.

Amanda passed again, and Sophie said, "Three no." When the rest of us had passed, Sophie recorded the bid. Then it was up to Marylou to lead. She played an eight of clubs.

I put my hand down on the table. Sophie took a moment to examine it before she pulled my jack of clubs from the board. Amanda carelessly pulled the queen from her hand and dropped it on the board. Sophie took the trick with the king and contemplated her next play.

Now that Amanda seemed a little more relaxed again, and her wineglass was almost empty, I decided it was time to prod her a little further. First, I got up from my chair and refilled her wineglass. She thanked me, and I sat down again, feeling a bit guilty about continuing to ply her with wine.

"My late husband left things in a bit of a mess," I said. Sophie shot me a quick glance. She knew Baxter had been very careful with money and investments, to the point that I had no financial worries. "I hate feeling like an idiot, but I've never had to think about these things before, and now I have to. Paul Hardy gave me his card last night when we met, and I was actually thinking about giving him a call."

"That might not be such a good idea," Marylou said, sounding alarmed. "I mean, if Janet was right about him, maybe you shouldn't even talk to him about anything to do with money."

"I'd like to be fair to him," I said. "Maybe he really is good at financial planning, and maybe Janet was just being vindictive for some reason." I shrugged. "But if there is something I should know before I call him, I sure want to hear it."

For a moment, Amanda didn't say anything. She gulped wine from her glass, then hiccuped. "Excuse me," she said. Her eyes appeared unfocused. "I can tell you what Janet was saying, but don't you dare tell anybody. If you tell anybody I told you, I'll swear it's a lie."

We all assured her that the story would go no further than my kitchen.

Blinking, Amanda turned to me. "Okay. This is what Janet told me. According to her, Paul sweet-talked a couple of widows into handing over their money to him to invest." She paused for another sip of wine and a couple of hiccups. "He lost most of the money, or so he told them, in a bad investment. But Janet said he really didn't lose the money, he just pretended to. It was right after that he bought himself and Shannon a new Mercedes each. Paid cash, too."

Appalled, I stared at Sophie and Marylou. If this was really true, then Paul Hardy was a criminal. And he well might have killed Janet McGreevey to stop her from spreading such talk around.

Amanda kept talking, her words becoming increasingly slurred. "Wasn't the first time, either, Janet said. Paul always goes after widows with money." She blinked at me. "So you'd better watch out, Emma. He'll be real pushy, trying to get you to let him handle your money for you."

"If Paul cheated those women out of their money, why didn't they take legal action, try to sue him or something like that?" Sophie asked. "Seems to me they could have made things pretty uncomfortable for him."

Amanda giggled again, and her giggles degenerated into hiccups. Sophie reached over and thumped her on the back, and the hiccups stopped abruptly.

"Thanks," Amanda muttered. "They were too ashamed, according to Janet. Janet said Paul slept with them. She said he does that all the time. He is good-looking, and he has a lot of women clients. Janet said he goes to bed with them, and then if something goes wrong, they're too embarrassed to admit they slept with him and gave him money."

"How did Janet find out about all of this?" Marylou asked. "If these women were too ashamed to do anything about it, then how did Janet hear about it? Surely they would've been too embarrassed to tell anyone."

"I don't know," Amanda admitted. "But Janet always knew things. She probably had people's houses bugged." That launched her into another fit of the giggles.

I resisted the urge to slap her. By now she was too drunk to play bridge, and I had no heart for the game right now. This was all pretty sordid, but that shouldn't have surprised me. In the mysteries with amateur detectives I read, the sleuths were always finding out dirty secrets like this about people. They had to, in order to get to the truth. But it was still unpleasant.

" 'Scuse me," Amanda said suddenly. "I think I'm going to throw up."

Before I could react, Sophie was out of her chair and dragging Amanda toward the bathroom just off the kitchen. Marylou and I stared at each other. I was sure her expression of dismay mirrored my own.

"Maybe I ought to just take Amanda home," Marylou said. "I don't think she's going to be in any shape to play bridge after this."

"Probably not," I agreed. "How far is her house?"

"It's in the next block, on the other side of the street. I can manage to get her that far."

"I'll go with you," I said.

Marylou shook her head. "No, I can handle her. I've done it before."

Moments after that, Sophie came back into the kitchen, towing a visibly suffering Amanda. "I think I'd better go home," Amanda said, whimpering. "I don't feel very good."

Marylou got up from her chair and went to Amanda. Wrapping her arm around the suffering woman, she said in a soothing tone, "It's okay, honey. I'll walk you home, okay?"

Amanda nodded, looking pitiful.

Judging from her expression, Sophie was grateful to relinquish her charge, and she went ahead of Marylou and Amanda to open the front door for them. I busied myself clearing the table, and I was tucking the cards into their boxes when Sophie returned.

"How about some coffee?" I said.

"Sounds good," Sophie responded. "Marylou said she was going home after she got Amanda settled. So it's just you and me. Want to play some canasta?"

"No," I said as I prepared the coffeemaker. "Not tonight. I don't think I feel up to much of anything."

"Don't start feeling sorry for Amanda," Sophie said, reading my thoughts. "She would have drunk the wine anyway, and she would have talked. That's the way she is, especially when her husband isn't around to stop her. So don't start blaming yourself or anything like that. I know you, Emma, and you're feeling responsible. But don't."

I held my tongue. Sophie did know me, and she knew how I was feeling at this moment. Perhaps she was right, but I couldn't escape feeling guilty over encouraging Amanda to drink and gossip.

We sat in silence, waiting for the coffee to finish brewing. When it was ready, I poured it out for us both and handed Sophie her cup. For once she added sugar and cream, stirring it in briskly. I decided not to comment on it.

"What about Paul Hardy?" I asked instead. "About what Amanda told us. You obviously know him better than I do. What do you think?"

Sophie shrugged. "He's attractive, and he knows it. He also has this kind of weasley charm, so I can certainly see him cozying up to little old ladies with more money than sense and talking them out of it." Her lips twisted in distaste. "But I can't quite imagine him going to bed with them, just to keep them quiet."

"The whole thing sounds pretty nasty," I said. "What I don't understand is, even if it's true, how on earth would Janet McGreevey have found out? Who in their right mind would have told her something like that?"

"Janet could appear sympathetic when she wanted to," Sophie said. "And she paid a lot of attention to people like the widows Amanda described. She lived and breathed two things, bridge and the blessed homeowners' association. She used the association as a battering ram sometimes, and if she got an idea that somebody was having money troubles, she'd find out why if she could."

I frowned, remembering the conversation that had taken place here in my kitchen a few days ago. "What about that poor woman Janet was talking about here? You remember?"

Sophie nodded. "Yes, I've been thinking about her." She took a sip of coffee. Then she looked at me with an enigmatic expression on her face. "Paul Hardy is her financial adviser."

Chilled by the possible implications, I stared back at her.

Chapter 11

"Do you really think . . ." I stuttered to a halt.

"I don't know," Sophie said. Her finger traced the circle around the edge of her coffee cup. "Marylou is a friend of hers. I don't really know her all that well."

I drank some of my coffee, grateful for the warmth. "Do you think Marylou knows anything about it?"

"Possibly," Sophie said. "Mrs. Anderson is certainly more likely to talk to Marylou about it than she would be to someone else. Like the police."

"I guess we can ask Marylou about it later," I said, not feeling very enthusiastic about the idea.

"We might not have to," Sophie said. "If there's anything to tell about this, Marylou will find out. She was planning to talk to Mrs. Anderson anyway, after Janet harangued her about it."

I didn't envy Marylou the task ahead of her. And I wasn't sure I wanted to see Paul Hardy again. Then I scolded myself for being too quick to judge. We had no idea whether any of the sleazy story Amanda had told us was really true. Perhaps Janet had made it all up simply to be nasty.

I voiced this thought to Sophie. Head cocked to one side, she considered the idea.

"It's possible," Sophie said. "Janet was definitely vindictive. If someone crossed her, she could be relentless. I just can't think of a reason she might have had it in for Paul, though."

"Did she have a happy marriage, do you think?"

Sophie laughed. "If that's a roundabout way of asking whether I think Janet cheated on Gerald, then the answer is yes. Gerald certainly cheated on her, and knowing Janet, she probably got even somehow."

"Then maybe she went after Paul, but he turned her down?" I said, thinking aloud.

"It's possible," Sophie said.

Loud music emanated from the handbag Sophie had dropped on the counter earlier.

"Excuse me," she said, getting up to retrieve her cell phone. She dug the phone out of her purse, flipped it open, and gazed at the screen. She punched a button before sticking the phone up to her ear.

"Hi, Nate," she said, "how are you doing?"

She listened for a moment. "I'm sorry to hear that." She paused again. "Why don't you come over and talk about it? Sounds like you could use some company right now."

Sophie looked at me, raising one eyebrow interrogatively. She wanted to know if he could come here. I sighed. *In for a penny, in for a pound,* I thought. "Sure," I said.

"Listen, Nate," Sophie said, "I'm not at home right now. I'm actually next door at my friend Emma's house. You remember her?" Sophie smiled reassuringly at me. "Yes, I'm sure she won't mind. Emma is very concerned, too. You just come on over here." She listened a moment longer, then ended the call with a final "Okay."

Sophie resumed her seat, placing her cell phone on the table. "He's coming right over."

"Why did he call you?" I asked. "I wasn't aware you two were that close."

"We aren't, I suppose," Sophie said. "But I don't think Nate has any other friends in the area."

If the manners I had witnessed last night were typical of Nate McGreevey, I wasn't surprised. My impression of him was that he wasn't comfortable around strangers.

Sophie read my thoughts a little too easily. "He's really a nice guy, Emma. He's a different person when he's not around his father or Janet."

"I should hope so," I said, a shade too tartly. Sophie frowned at me. "But you're right, I shouldn't judge him on just that one meeting. I could tell he didn't care for his stepmother."

"I think *despised* is probably a better word," Sophie said. "Janet tried to mother him, and he resented it. Plus he could see how other people felt about her. That certainly didn't help."

"Why on earth did his father ever marry her?" I asked. "How long were they married? I think Nate said something about his mother dying when he was ten."

"Yes, that's right," Sophie said. "I believe Gerald and Janet married when Nate was around fifteen, so that means they were married sixteen years or so."

"Maybe she was different back then," I said without much conviction.

"I should hope so," Sophie responded, wrinkling her nose. "Gerald is not a stupid man. He is a lech, but he's not dumb."

The doorbell rang, and Sophie stood up. "I'll go," she said, "if you don't mind."

I waved a hand. "Be my guest."

I sat at the table waiting. It took them longer than was necessary to return to the kitchen, and I was getting impatient and annoyed when they finally walked into the room.

Sophie held Nate's hand firmly in hers and almost pulled him into the room. "Tell him it's okay, Emma."

I stood up and walked toward them. I held out my hand. "Of course it's all right, Nate. You're welcome here."

The strain was evident on his face. I hadn't had

time to pay much attention to him last night, other than to notice how tall and thin he was. Now I could see why he had attracted Sophie's interest. He was good-looking in an understated way, though he needed to put on some weight to stop appearing gangly and ill-nourished. His eyes were a dark violet and ringed by thick lashes, but at the moment they gave evidence of his troubled state.

"Thank you, Emma," he said, relaxing slightly.

"Come and have a seat. What can I offer you to drink?"

Following Sophie to the table, Nate laughed. "I'd love a shot of scotch, but I've been sober for five years. No point in blowing it now." He smiled faintly. "How about some coffee instead?"

The pain in his voice touched me, but I left it to Sophie to console him. She patted his hand, lying on top of the table, and he gazed gratefully at her. I busied myself with pouring coffee for him.

"How do you take it?" I asked as I set the cup down.

"Black is fine, Emma, thank you," he said. He lifted the cup to his mouth and drank from it. "And thank you for inviting me over. I'm afraid I wasn't at my best last night when we met, and I sincerely regret it if I was rude to you."

Those beautiful eyes stared right into mine, and all I could read there was sincerity. "Not at all," I said. "I didn't think you were rude." *At least not to me,* I added silently.

"I hated Janet," he said abruptly. "But I didn't kill her. I swear to you, I didn't do it."

He was facing Sophie when he uttered that last sentence, and Sophie gave him a smile that had bewitched many men, young and old. I had seen it happen more times than I could even begin to remember. Nate devoured that smile with his eyes, and even an idiot could see that he was desperately in love with Sophie. Now I knew whom he had been looking at last night.

I suppressed a sigh. This situation could get very awkward. Nate appeared sincere when he said he didn't kill his stepmother, but I had to reserve judgment. Sophie, normally cynical about almost everyone and everything, appeared to believe Nate implicitly. Not unusual for her, as I knew all too well.

"Who do you think did do it?" I asked. That sounded a bit brutal, but I thought someone needed to take control of the conversation.

Startled, both Nate and Sophie shifted their attention to me.

"God knows," Nate said with bitterness. "Everyone hated Janet. I'm surprised there wasn't a long line at the door, people just waiting for their chance."

"I have to admit that she struck me as a very unpleasant woman," I said, keeping my tone as neutral as I could. "But being unpleasant doesn't make people want to kill you."

"Janet was a stone-hearted bitch," Nate said, and both Sophie and I flinched at the viciousness of his words. "I'm glad she's gone."

"You have to be careful about saying things like that," Sophie said gently. "I understand how you feel, Nate, I really do. But you can't go around talking like that, or the police really will think you did it."

Nate laughed. "They already do." He ran a hand through his short, dark hair, leaving it spiked up in several places. Sophie reached out, as if to smooth it down again, but then she pulled her hand back. I didn't think Nate noticed. "I don't know why they didn't go ahead and arrest me when I was down there giving a statement. I could tell that Lieutenant Burnes considers me the chief suspect."

"Why you?" I asked. I wanted to keep him from getting wrapped up in self-pity. Sophie was obviously too sympathetic not to encourage him. While I felt sorry for him, I knew all too well that self-pity was counterproductive, if not destructive.

"Why *not* me?" Nate asked, then had the grace to

look abashed. "Sorry. I've gotten into the habit of feeling really sorry for myself, and I know how stupid that is." He flashed a smile, and in that moment I understood Sophie's attraction to him. That smile made him a different person.

"It's easy to do," I said. "But you're right. It doesn't help the situation."

"No," Sophie said, "and Emma and I don't think you killed her. So you don't have to feel like that with us. We want to help you, Nate, any way we can."

"Thank you," he said. His eyes were locked on her face, as were hers on his. I was going to have to pour cold water on both of them if they kept this up.

"Given the fact that a lot of people had reason to despise Janet," I said firmly, regaining their attention, "we would still have to prove that someone hated her enough to murder her. Who had the most compelling motive?"

Nate shrugged. "I don't know. She was nasty to a lot of people."

"It had to be someone who was in the house last night," Sophie said. "That narrows it down."

"Yes, it does," I said. "Leaving out the three of us, who of the people in the house last night might have done it?"

Nate peered into his coffee cup. "Could I have some more coffee?" He held out his cup to me. Nodding, I took it and got up from the table to pour him some more. At this rate, I'd have to make another pot.

No one spoke until I gave Nate his cup back to him. "Thank you. Who might have done it?" He laughed suddenly. "First off, there's my father. I know he wanted to be rid of her."

"Surely he could just have divorced her," I said. "He wouldn't have to kill her." I kept my tone even, but I was rather taken aback by Nate's blunt accusation against his father. This was beginning to remind me, all too uncomfortably, of my relationship with my own parents. I eyed Nate with renewed interest.

Nate drank some coffee. He set the cup down, and like Sophie had done earlier, he traced the rim of it with one finger. "They came close to getting a divorce a couple of years ago, and I really thought Dad was going through with it. But they didn't."

"Why not?" Sophie asked.

"I think it had something to do with money," Nate said, beginning to sound like he wished he hadn't started this thread of the conversation. "Janet inherited a lot of money from one of her aunts a few years ago, and I think Dad must have used a good bit of it. Janet wasn't too happy about that."

"Surely he could have repaid her, somehow," Sophie said.

Nate shook his head. "No, Dad had a gambling problem a few years ago. I mean, he's over it now," he added hastily, seeing the shock on Sophie's face, "but it really was a big issue between them. If they had gone through with the divorce, Janet would have sucked him dry, taken everything he had because of that money of hers he lost."

That put a different spin on the situation. The amount of money Gerald McGreevey had gambled away must have been pretty substantial. With large amounts of money involved, murder might have been a solution preferable to divorce.

Nate stifled a sob. "That's why I think my dad could have killed her." He buried his head in his arms on the table. While Sophie did her best to comfort him, I sat, appalled and fascinated at the same time.

Was the answer really that simple?

Chapter 12

I rubbed my eyes and forced myself to concentrate, yet again, on the intricacies of bidding. My brother Jake had recommended the book, and I had no doubt it was helpful. At the moment, however, bidding didn't seem nearly as interesting as the events of the past two days.

I put the book on the bedside table, and Olaf took that as a signal to climb onto my chest. Hilda, nestled comfortably in my lap, protested as Olaf's tail flicked her face.

"Settle down, you two," I told them sternly, reaching to tuck Olaf's tail out of Hilda's way. With the two cats attached to me like this I was pinned to the bed. Eventually I would have to shift them both off me so I could turn out the light and go to sleep, but for now I felt cozy and comforted to have them so close.

Leaning back against the nest of pillows supporting me, I closed my eyes. The evening had been eventful and interesting, and I needed to think about it all, to try to put things in order in my mind. Though I had involved myself with the amateur murder investigation against my better judgment, I had to admit I was very curious.

Nate hadn't lingered long in my kitchen after his

dramatic announcement that he was afraid his father could have killed Janet. I think he was so embarrassed by what he had said that he couldn't get away fast enough. Sophie did her best to comfort him and to assure him that neither she nor I thought badly of him for what he had said.

I had added my voice to hers, although quite a bit less forcefully, and I was sure that Nate had realized it. It wasn't that I didn't like Nate or have some sympathy for his situation, but I had the sneaking suspicion that much of it had been an act purely for Sophie's benefit. He was so enamored of her and so desperate for her attention that I think he was in danger of overplaying his hand.

If he wasn't putting on an act, however, then he was very badly frightened about something. Was he afraid of his father? Or afraid *for* his father? The next time I was around Nate, I would have to observe him carefully.

In the meantime, Nate definitely had my sympathy where his father and stepmother were concerned. The two people who had donated sperm and eggs to create my brother Jake and me had had little interest in parenting, other than the fact that persons of their station in life were supposed to have children. I know I make it sound like Jake and I were born in test tubes, but our mother actually did give birth to us. Once she had produced a child of each gender, however, she had surgery to prevent any further pregnancies. She herself told me this on my fifth birthday, when I told her I wanted a baby sister to play with. Looking back, I'm rather astonished at the fact that she was even in the country for my birthday. That was one of the few such occasions she had been.

Given all this, I was not really surprised by the fact that Nate sounded disconnected from his father and his stepmother. I was the last person to expect a child to offer blind, loving loyalty to a parent, but I suppose part of me was shocked because I wanted to believe that somewhere, children and parents had more care for one another.

Nate's situation was an important part of his attraction for Sophie. Her parents had been no more devoted to her and her siblings than mine had been to my brother and me. Luckily for us, however, we had given each other the kind of love and support that a family should.

Nate aroused all of Sophie's protective instincts because he reminded her, at least subconsciously, of herself. Every single one of her boyfriends and both of her husbands had been very much like Nate, attractive and needy. Whether there was anything more to Nate had yet to be seen. For Sophie's sake I hoped there was more to him. She deserved the best, but she rarely got it with the men she chose.

Enough of this, I told myself. I seldom let myself spend much time thinking about my parents, or Sophie's. Still, the comparison to Nate's situation was useful, and I thought I understood him a little better now.

Even if Nate were exaggerating his anxieties over his father's role in Janet's death to gain Sophie's attention, there was real fear at the bottom of it. I had thought this already, but I became more convinced of it. Frankly, who had a better motive to kill Janet than Gerald McGreevey? If, as Nate had told us, divorce would have been difficult because of money issues, he might have opted to take an easier way out. Accidental poisoning via peanuts would be simple to arrange, and so it had proven.

I forced myself to relive those moments when Gerald was ministering to his stricken wife on the floor of the McGreevey kitchen. Part of the time he'd had his back to me, and I hadn't been able to see what he was doing. And there I was, rooted to the floor, not being of any help whatsoever. Could I have done anything to help, something that might have changed the outcome? I wasn't sure.

Had Gerald acted as quickly as he should have? Or had he purposely delayed getting Janet the antidote she needed?

That was a chilling thought. If Gerald hadn't put the peanuts in the spinach dip himself, he might have seized the opportunity to be certain that his wife didn't survive someone else's intention to kill her.

If he hated his wife enough, and if he were cold-blooded enough, he could have done exactly that. I remembered that it seemed to take a few minutes to find Janet's epinephrine.

That in itself was odd. Why hadn't she had it on her person? Gerald had looked for it on her, I recalled. And surely someone who suffered from such a deadly allergy would have kept the antidote with her at all times, just in case. Janet hadn't struck me as the kind of person to be careless of a detail like that.

No doubt the police had already considered this. I wondered what Lieutenant Burnes really made of this whole situation. He had been extremely affable, actually rather laid-back, during our conversation today. Somehow I had expected a homicide detective to be more intense, but perhaps he wasn't really convinced that this was a case of murder.

What else could it be, though? A practical joke gone horribly wrong?

I could see someone thinking it would be funny to make Janet slightly ill to pay her back for being so obnoxious, but surely the people at the bridge party realized that it was too dangerous to play a trick like that. It would have to be someone pretty stupid to try it.

Why did the face of Dan Connor immediately pop into my mind's eye? He hadn't impressed me as being particularly bright, and I had little difficulty seeing him as someone who enjoyed playing stupid practical jokes.

This was all useless speculation, and my head was beginning to ache. I gently removed Olaf from my chest and shifted Hilda off my lap so I could reach the bedside lamp. I switched out the lamp and nestled down in the bed. After brief, but vocal, complaints Hilda settled herself into her accustomed place beside my pillows, and Olaf stretched out atop the blanket-covered trunk at the foot of my bed.

I tried to clear my mind as an inducement to sleep, but for the moment it wasn't working. A new thought struck me. Motive was important in murder cases, but opportunity was just as important, especially in this case. Who had an opportunity to put the ground peanuts into the spinach dip?

After mulling this over for a few minutes, I decided this question was something I needed to discuss with Sophie and Marylou. Marylou was the one with the best opportunity to spike the spinach dip, but I pushed that thought uncomfortably aside. I just couldn't see kindly Marylou as a killer. Maybe I should talk it over with Sophie first.

Decision made, I was able to relax, and eventually sleep came.

Thanks to my feline alarm system, I woke early the next morning. Dislodging Olaf from my chest as I sat up in bed, I glanced over at the time on the cable box. Six fifteen. Well, it was certainly better than five thirty, the time Olaf generally preferred.

I went to the window and looked out into the backyard. The sky was clear, and the sun was on the rise. Suddenly, outside looked terribly inviting.

Before I could change my mind, I quickly swapped my nightgown for jogging pants and an old Rice University jersey and slipped on my walking shoes. Downstairs, I checked to be sure Olaf and Hilda had enough food and water to ensure their survival until I was back from my walk. I grabbed my keys and stuffed them in my pocket, then took a bottle of water from the refrigerator. I let myself out the front door and paused on the doorstep to breathe in the fresh cool air of morning.

This was only my third morning walk since I had moved into the neighborhood, and I was still getting used to the immediate area. The bayou was only a couple of blocks away, and it was a favorite place for the locals to walk, jog, and bicycle. After doing some stretches to get my legs ready, I set off at a leisurely pace for the bayou.

As I waited for the traffic light to change, I saw only two other people walking along the bayou at the moment. Farther down, someone was cycling rapidly away.

I crossed the street when the light changed and walked up to the paved track running along the bayou. I stretched again, just to make sure my legs felt loose and warmed up, then began walking briskly along the track, the rising sun at my back.

As I walked, I took a few sips of water from the bottle. Thus far I hadn't encountered anyone, but, glancing ahead about fifty yards, I could see a jogger approaching me at a fast pace. Something about the woman's figure seemed familiar.

The gap between us closed quickly, and soon she was near enough for me to see her face. Had I met her somewhere before? Her red hair was pulled back in a ponytail, and her face was devoid of makeup. But her considerable bosom jounced as she jogged, despite the athletic bra she wore.

Bootsie Flannigan, of course. Without the bouffant hairdo and makeup she appeared quite different, but there was no mistaking the bosom.

She had apparently recognized me, too, because her pace slowed as she came closer. I put a smile of greeting on my face and prepared to say hello, at the very least. I was not at my best first thing in the morning, but somehow I doubted Bootsie would jog on by and let me walk in peace.

"Good morning, honey," Bootsie said, coming to a halt about ten feet ahead of me. Her chest heaved a bit, and she wiped a sweatbanded wrist across her forehead. "Emma, isn't it?"

"Good morning, Bootsie, how are you?" I walked closer.

She pulled a water bottle from the holder at her waist and drank deeply before replying. Shoving the bottle back in its holder, she laughed. "I'd be doing a heckuva lot better if I didn't have to haul my rear end out here every morning and sweat like a stuck pig."

I had reached her now, and I stopped a couple of feet in front of her. "I know what you mean, but it looked like such a beautiful morning, I had to be outside for a while."

"Come on," she said, "let's walk." She turned and headed back in the direction from whence she had been jogging, and I fell into step beside her.

"So you go jogging every morning," I said. "I admire your discipline."

Bootsie laughed. "It ain't discipline, honey, it's self-preservation. The way I like to eat and drink, I got to do something to keep from being as big as the side of a barn."

"Even so," I said, smiling at her self-deprecating honesty, "I admire you for doing it." I drank more water.

"How are you settling in?"

"Fine so far," I said, "though I still have plenty of boxes to sort out."

"Moving's a bitch, isn't it?" Bootsie laughed.

"It's not my favorite thing to do," I said.

"How did you come to pick our neighborhood?"

Amused by her friendly curiosity, but hoping she wouldn't press me for too many details, I said, "Sophie Parker is my best friend, and when I wanted to move to a new neighborhood, she told me the house next door to her was on the market. I came to see it, and I liked it and the neighborhood. So that was that."

"I like Sophie," Bootsie said. "That girl has balls."

Startled into laughter, all I could mutter was "uh-huh."

"You know what I mean," Bootsie went on. "She knows her own mind, and she ain't afraid to speak it. She's a lot like me." She laughed. "And that ain't as bad as it sounds."

I couldn't think of a suitable rejoinder for that, so for the moment I didn't say anything. I glanced sideways at her, only to find her eyeing me with a speculative gleam in her eye.

"It's okay, honey," she said, "you don't have to worry about offending me. It takes a lot to get through this thick old hide of mine."

"I'll keep that in mind," I said, my tone dry.

Bootsie punched me lightly on the arm. "I like you, too, even though I don't know you very well yet. But I reckon if you're Sophie's best friend, you must be A-OK."

"Thank you," I said. "I appreciate the commendation."

I decided it was time to direct the conversation into another channel. "You must be pretty upset about what happened the other night."

"What?" She stumbled but quickly regained her stride. "Oh, you mean Janet."

"Yes. You've known her for a long time, haven't you?" I tried to keep my tone as nonchalant and innocent-sounding as possible.

"Yeah, I did," Bootsie said. "And I disliked her the whole time."

"Really?" I said. "Seems to me that just about everybody disliked her."

"Is the pope Catholic?" She snickered. "Honey, that woman had a gift for irritating the hell out of anyone she ever met. And it usually didn't take her more than five minutes to do it."

"I'm surprised people put up with her, then."

Bootsie sighed heavily. "If it hadn't been for Gerald

and Nate, I don't reckon anybody would have. I'll never understand what Gerald saw in that woman."

Something in her tone intrigued me. She sounded bitter. I wondered if she'd had designs on Gerald herself at some point.

"It's often difficult, from outside a relationship, to understand what makes two people choose each other," I said. People had often wondered, and not too politely, why I had married a man nearly twenty years older than I was.

"Like me and Dan," Bootsie said unexpectedly. "I know people snicker at us behind our backs, but I don't give a rat's ass what they think."

"Good for you," I said, feeling slightly guilty for having rude thoughts about that very thing. She was right. It wasn't anyone's business but theirs, and I knew all too well how galling it was to have others sneer at you, despite the fact that they really knew nothing about the relationship.

"Good morning, ladies," a voice called out behind us. I turned to see Carlene Newberry approaching us at a steady clip.

Beside me, Bootsie muttered, "Oh, go away, bitch."

This should prove interesting, I thought as I waved at Carlene.

Chapter 13

"Emma, how are you?" Carlene smiled as she came to a stop in front of Bootsie and me. "Morning, Bootsie. It's just as well I ran into you. I need to talk to you about something."

"Is it something private?" I asked. "If you like I can walk on while you talk."

Carlene put a restraining hand on my arm. "Heavens, no, Emma. Let's all walk together, shall we?" She stepped between Bootsie and me, and we fell into stride along with her.

Neither of them spoke, though I had expected Carlene to talk to Bootsie about whatever it was she wanted. When the silence lengthened, I decided to break it.

"We were talking about how awful it was," I said, "you know, the other night at the McGreeveys' house. Poor Janet."

Carlene snickered. "I'm sure you do think it was awful, Emma, and I suppose it was. If it had been anyone other than Janet, I'd probably be more grief-stricken, but frankly, I'm not."

I hadn't liked the woman myself, and I admitted it freely, but it struck me as rather cold and callous—and sad—that no one appeared to be mourning her. And if it were true that Carlene was having an affair with Gerald, it seemed even worse for Carlene to be talking this way.

Carlene must have read some of my feelings in my face, because her expression hardened. "Look, Janet never understood the most basic thing about friendship, that you have to genuinely care about someone else's well-being besides your own. She had no idea what empathy was."

"Ain't that the truth?" Bootsie said. "What did you want to see me about, Carlene?"

Carlene had set a brisk pace, and I was getting a bit winded. I deliberately slowed down, and Carlene adjusted her gait to mine. Bootsie followed suit. I drank some water while they talked. The sun was really warming up the day.

"Gerald asked me to help him plan the service," Carlene said. "Of course, we don't know just when they'll release the body, but he wants to be prepared."

"What do you want *me* to do?" Bootsie asked. Her tone was decidedly peevish, and I couldn't decide whether she was hurt that Gerald hadn't asked her or because he had asked Carlene instead.

"Gerald really should have asked you, and I told him that," Carlene said in a tone intended to mollify. "After all, you were probably Janet's *oldest* friend."

Except for that slight emphasis on the one word, Carlene sounded perfectly warm and sincere, but I could tell from Bootsie's sharp intake of breath that the hit had registered. I was witnessing some very interesting dynamics between these two—and that was no understatement.

"Yeah, I knew Janet longer than anybody, even longer than Gerald. Hell, I was the one that introduced them to each other." Her tone indicated she was none too happy about that fact.

"And that's why I think you should really be helping Gerald with all this," Carlene said sweetly. "But he's been so distracted by everything, I don't think he's really thought things through properly. So would you mind helping me?"

"I guess not," Bootsie said. "What can I do?"

"Will you go with me to the funeral home?"

Bootsie said she would, and for the moment, they discussed their respective schedules to pick out a time convenient for them both. When they had finished, Bootsie turned abruptly away and started walking in the other direction. "See you later," she called over her shoulder. "Bye, Emma."

"Bye, Bootsie. Have a good one," I called after her.

"That woman," Carlene said good-naturedly. "She really is something else."

"I don't know her all that well," I said, trying to keep a note of censure out of my voice, "but I like her. She's very down-to-earth."

Carlene laughed. "Well, if that's a polite way of saying she's vulgar, then I'd have to agree." She laughed again, but when I didn't join in, she said, "Sorry, Emma, I shouldn't be such a cat about her, but she always acts like I've got dog poop on my shoes whenever I'm around her."

"I noticed," I said dryly. "But surely you don't care all that much whether she likes you."

"Not really, I suppose," Carlene said, shrugging, "but it does make things awkward sometimes. We always end up at the same neighborhood bridge parties, and it would be easier if she were friendlier."

I forbore to ask why Bootsie didn't like her, but Carlene was apparently in a chatty, confiding mood this morning.

"She's jealous of me," she said.

"Because you're younger and more attractive?"

Carlene cut me a sideways glance. I hadn't meant that to sound catty, but I couldn't help it if she took it that way.

"That may be part of it," she said, her tone suddenly cooler. "But mostly it's because of Gerald."

"Just because you work with him?" I wasn't about to accuse her of having an affair with Gerald, though I wondered what Sophie would have done, were she in my place. She might very well have said something about it.

By now we had reached a major intersection, and rather than crossing it and continuing down along the bayou, we turned and headed back. I was feeling ready for some caffeine and some breakfast, and Carlene probably had to go to work.

"Partly that," she said. "She thinks I have my cap set for Gerald." She laughed. "Isn't that the way they used to put it in romance novels?"

"Yes, it is," I agreed. "Have you?"

"Well, you certainly don't pull any punches," Carlene said with a short laugh.

"I know that was rather rude of me," I said, half apologetically, "but I can't help wondering." I didn't add, *especially after the way you behaved the night Janet died.*

Carlene laughed again. "I can see now why you and Sophie are such good friends. Sophie always shoots straight from the hip, and I guess you do, too."

"Maybe," I said, "but you still haven't answered my question."

"I work pretty closely with Gerald," she said, "and I have to admit I find him attractive. But, no, I haven't set my cap for him." That made her laugh again. "I just find it amusing that Bootsie thinks I have."

"Why should it matter to her?" I thought I knew the answer, but perhaps Carlene would confirm it.

"There's no reason you should know it," she said, "unless one of the neighborhood gossips—like Marylou Lockridge, for example—told you the story."

"No, no one's told me anything," I said.

Carlene paused for a drink of water. Placing her bottle back in its holster, she said, "Years ago, Bootsie and Gerald's first wife, Nancy, were really close. When Nancy died, Bootsie, who was single at the time, stepped in and helped out a lot, especially with Nate. I figure she must have been half in love with Gerald already, but I don't think it was long before she started casting herself in the role of the second Mrs. McGreevey."

"Why didn't it happen?"

"Bootsie introduced Gerald to Janet, who was somebody she knew from working on one of the committees for the Houston Rodeo. And for whatever reason, Gerald and Janet started dating, and then they got married."

"And Gerald never realized Bootsie was in love with him?" Surely Gerald McGreevey wasn't that dense? Or perhaps he simply hadn't cared.

Carlene shrugged. "You never can tell with Gerald. Bootsie can be pretty cloying, if you give her a chance. Give her an inch, and she'll take three miles. Gerald hates that."

"So Bootsie was out, and Janet was in," I said.

"Yep, and it didn't hurt that Janet came from a pretty well-to-do family," Carlene said.

"My, my, Carlene, you do sound cynical," I said lightly. "You mean it wasn't a love match?"

"About the only person in this world that Gerald loves is Gerald," Carlene said, endeavoring to match my light tone, but failing ever so slightly. I thought she cared a lot more about Gerald than she was willing to admit. "I've worked with him for almost seven years, and believe me, I know how he is. I have no illusions about him."

"I'll take your word for it," I said. By now we were approaching the intersection where we could cross back to our neighborhood. "I get off here, I'm afraid. Are you coming?"

"No," Carlene said, "I'm going to run for a few minutes, I think. See you later, Emma." With that, she turned and ran off, back down the way we had just come.

As I crossed the street and headed for home, I

mulled over the events of the morning so far. I might have to come out for walks every morning, if they were all as productive as this one in terms of exposing neighborhood skeletons in the closet. When I told Sophie about all this she would be sorry she hadn't been in on any of it, but even juicy secrets couldn't induce her to get up and walk this early in the morning. Besides, she had that invisible treadmill, the one she insisted she used but that I had never seen.

I smiled. I had no idea how she did it. Maybe her metabolism just functioned at a much higher rate than mine, but she did manage to keep to an appropriate weight without seeming to exert herself. She probably just pretended to exercise on that invisible treadmill so as not to make me feel bad. Sophie could be very sweet when she wanted to be.

And, speak of the little dickens, there she was, waiting outside my front door when I walked up the street.

"Where have you been, Emma? I must have knocked for five minutes on the back door before I realized you weren't home. I was starting to get worried." From the petulant tone in her voice, I almost expected her to stamp her foot at me, the way she did when she was eight years old.

"Good morning to you, too," I said, raising my voice slightly as I approached her. I fished my keys out of my pocket. "Remind me to give you a key to the back door and this one."

"Sure," Sophie said. "But don't tell me you've actually been out exercising this morning."

"Okay, I won't tell you," I said. I unlocked the door, opened it, and motioned for her to precede me. I was about to shut the door when someone hailed me from the front walk.

"Morning, Emma," Marylou Lockridge said, huffing up to the door. "Mind if I come in, too?" She held up a plate. "I've got a fresh batch of coffee cake."

"Well, of course," I said, "come on in." I let her pass by me, and then I shut the door. "Goodness,

Marylou, have you already been up and baking this morning?"

"Oh, sometimes I don't sleep too well," she said with a little laugh, "and then I just get up and start cooking or baking. Something to keep my mind and hands occupied."

I laid a comforting hand on her arm as we walked toward the kitchen behind Sophie. She didn't have to explain any further. I knew just what she meant. Since Baxter died, I often found myself sleepless in the early morning hours. When I did, I had to get up and away from the bed, all too aware that he wasn't there beside me. Instead of baking, however, I cleaned.

"Y'all sit down, and let me get you some coffee," I said. "And I'll get some plates for that coffee cake. I can already smell it. Do we need a knife to cut it?"

"No," Marylou said with a chuckle, busy unwrapping it, "it's already cut and ready to eat."

"Morning, Marylou, how are you?" Sophie asked. She looked perfectly perky in her turquoise velour warm-up pants and a jade-green top. Her hair was perfectly styled, and she could have just stepped out of an ad for a health club. I shook my head admiringly. She always looked absolutely perfect.

Marylou and I, on the other hand, were far more ordinary. I figured my hair was probably sticking up the way it always did when I exercised, and I wiped my face with a paper towel. I was still glowing from my walk, and I drank more water in an effort to cool down. Marylou was slightly better groomed than I was this morning, but the shadows under her eyes gave evidence of her interrupted sleep.

I washed my hands and dried them while Sophie and Marylou chatted in desultory fashion behind me. Then I prepared for the coffee by retrieving mugs from the cabinet, spoons from the drawer, and cream from the refrigerator.

Taking a place at the table, I reached for a slice of Marylou's coffee cake. It was warm in my hand, and the most heavenly aroma of mingled cinnamon and nutmeg drifted up to my nose. I took a bite, savoring the taste. "Marylou, this is delicious," I said. "You definitely have the touch when it comes to baking."

Marylou beamed at me. "Thank you, Emma. I'm not very good at a lot of things, but I do like to bake."

"Do you ever take orders?" I asked. "I'm hopeless when it comes to baking, but I'd love to have something like this to take to my brother and his partner. They would absolutely adore this coffee cake."

"Good gracious, Emma," Marylou said, "you don't have to pay me to bake something for you. I wouldn't hear of it. I'd be happy to do it for you."

"Thank you," I said, not surprised that she was refusing any kind of payment for her skills. I'd find some way around that. "But the least I can do is buy the ingredients, and if you'll write down what you need, I'll get it all the next time I go shopping."

"I'll do that," Marylou promised.

Sophie, having brought the coffeepot to the table, commenced pouring coffee for all of us. "And you might as well make up your mind, Marylou, to let Emma pay you. She's as stubborn as a mule when it comes to things like that. If you don't let her do something, she'll feel like she's taking advantage of you."

"That's just plain silly," Marylou said. "What else have I got to do but bake something for a friend?" She offered me a mock glare. "And don't you dare try to pay me, Emma."

"We'll see," I said, then decided to change the subject. "Let me tell you about my morning."

"What happened?" Sophie asked. "Couldn't have been much, because you were just out taking a walk." She blew on her coffee, then took a sip.

"That's where you're wrong," I said sweetly. "I ran into Bootsie Flannigan on my walk. And then Carlene Newberry popped up. Very interesting undercurrents between those two, let me tell you."

"We know that already," Sophie said. "But what happened?"

I related the gist of the conversations I'd had that morning, and Sophie actually remained quiet for once. Marylou hung on my every word.

"I had no idea that it was Bootsie who introduced Gerald and Janet," Sophie said. "Very interesting. Poor Bootsie. I'm sure if she'd had any idea what was going to happen, she would have kept Janet as far away from Gerald as she could."

"Exactly," Marylou said. "Now, I never knew Nancy, Gerald's first wife. I only moved into this neighborhood about five years ago, when I married Mr. Lockridge, but some of the women who've lived here a long time told me what a lovely person she was."

"And that makes it even stranger that Gerald would marry someone like Janet," Sophie said. "What on earth did he see in her?"

"According to Carlene," I said, "it was money. She said Janet came from a well-to-do family, and Gerald basically married her because of that."

Marylou nodded. "It's true, Janet's family was very well off. I think when her parents died she and her sister inherited a lot of money and some property."

"She has a sister?" I asked, surprised. "This is the first time I've heard anyone mention her."

"I hardly ever heard Janet mention her, actually," Marylou said. "I don't think they got along at all. Plus I think she lives in Denver, or maybe San Francisco." She shook her head. "Anyway, she and Janet didn't see each other very often, I don't think."

Sophie laughed. "Then this sister must be a really nice person, if she didn't want to have anything to do with Janet."

"Sophie," I said, mock-severely, "I'm going to have to give you a big bowl of milk for breakfast."

She purred at me. I looked at Marylou and rolled my eyes. Marylou laughed.

After pretending to drink cream right out of the pitcher, Sophie turned serious. "So, Marylou, do you think that Bootsie has been carrying a torch for Gerald all this time?"

"Probably." Marylou sighed. "The poor woman. And Gerald treats her like one of the boys, most of the time. Good ol' Bootsie, what a gal. You know what I mean."

Sophie and I nodded. We had both had plenty of experience with that kind of treatment from our brothers. In my case, at least, it was done with great affection, and not contempt. Somehow I didn't think Bootsie was that lucky.

"What's our next move?" Sophie sat forward in her chair, both elbows inelegantly propped on the table. "How about another bridge party?"

"So soon?" I asked, suppressing a sigh. It would be one thing if we were actually playing bridge and having fun, but it was something else if the next bridge party went like the one we'd had with Amanda Graham.

"Oh, lighten up, Emma," Sophie said. "How else are we going to poke our noses into everybody's business?"

I threw my hands up while Marylou laughed. "Okay, I give. More bridge. But who this time?"

Marylou and Sophie spoke in unison. "Bootsie."

Chapter 14

Olaf hopped into the box the minute I opened it.

"How am I supposed to unpack this box if you want to play in it?"

Olaf blinked at me for a moment. He bent his head and sniffed at the contents of the box—books—and then he hopped out. Olaf loved books—if he could sleep on top of them or chew on them. Years ago he had ruined several collectible books before I had learned not to leave them with any corners or edges exposed on a shelf or table.

Hilda, stretched out across the back of the sofa nearby, regarded us both with marked disinterest. Olaf took up position on the floor near the box, his tail twitching like a semaphore behind him.

"Thank you, Olaf," I said before reaching into the box. It contained the pride of Baxter's extensive collection of first edition mysteries. These were destined for the glass-fronted bookshelves Baxter had bought especially for them. I pulled the first two books from the box—dust-jacketed copies of Margery Allingham's *The Tiger in the Smoke* and *The Estate of the Beckoning Lady.* I regarded them for a moment.

I met Baxter eleven years ago at a book signing at the local mystery bookstore. One of my favorite English mystery writers, Robert Barnard, was speaking there, and I didn't want to miss him. By the time I reached the bookstore, most of the seats for the event were taken, and I chose one next to an attractive older man. He smiled as I sat down, and I was immediately struck by the way that smile lit his eyes. I think I fell in love with him that very moment, though I didn't realize it until later.

Throughout the program I kept stealing glances at the man next to me, and often I found him regarding me with that same sweet smile. I did my best to focus on what the author was saying, but to this day I couldn't tell you much about what Mr. Barnard told us that night. I do remember the wonderful twinkle in his eye, however, when I told him how much I enjoyed his books. He was appreciative of the stack of hardcover books I had brought with me to have signed.

While the smiling stranger and I waited for our turn to have our books signed, he started chatting with me. First he asked me whether I had read Mr. Barnard's new book yet, and I had to confess I hadn't.

"It's excellent," he told me. "Have you read many of his books?" He gestured to the bag I had with me. "I see you've brought a few to have signed."

"Yes," I said, "I've read everything except this new one. He's one of my favorites." I paused a moment. "I love English mysteries."

"As do I," he said. He had a lovely baritone voice. "P. D. James, Ruth Rendell, Kate Charles, Frances Fyfield, Reginald Hill—among the current writers, that is. But I do love the classics, too, like Margery Allingham and Agatha Christie."

"Margery Allingham is one of my favorites," I exclaimed. "And I love all the others you mentioned, too."

"Then you are obviously a woman of taste and perception," he said, his eyes dancing wickedly. That's when I knew he was flirting with me, and for once in my life, I didn't bolt for the nearest exit like I usually did any time a man evinced interest in me.

"Baxter Diamond," he said, holding out his hand.

"Emma Brett," I said, offering my own. His hand felt warm and strong as it clasped mine.

"I haven't had dinner yet," he said. "I know I'm being extremely presumptuous, Emma, but perhaps you would join me for dinner after this is finished?" He quirked an eyebrow toward the front of the store where Mr. Barnard was signing books and talking to his readers.

"I'd love to," I said, then immediately cursed myself for sounding so eager. At this rate he would think I was desperate for attention. *Slow down, Emma,* I told myself sternly.

To my relief, he smiled and said, "That would be lovely."

After the signing I followed Baxter's car in my own to a neighborhood restaurant, the Raven Grill. Over a delicious dinner Baxter and I took turns talking about ourselves. I found out he had been married before, to a woman who had died of cancer fifteen years before. They never had children, and he was forty-eight years old.

At the time we met I was just about to turn thirty. I had always been drawn to older men, and he had a quiet air of confidence and repose that attracted me strongly. By the time we were ready to leave the restaurant I felt more comfortable with him than I ever had with any man other than my brother. I gave him my phone number without hesitation, and I was on tenterhooks the next day until he called me.

We were married three months later. My brother, who had taken to Baxter immediately, gave me away. I had invited my parents to the wedding as a matter of form, but my mother, calling from London, told me, "I'm so sorry, Emma, but we simply can't get away to be there."

Frankly, I was relieved. No bride likes to be upstaged at her own wedding, and my mother could not bear *not* being the complete center of attention. My father sulked if he thought anyone was flirting with my mother, who taunted him deliberately with her latest conquests, and the whole mess resembled a very bad stage farce. Being the offspring of walking clichés was rather tiresome.

I hugged the books to my chest and tried to keep the tears at bay. Married life with Baxter had been everything I had ever dreamed about. We did have the occasional argument, sometimes quite a vigorous one, but we never went to bed angry with each other. Everything seemed perfect—until the day six months before when the police called to tell me he had been killed in an accident on the Gulf Freeway.

I breathed deeply several times to steady myself, then began calmly placing the books in the bookcase. I arranged them as Baxter would have, by author and then by title, and when I had finished, I closed the doors of the bookcase and leaned against them. I never felt closer to him than when I was near the books that we both had loved. The shared passion that first drew us together comforted me now.

After a while I turned back to the empty boxes. Olaf had taken up residence in one, so I left that one for him to nap in for a few days. I broke the others down and took them out to the garage. I would soon have to take a load of cardboard to the recycling place, I thought, eyeing the stack of flattened boxes.

Deciding that I'd had enough of unpacking for the day, I prepared a sandwich and some tea for lunch. I took them upstairs to the room I had designated my study and sat down at the computer. I would check e-mail, then play a little bridge to prepare for tonight. I wasn't really looking forward to bridge with Bootsie and Dan the boy toy, but I resigned myself to it.

Hilda followed me upstairs and sat beside my chair, chattering at me, trying to claim my attention. I scratched her head and ears with my left hand while I ate my sandwich and operated the computer with my right. Eventually she decided she'd had enough attention, and she curled up in a spot she liked in the corner and went to sleep.

The few e-mails I had received I dealt with quickly; then I opened the bridge game and played a couple of rubbers. When I next looked at the clock, it was a little after two.

Yawning a bit, I shut down the computer before taking my glass and plate back downstairs to the kitchen. I did a little stretching to work the kinks out of my back and neck.

What should I do now?

Spying the list of ingredients Marylou had given me, I decided I might as well go to the grocery store. Jake and Luke had invited me and Sophie for dinner tomorrow night, and I wanted to have the coffee cake to take to them. Marylou had assured me she would be happy to bake it tomorrow.

I ran back upstairs to change clothes and apply a little makeup. When I ran errands, I didn't like leaving the house unless I looked halfway presentable. I supposed I was that much like my mother.

There were a couple of grocery stores nearby, and I drove to the one Sophie had recommended, just on the other side of the bayou from my neighborhood. The parking lot was pretty full, but I found a space near the street and parked. The cold air blasted me as I walked inside and claimed one of the few carts waiting there.

I extracted my shopping list from my purse, then carefully closed the purse and set it in the seat of the cart. A friend had once had her wallet lifted from her open purse at a grocery store when her back was turned, and ever since then I had been very careful with my own.

This was only my second visit to this particular store, and I took my time walking around, orienting myself to the arrangement. As I went through I found various items on my list and added them to the basket.

Coming around the end of the pet food aisle, where

I had found food for Olaf and Hilda, I bumped into another cart.

"I'm sorry," I said to the other woman. "I didn't see you in time."

"No problem," she said. "I wasn't watching where I was going." She smiled to show that she wasn't annoyed.

We started to pass each other, but then recognition dawned for us both at the same time. "I'm sorry, Shannon, I didn't realize for a moment it was you."

Shannon Hardy laughed. "I know. Me too. Emma, right?"

I nodded.

"How are you settling in to the neighborhood?" she asked.

"Pretty well so far," I said. "I'm still getting used to this store, though. I don't know where everything is yet, but I'm getting there."

"I shop here all the time," Shannon said, "so if there's something you haven't found, I can probably tell you where it is."

"Thanks," I said. I glanced at my list. "I haven't found the flour and spices yet."

"Come on," Shannon said, pushing her cart forward. "They're a couple of aisles over."

I followed her, and she led me to what I needed. "Thanks, I appreciate it."

"Are you going to bake something?" Shannon asked, eyeing my choices with interest. "I'm terrible at baking, but luckily Paul doesn't care. He doesn't much like cakes or pies."

I laughed. "I'm not very good at baking, either. I'm buying the ingredients for a coffee cake, and Marylou Lockridge is going to bake it for me. She's wonderful at it."

Shannon's eyes grew round. "Marylou Lockridge!" She almost squeaked the words, her voice had risen so high. "I wouldn't let her bake anything for me if I were you, Emma."

"What do you mean?" My voice must have sounded harsher than I intended, because Shannon drew back slightly.

"I probably shouldn't say anything," Shannon began, and that of course meant that she was going to say something, and probably something I wouldn't want to hear. "But, after all, it was Marylou's spinach dip that killed Janet McGreevey."

"Marylou wasn't responsible for that," I said firmly. "Someone else put the peanuts in the spinach dip."

Shannon leaned closer and dropped her voice to almost a whisper. "I wouldn't be so sure of that if I were you." She glanced around. "They say she poisoned all three of her husbands, you know."

Chapter 15

I couldn't help myself. I burst out laughing. The thought of dear, sweet Marylou Lockridge as a serial poisoner was just too funny.

Obviously affronted, Shannon drew back and folded her arms across her chest. She looked a bit like a short-haired, Malibu Barbie about to have a tantrum.

"You can laugh if you want to," she said, almost spitting the words at me, "but you just ask around the neighborhood. All three of her husbands have died under odd circumstances."

She really was serious. Or at least she appeared to be. I wondered if she had heard the talk about her husband, and his putative motive for murdering Janet McGreevey. Maybe this was her way of deflecting interest from him.

I stopped laughing, regarding her warily. "Sorry, I didn't mean to laugh at you like that. It just took me by surprise." I paused for a breath. "I'll admit that I don't know Marylou very well, and I certainly don't know her life story. But I just can't see her as a poisoner. You have to admit it's a stretch."

"I know," Shannon said, slightly mollified now. "She looks like everyone's picture of their favorite grandmother. All sweet and cuddly and all that." Her eyes narrowed. "But she can be pretty tough, believe you me."

"I guess I'll have to keep my eye on her," I said with a straight face, though I could feel the laughter welling up again.

"You do that," Shannon said. She smiled, and her smile looked about as real as Malibu Barbie's. "Well, it's been real nice talking with you, Emma, but I'd better get on with my shopping. You'll have to come over some night for bridge, okay?"

"I'd like that," I said, trying to match her faux-sincere tone. "We'll chat later." I waved at her as she pushed her cart away toward the front of the store.

I headed my cart in the other direction. I didn't want to run into her again before I finished shopping.

I concentrated on finding the remaining items on my list, and to my relief, there was no sign of Shannon in the checkout lines when I was ready to pay for my groceries.

While I waited in line, I mulled over what Shannon had said to me. Though I was highly suspicious of her motives in telling me such a tale, I couldn't dismiss what she had said completely. I liked to think of myself as a fair judge of character—no doubt everyone likes to think that—and I had taken to Marylou pretty quickly. That in itself was unusual. I'm not one to warm up fast to strangers.

I knew, however, that a killer could be lurking behind the most innocent of faces. Add to that the fact that I really didn't know Marylou very well, and I was left with a tiny bit of doubt gnawing at me.

I started unloading my cart on the belt, and the checker scanned the items as they reached him. He smiled at me, and I smiled vaguely back, still lost in thought.

I couldn't very well come right out and ask Marylou if she had poisoned her husbands. Nor did I think I could tell her what Shannon had said, even as one friend to another.

"Guess what people are saying about you, Marylou?" Or maybe, "Marylou, did you know people are saying you murdered all three of your husbands?"

No, I couldn't do that. It was too weird.

The checker claimed my attention, and I fumbled in my wallet for my debit card. I swiped it through the machine, then followed the prompts till the process was complete.

After the cold air of the grocery store, I welcomed the heat of the day outside—for about three minutes. Then the sweating started. Reaching the car and unlocking it, I cranked it and turned the air-conditioning on full blast before loading my groceries in the trunk.

There was a place for carts close to my car, and I kept an eye out while I pushed the cart into it. I imagined how stupid I would feel if someone jumped into my car and drove off in it while I was disposing of the cart. If I didn't hate it so much when people left carts willy-nilly around the parking lot, I wouldn't have bothered with mine. But I just couldn't leave it out in the lot.

Thankful that no one had stolen my car while I was obeying my compulsion, I got in the car and drove home, enjoying the cool air inside.

As I unloaded the groceries at home, I decided I would talk to Sophie about what Shannon Hardy had told me. Sophie had known Marylou for almost two years now, and she was a pretty shrewd judge of character—at least where women were concerned.

Not a minute after I finished putting away the last of the groceries, I heard a knock at the back door. I went to answer it for Sophie, of course.

"Hi, Emma," she said. "Been shopping?"

"Yes," I said, "I went to the grocery store. I wanted to get the ingredients for the coffee cake. Marylou said she would bake it for me tomorrow afternoon so I can take it with me tomorrow night."

"What time do you want to leave?" Sophie dropped down into a chair.

"How long do you think it will take to get to the Heights from here, especially with the evening traffic?" I hadn't been to Jake's house since I had moved.

"I'd say at least thirty minutes," Sophie said, considering, "but probably more like forty-five. You know what traffic is like on the Loop in the evening."

"Good point," I said. "Then why don't we leave about six fifteen? Some of the traffic may have cleared by then."

"Sounds good."

"Would you like something to drink?"

"No, thanks," Sophie said. She seemed a bit too quiet. I wondered what was going on. I knew better than to inquire, however. She would tell me when she was ready.

I fetched a bottle of water from the fridge and brought it with me to the table. I drank about a third of it before setting it down, then smiled at Sophie. "Sorry, but I needed that. It's so humid outside today, and I was really thirsty."

"Would you like to go for a swim?"

Sophie had a beautiful pool, and I was tempted for a moment to say yes. The thought of immersing myself in the water was appealing. But if I swam, I'd have to wash my hair afterward, and I didn't want to bother with it today.

"Thanks, but not today," I said. "Maybe tomorrow, though."

Sophie shrugged. "Sure, just help yourself. Go swimming whenever you like. If I'm not there, Esperanza will let you in."

"I will, thanks," I said. "Now, I've got something interesting to tell you."

She immediately sat up and looked more alert. "What?"

"I ran into Shannon Hardy at the grocery store— literally." I laughed. "And she told me the most outrageous thing."

"What was on Barbie's mind today?" She noted my

expression. "Sad, but true, I know. Don't tell me you didn't think the same thing."

"Touch." I grinned. "She told me that 'people say' Marylou poisoned all three of her husbands, and she thinks Marylou poisoned Janet, too."

I expected Sophie to respond with laughter, the way I had. When she didn't, I was taken aback.

"Don't tell me you believe it," I said.

"No, of course I don't believe it," she said, almost snapping at me. "Not really. But Shannon wasn't making it up, Emma. People have said that. About the husbands, I mean. Not about Janet." She frowned. "At least not yet."

"I just can't believe Marylou is a poisoner," I said. "But apparently other people do. Why?"

"Marylou was married for thirty-two years to the first husband," Sophie said. "He was the love of her life, she told me. They got married the day after they graduated from high school. When he died about fifteen years ago, their kids were grown and out of the house. Marylou started dating after a while, and she met someone she liked. They got married. He died of a heart attack six years later."

"That sounds perfectly natural to me," I said.

Sophie arched an eyebrow at me. "Yeah, you'd think so, wouldn't you? But the thing is, he was really overweight, and Marylou told me he would eat a whole cake a day if she didn't watch him."

"So, what? She fed him to death? Is that it?" I was appalled.

Sophie shrugged. "That's one interpretation I've heard. He ate so much and got so overweight his heart finally gave out."

"What was the alleged reason for her wanting him dead?"

"Marylou said he could be violent, and she got to the point that she was afraid of him."

"Why didn't she just leave him? She's a smart woman. Surely she knew she had options."

"Again, yes, that's the logical thing, but there were complications."

"Like what?" I was struggling with these revelations about Marylou. Had I misjudged her?

"He was a gambler, and he had run up a lot of debts. Marylou said that, after he died, the only thing that saved her from losing the house—it was in his name—was a huge life insurance policy he had. He didn't have any kids, so she got everything. She was able to pay off his debts and keep her house."

I shook my head. "Sounds like a really bad movie of the week."

Sophie just rolled her eyes. "Doesn't it just? I couldn't believe it when Marylou told me the story. I swear I've seen something like it on Lifetime or one of the cable channels."

"Poor Marylou," I said. "How awful for her."

"Yeah," Sophie said, "but it sorta gets worse."

"How so?"

"Husband number three, Mr. Lockridge," Sophie said. "He was another one who seemed really nice—until they got married. Then he turned into a tyrant. Made her sell her house and move into his, the one next door. He was possessive, didn't like Marylou going anywhere or doing anything unless he gave his approval. But the saddest thing is, Marylou really loved him."

I very carefully didn't look at Sophie. She was talking about Marylou, but she could just as easily have been talking about herself and the marriage now ending in divorce.

"How awful," I said.

"It's okay, Emma," Sophie said, not deceived. "I'm handling it just fine. You don't need to worry about me."

I met her gaze and was reassured by what I read there. She did seem to be handling her situation well, but she obviously didn't want to dwell on it. "Okay, so what happened to Mr. Lockridge?"

"One night when Marylou was out playing bridge, he choked on something. He was home by himself when it happened, and he tried calling 911, but by the time the paramedics reached him he was dead."

"Then how could people say Marylou poisoned him? That's just vicious nonsense."

"You know how rumors spread. It doesn't matter what the facts are, things are going to get distorted," Sophie said. "The thing is, the deaths of husbands number two and number three were pretty convenient for Marylou—if you want to look at it that way."

"I suppose so," I said. "But frankly I think it's all nonsense. Now that you've told me about it, I'm relieved. I don't believe Marylou's a killer."

"I don't either," Sophie said, "but I guess it's better that you know what the rumors are based on."

"Definitely," I said. "Now, do you think we should say anything to Marylou? I mean, about what Shannon said to me? I don't want to."

"I don't think you need to," Sophie said, frowning. "Marylou is perfectly aware of what people have said in the past, and she's not going to be that surprised to know that people are saying it now."

"The really absurd thing is people saying she murdered Janet McGreevey," I said.

"Not really, if you look at it from their point of view," Sophie said.

"What do you mean?"

"Oh, you know," Sophie said airily, waving a hand around, "she's in the market for husband number four, and she wants Gerald McGreevey. So just get Janet out of the way, and there you are."

"That's utterly ridiculous," I said; then I laughed. Sophie just shrugged.

"Anyway, I'll bet you that's what some people are saying," she said.

"Maybe so, but I think the police will have to look elsewhere for Janet's murderer."

Sophie looked away from me, but not before I caught the odd expression on her face.

"Okay," I said, softening my voice, "what's going on? Are you ready to tell me what's bothering you?"

She turned back to look me in the face. "You know me too well sometimes, Emma. And that can be a pain." She paused. "But you're right, something is bothering me, and you're the only person I can talk about it with. I know you'll understand." Her eyes pleaded with me to listen and not criticize.

I reached across the table and grasped one of her hands, giving it a quick squeeze. "Of course I will, sweetie, just tell me. Tell Auntie Em."

We both laughed at the pet name she had given me the first time we had watched *The Wizard of Oz* together many years ago.

"It's Nate," Sophie said, and I had to admit I wasn't surprised. Whenever Sophie acted like this, there was usually a man involved.

"What about Nate?" I had to tread warily here. I was afraid she had rushed into something before she was really ready. Heck, her divorce wasn't even final yet.

"He confided in me," Sophie said. "And now I'm worried that he really did have a motive for murdering Janet."

Chapter 16

"Can you tell me what it was he confided in you?" I asked. "Whatever it was, it's obviously bothering you."

"He didn't ask me *not* to tell you," Sophie said slowly. "So I suppose it's okay." She looked away from me for a moment. "I'm really worried, Emma."

"Then what did he tell you?" The more matter-of-fact I tried to be, the better it would be for her. She didn't handle emotional upsets all that well, though goodness knows, she's had plenty of experience with them.

"He really is a nice guy," she told me, face and voice as earnest as I had ever experienced with her. The trouble was, I had heard those words from her before, and always about a boy, or a man, who really wasn't that nice in the long run. "I mean it, Emma, he really is. He's different from all the others."

"I'm willing to give him the benefit of the doubt," I said. "Just tell me what he told you."

Hilda appeared suddenly at my side and began talking to me. As usual she managed to pick an inconvenient moment for me when she decided she needed attention. Standing on her hind legs, her front legs braced against the side of the chair, she butted my leg with her head. I reached down to rub her ears in the special way she liked, and she kept up the chatter.

"Sorry," I told Sophie, who appeared slightly annoyed over this distraction. Hilda was still muttering away.

"That cat," was all she said for a moment. She raised her voice slightly to be heard. "Nate asked his father for some money because he wants to quit his job and go to graduate school full-time."

I shrugged. "That doesn't sound like much of a motive to me." All at once, Hilda decided she'd had enough attention. She dropped to all fours and padded away. Such a little princess she was.

"The bad part about it," Sophie said, "is that Janet had a fit about it. She didn't want Gerald to give Nate the money, and she was really nasty to Nate."

"Why should she care?"

Sophie sighed deeply. "Because she and Gerald had already spent a lot of money on Nate. They bought him his own business when he got out of college, but that failed. Then they gave him the money to start up another one."

"And that one failed, too," I said when Sophie fell silent.

"Yes," she said, "but it wasn't really Nate's fault. A lot of dot-com businesses failed then, so it wasn't just Nate."

"And so now he wants to go to graduate school?" I wasn't about to get into a discussion with her over what seemed to me Nate's obvious lack of business acumen. "What does he want to study?"

"He wants to be a librarian," Sophie said. She had such a funny look on her face I almost laughed. Frankly, I wasn't expecting something that practical— or useful—from Nate.

"Good for him," I said, and I meant it.

"He's been working in one of the branches of the public library system," Sophie said, "and he really likes it a lot. But to get a decent salary and everything, he needs to have the master's degree."

"That all seems perfectly respectable to me," I said.

"Why wouldn't Janet want him to be something good and useful like a librarian?"

Sophie made a nasty face. "Janet thought only women should be librarians. She said everyone would think he was gay if he became a librarian."

"You know, I'm finding it even harder than I did before to regret that someone murdered that woman," I said.

"Tell me about it," Sophie muttered. "The reason I want to find out who did it is so I can give them a gold medal."

"I don't think the police will take the same view," I said.

"No, probably not," Sophie said, laughing suddenly. Then she sobered. "The point is, Nate and Janet apparently had a *huge* fight over this. Nate really let her have it, telling her how much he'd always despised her, and she gave it right back to him. Told him she wanted him out of the house and that she'd see that his father never let him have a dime, and so on and so on."

"When did this happen?"

"Two days before Janet died," Sophie said.

"When I met Nate that night at the bridge party," I said, "I could tell he didn't care much for her. But he was still living in their house, wasn't he?"

"Only till the end of the week," Sophie said. "Janet had told him he had that long to find an apartment. Otherwise she was going to dump all his things in the bayou and have the locks changed on the house. She would have done it, too."

"The important thing is, did Nate really believe she would have done it?"

Sophie nodded. "Oh, he believed all right. She did it to him once before, about five years ago."

"Good grief! That woman was absolutely nuts." And I thought my parents were bad. I mean, they would never win any contests for parenting skills, but even they weren't this crazy.

"I know," Sophie said, easily reading my thoughts.

"Makes you appreciate your own parents a little more, doesn't it? Even mine aren't as nutty as Janet was." And that was saying something. Sophie's parents were fruitcakes—very amiable, but still fruitcakes.

"I take it you're having second thoughts now about Nate's being innocent," I said.

"I don't know, Emma," Sophie said. "He got so upset just telling me about it. He might have been so angry at her that he did something really stupid. Maybe he wanted to make her sick, punish her a little, but it went too far."

"That could be," I said slowly, thinking of my own idea that Gerald McGreevey might have deliberately delayed giving Janet the antidote she needed.

"What is it?" Sophie asked. "You know something. Tell me."

I shook my head. "I don't really know anything. It's just an idea I had."

"Well, what is it?" Sophie was determined to have an answer from me.

I gave it to her. When I had finished, she sat back in her chair and regarded me quietly.

"That makes a lot of sense," she said finally. "I have no trouble believing that Gerald is a cold-blooded bastard. But how could anyone ever prove he didn't give her the medicine quickly enough on purpose?"

"I don't know," I said. "I don't know that anyone can, and that means if the police—or if we—figure out who put the peanuts in the spinach dip, that person is going to be the one who's charged with murder. Not Gerald, even though he could be as morally responsible as the other person."

"It really is nasty, isn't it?" Sophie said. "But we have to find out who did it. We can't have it hanging over us without resolution."

"No, you're right," I said. "We're doing our bit, although I doubt Lieutenant Burnes would be all that grateful for our help, if he knew what we're up to."

"Probably not." Sophie laughed. "Even Jessica Fletcher had trouble with the cops sometimes. They didn't all just sit back and let her do their jobs for them."

The doorbell rang. I stared at Sophie. "I wonder if it's Marylou."

"Probably," Sophie said. "Oh, good grief, Emma, just go open the door. She's not going to know we've been talking about her."

"You're right," I said, pushing myself up from my chair. "I'm being silly."

"I'd better go home," Sophie said. "I've got things I need to do."

"You sit right there," I said. "If you leave now, I'll wring your neck later."

She laughed at that. I hoped she would still be in the kitchen when I returned.

Marylou was indeed standing on the doorstep. I could see her through the peephole. Her hand was raised to the bell when I swung the door open.

But she wasn't alone. Standing behind her was Gerald McGreevey.

I was so surprised by his appearance at my door that for a moment I couldn't say anything. Marylou, bless her heart, saved me from looking like a total fool.

"Emma, dear, I hope you don't mind us dropping by like this," she said. I motioned for them to enter, and she and Gerald stepped past me into the hall.

"Of course not," I said. "Please, do come in. Gerald, how are you doing?"

Given what I had been thinking about the man, I found his presence in my house disconcerting.

"I'm doing okay, Emma," he said, "thank you. It was such a shock, but thanks to the kindness of my friends and neighbors, like Marylou here, I'm getting through it." He put an arm around Marylou and gave her a quick hug. Marylou smiled up at him.

That bothered me a little. I was all too aware of

the conversation Sophie and I had been having, and seeing Gerald and Marylou together like this was a bit much on top of that. I was suddenly having the most awful doubts about Marylou. Was I imagining that she was gazing at him adoringly?

Then I realized I was standing there like a complete idiot. "Forgive me, I'm forgetting my manners. Come with me, and let me offer you something to drink." They followed me down the hall.

"That would be nice," Marylou said. "Emma's kitchen is so pleasant, Gerald. We've been having such a lovely time getting to know each other, just sitting around the table and chatting."

To my relief Sophie was still there. In the time since I had gone to answer the door, she had helped herself to some of the diet green tea I had in the fridge.

"Hi, Gerald," Sophie said, darting a quick glance at me. "How are you doing? Afternoon, Marylou."

"I'm doing okay, Sophie, thank you," Gerald said. He pulled out a chair for Marylou in very courtly fashion before seating himself.

"What can I offer you to drink?" I asked. "Coffee, tea, a soft drink? Or water?"

"How about a little bourbon?" Gerald asked.

I was taken aback by that, but then I realized he was joking.

"Sorry, Emma," Gerald said. "Just kidding. A soft drink will be fine for me."

"Good," I said, laughing a little, "because I'm pretty sure I'm completely out of bourbon." In fact, I had very little of an alcoholic nature in the house, except maybe a bottle or two of wine. Neither Baxter nor I had been drinkers, other than wine with dinner sometimes.

"I'll have some of what Sophie's drinking," Marylou said. "Is it that green tea you were telling me about?"

"Yes," I said. "It's very good, and it's good for you, too."

I brought them their drinks, and some green tea for

myself, then sat down at the table. I was rather at a loss for conversation, but luckily for the speechless hostess, Sophie jumped right in.

"Have you heard anything about when you can hold the funeral, Gerald?"

"Not yet," he said, looking woebegone. "Poor Janet. As if all this weren't terrible enough, we can't even hold a proper funeral for her. But I'm hoping it won't take too long."

"I saw Carlene this morning," I said, "and she said she would be helping with the arrangements."

"Such a sweet girl," Marylou said, never taking her eyes from Gerald's face. "I know you must find her a great comfort, Gerald."

I couldn't help darting a sideways glance at Sophie. What was going on here? Surely I wasn't imagining the barb in that last remark. Sophie blinked at me, then looked away.

"Oh, she is, she is," Gerald said. "Carlene is one of those people you can always rely on. Sensible, keeps her head in a crisis, and very detail-oriented." He laughed. "She's much better at organizing things than I am."

"She seems very capable," I said. "Not to mention beautiful and intelligent."

Gerald laughed again, though Marylou looked a bit pained.

"Yes, she is all those things, and more," Gerald said.

"We're all very sorry for what you and Nate are going through," Sophie said. "I know you must find this all very trying."

Gerald heaved a heavy sigh and put on a very tragic face. "Yes, it is. Especially when I know it's all my fault."

Marylou patted his hand, while Sophie and I sat, stunned, staring at him.

"What on earth do you mean?" I was finally able to speak.

"Go ahead, Gerald," Marylou said, "tell them what you told me." She looked at Sophie and me. "The poor dear was so upset, but I told him it would do him good to talk about it with us."

"About what?" Sophie asked.

Gerald sighed again. "The afternoon of the bridge party, I told Janet I wanted a divorce, and she staged this awful stunt to get back at me. But it went a little too far, and she killed herself by mistake."

Chapter 17

Neither Sophie nor I said anything after Gerald's bald announcement. Had the man completely lost his mind?

"Isn't it terrible?" Marylou smiled sweetly as she patted Gerald's hand. "Poor Gerald has been agonizing over this, but I told him he had to tell people about it. Particularly the police."

"I feel so terrible about the whole thing," Gerald said, and he attempted to appear pitiful and emotionally worn, but he didn't pull it off as far as I was concerned.

I watched Marylou, appalled by her behavior. Surely she wasn't believing any of this taradiddle?

Then she caught my eye, and I would swear she winked at me. Then she was gazing adoringly at Gerald again. It happened so fast, though, I couldn't be certain what I had seen.

"Janet certainly chose a bizarre way to get back at you," Sophie said. "Not to mention dangerous."

"Obviously," Gerald said. "But Janet wasn't always the most intelligent of women, particularly when she was upset. She was very stubborn, and once she made up her mind about something, nothing could shake her."

"Oh yes, Janet could be very pigheaded," Marylou chimed in. "And spiteful."

"Still, to think she would choose such a risky way to get back at you," I said.

My tone must have sounded too skeptical because Gerald shot me a quick, appraising glance. Then his expression turned sorrowful once more.

"The reason I know Janet must have planned it," Gerald said, "is that her epinephrine wasn't on her. She usually had the thing on a cord around her neck. But she wasn't wearing it that night." He shook his head in puzzlement over Janet's behavior.

"That's even stupider," Sophie said. "It was Nate, wasn't it, who found it?"

"He found one of them," Gerald said. "He ran up to our bedroom and found the spare one. I found the other one later, and it was right there in the kitchen." He paused dramatically. "It was in the silverware drawer."

"How tragic it all is," Marylou said. She turned sorrowing eyes to me and Sophie, tears beginning to trickle down her face. "Poor, stupid Janet. Hoisted by her own petard, you might say."

"Er, yes," Gerald said, with an odd look at Marylou. "I'm sorry, I really shouldn't be burdening you ladies with this, but Marylou insisted you would want to know."

"Thank you for telling us," I said, working hard to keep a straight face. I didn't dare look at Sophie. Did the man really think we'd be taken in by this farce?

"I should be going," Gerald said, standing up. "Thanks for the drink, Emma. There are things I should be doing, so if you'll excuse me."

"I'll show him out, Emma," Marylou said, rising from her chair.

"Thank you," I said. Sophie and I watched them disappear down the hall, heads bent together, Marylou murmuring something to Gerald as they went.

"What do you make of that?" I asked Sophie in an undertone.

"Absolute crap," Sophie said. "The man must think we're all idiots."

"Marylou certainly seems to be buying into it," I

said. "Maybe she really is after him. What do you think?"

Sophie shifted her head slightly in warning, and I turned to see Marylou approaching the table. She dropped down somewhat heavily into her chair and faced us with a bright smile.

"Isn't that about the biggest load of bull twaddle you've ever heard?" she asked.

Without even looking at each other Sophie and I both burst out laughing. "Thank goodness," I finally managed to say. "You really had us worried there for a minute, Marylou."

A pained expression crossed Marylou's face. "Now, Emma, surely you realized I was just playing along with him. You didn't really think I believed him, did you?"

"You were pretty convincing," I said apologetically.

"Sophie?"

"I knew you were acting the whole time," the little rat said. If I could have kicked her under the table, I would have, but her legs were too far away. I settled for glaring at her. "After all, Emma doesn't know you as well as I do." Butter wouldn't melt in her mouth— oh, she was good, I had to give her that.

"I'd say I'm not the only one who can be convincing when she wants to be," Marylou said, and we all laughed.

"Seriously, now," Sophie said when the laughter had died down, "why do you think he came up with that stupid story?"

"I can think of two reasons right away," I said. "One—he's trying to protect himself because he deliberately delayed getting Janet the help she needed, whether he's the one who poisoned the spinach dip or someone else did. Two—he's trying to cover for someone else, like his son."

"I hadn't thought of that first one," Marylou said slowly, "but you're right. I can definitely see Gerald taking advantage of the opportunity to rid himself of

Janet. I can also see him putting the peanuts in the spinach dip in the first place. I think he was prepared for what was going to happen."

"Otherwise, why would Janet's epinephrine have been missing?" Sophie said.

"Exactly," Marylou and I said in unison.

"Of course," I said, trying to think it out as I spoke, "we really only have Gerald's word for it that Janet didn't have one of those pen things on her when she collapsed."

"What do you mean?" Sophie asked.

I visualized the scene that night. "I was the one closest to them, and Gerald was crouched so that he was effectively shielding Janet's body from view. He could very quickly have found the pen in her skirt pocket and palmed it. Everyone was hanging back out of the way, and he might have counted on that."

"And then later on he could easily claim to have found it in the silverware drawer," Marylou said, "and no one could really dispute him."

The cold-bloodedness of it affected all three of us. No one had anything to say for a few minutes. We simply stared at one another, appalled.

"I think that's what must have happened." Sophie finally broke the silence, and her voice sounded harsh and strange. She cleared her throat. "I just can't see Janet forgetting to have that thing with her. Surely someone as allergic as she was would never be without one close at hand."

"You're right," Marylou said. "She usually wore it on a cord around her neck. I've seen it many times. I don't think she'd go anywhere without it."

"Even in her own home?" I asked. "Would she feel it as necessary at home?"

"It was probably a habit," Sophie said. "I mean, she would have had it with her out of habit, if nothing else."

Marylou nodded. "Sophie's right. Janet would have

put it in her pocket or around her neck without even thinking twice about it, because that's what she always did."

"I agree with both of you," I said. "So, if Janet had the device with her when she collapsed . . ."

"Ergo, Gerald must have been lying about not being able to find it on her," Sophie said. "He must have palmed it and stuck it in his pocket, like you said, Emma."

We nodded at one another.

"But does that mean Gerald was the one who put the peanuts in my spinach dip?" Marylou asked.

"That's the difficult question," I said. "He certainly had the motive."

"But he's not the only one," Marylou said.

"No, there are others who seem to have motives, and strong ones," I said. "Paul Hardy is a possibility, because Janet may have been spreading nasty talk about him."

"And Bootsie Flannigan because she wants Gerald for herself," Sophie said.

"And Nate McGreevey," I said, watching Sophie as I spoke. "He hated his stepmother, and with her out of the way, he might be a lot happier."

Sophie frowned, but she didn't rush in to defend Nate as I halfway expected she would.

"There's also Carlene," Marylou said. "She didn't like Janet either, and I think she's interested in Gerald herself."

"She's a hard one to read," I said. "I think she's probably ruthless enough to do it, if she perceived Janet as an obstacle in her way."

"Oh, most definitely," Marylou said. "I'd say she can definitely be ruthless."

"Anybody else?" I said. "Among the others who were there that night? Shannon Hardy, the Grahams?"

"And don't forget me," Marylou said, chuckling. "You and Sophie don't count, although I suppose we should consider Sophie, too. After all, she knew Janet well enough to hate her, too."

Sophie had a pained expression on her face, but before she could speak, I said, "Thanks for striking me off the suspect list, Marylou. But why would you want to kill Janet?" I didn't look at Sophie after I asked the question. "Surely you shouldn't be on that list either?" I laughed.

"Thank you, Emma," Marylou said. Her face darkened. "It's okay. I know what has been said about me in this neighborhood. I know some people think I'm a poisoner."

Neither Sophie nor I said anything, because to do so would have insulted Marylou's intelligence. She knew that, by this time, we had both more than likely heard the stories, too.

"I can't deny that I made mistakes with my second and third husbands," Marylou said, "but I did care about both of them, believe it or not. They weren't perfect, and I probably would have been happier without marrying them. But I didn't kill either one of them."

"We know that, dear," Sophie said gently. "You don't have to defend yourself to us." I added my voice to hers.

"Thank you," Marylou said. "But of course the neighborhood rumor mill would have you believe I want Gerald to be my fourth husband." She laughed, loud and long, startling both Sophie and me. "I should take that as an insult, but with the mistakes I made with Two and Three, I shouldn't be surprised people would think I had another jackass lined up for Four."

She laughed again, and her laughter was so infectious that Sophie and I couldn't help ourselves. Soon all three of us were wiping our eyes. My sides hurt by the time we finally stopped.

"Well, we certainly strayed off the subject," Sophie said, "and we still don't have any good answer."

"To what?" I asked.

"To who had the strongest motive for murder," Sophie answered.

"And we don't know if we have a complete list yet," Marylou added. "Eric and Amanda Graham might have had some problem with Janet that we don't know about. I mean, almost everyone had a problem with Janet at some point or another, and I can't think they escaped."

"I wonder what it could be," Sophie mused.

"I don't know," Marylou said, "but I imagine we can find out."

"Over the bridge table," I said.

"Certainly," Marylou said. "And tonight, if I'm not underestimating my guests."

"Bootsie, you mean," I said.

Marylou nodded emphatically. "Oh yes, if there's any dirt about the Grahams and Janet, Bootsie will know."

"And she'll be happy to tell it, too," Sophie added.

"Goodness, look at the time," Marylou said, getting up from her chair. "I'd better run on home and start getting ready for this evening's little bridge soiree."

"I'd better go home, too," Sophie said. "I have a few things I need to take care of, like talking to my lawyers." She made a face.

I patted her hand. "If there's anything I can do, let me know."

"I will," Sophie said. "See you at seven, Marylou." She disappeared out the back door, shutting it quietly behind her.

"Is there anything I can bring?" I asked Marylou, accompanying her to the front door.

"No, I have everything I need, dear," she said. Her eyes twinkled. "Just keep your eyes and ears on alert tonight."

"I will," I promised. I opened the door and waved her out. "See you later."

Back in the kitchen, I glanced at the clock. I had a couple of hours before I needed to start getting ready for the bridge game. I had some correspondence that needed attention, and I might as well go to my study and deal with it.

As I climbed the stairs I thought about the bridge party ahead of me. Would Bootsie reveal anything useful?

If nothing else, with Bootsie and Boy Toy on hand, it wouldn't be dull.

Chapter 18

Ten minutes before seven, Marylou, Sophie, and I were sitting in Marylou's comfortable, spacious living room, waiting for Bootsie and Dan to arrive.

"He doesn't always come with her," Marylou said, "and you never know till the last minute. Sometimes he sulks and won't go anywhere."

"It wouldn't hurt my feelings if he stayed home," Sophie said. "Someone should have poured a little Clorox in that gene pool a long time ago."

"He's certainly pretty to look at," Marylou said, grinning, "but he spoils it all by opening his mouth."

"Is he really that dumb?" I asked. "I didn't get much chance to find out the other night."

Marylou and Sophie exchanged glances. "He's not really dumb," Marylou said.

"He's just one of those guys who never quite gets it," Sophie said. "You know what I mean?"

"You mean too self-centered to understand that someone else might have a different point of view?" I asked.

They both nodded. "He thinks he's smarter and slicker than everyone else," Sophie said, "but he's not. Of course, you could never convince *him* of that."

"I don't think I really care to try," I said, and Sophie snorted with laughter, while Marylou nodded.

We waited, and then we waited a few minutes more.

I had begun to think Bootsie had completely forgotten about tonight, but the doorbell rang at nearly a quarter past seven. Marylou rose to answer it.

"This means Dan must be with her, because Bootsie's usually on time when she's on her own," Sophie said, rolling her eyes at me. "Oh frabjous day."

We rose to greet the new arrivals as Marylou ushered them into the living room.

"Hi, Emma, hi, Sophie," Bootsie said gaily. "How are y'all doing this evening?"

"Fine, Bootsie," I said, with Sophie echoing me. "How are you doing? Good evening, Dan. Nice to see you."

Dan smirked at us. "Howdy, ladies. Good to be seen by you." He laughed at his own witticism as he preened for us, a backpack slung over one shoulder.

I avoided looking at Sophie, fixing my gaze on Dan instead. I had to admit he made a very attractive picture. His jeans could have been painted on, and they outlined his lower body all too well. I hastily centered my gaze farther north. His upper body was every bit as impressive. The black shirt he wore clung to his chest and arms, leaving little to the imagination.

He caught me looking and smirked at me again. I smiled briefly before turning to Bootsie. Her outfit mirrored Dan's, right down to the cowboy boots she wore, except hers were bright red and his were black. With every breath she took, her impressive bosom threatened to escape her low-cut shirt.

By contrast Marylou, Sophie, and I could have passed for nuns in our casual tops and pants. For once even Sophie had worn subdued colors.

"What can I get y'all to drink?" Marylou asked.

"Some wine if you have it," Bootsie said, "or tea, if not."

"Same here," Dan said.

"I have some nice white wine chilled," Marylou said. "I'll be right back."

Bootsie dropped her purse on the sofa and regarded

Sophie and me. "I didn't realize there was going to be five of us tonight. I guess Dan could have stayed home."

"Oh, it's no problem," I said, smiling. "We've already worked it out. I'm going to take turns with Marylou. Or I may just sit and watch. I've got a little bit of a headache."

"Sorry to hear that," Bootsie said.

Dan had followed Marylou to the kitchen with his backpack. When they returned, his backpack was gone, and he carried his own drink and Bootsie's. "Here you go, honey," he said.

Marylou had followed with a large tray of munchies—cheese, crackers, some sausage rolls, and some fresh grapes. She set the tray on the coffee table. "Now, everyone just help themselves." She pointed to small plates and napkins on the table. "And if you need anything else, just ask."

"Let's get started," Sophie said. She stood at the card table that Marylou had placed in the center of the room. "Shall we draw for partners?"

"What about Emma?" Dan asked when I didn't approach the table with the others.

"I'm going to sit out the first rubber," I explained.

Dan shrugged. "Whatever."

Sophie ended up with Dan as her partner this first rubber, and I could tell she was ecstatic. I sat on the sofa near the card table a little behind Marylou and watched the game.

Marylou dealt, and she opened at one no trump. Dan, sitting to her left, doubled. Bootsie passed, grimacing as she did so. Sophie, after staring at her cards for a long moment, responded to Dan's double with a bid of two spades.

Marylou passed, and so did Dan. Sophie, from my vantage point on the sofa, appeared to be shooting daggers at Dan. I did a rapid calculation in my head. If Marylou opened at one no trump, that meant she probably had at least fifteen high-card points and a balanced hand. For Dan to double that, he must have a strong hand, at least fifteen points himself.

I was still unclear on some aspects of bidding. There might have been another reason Dan doubled. I'd have to ask Sophie later. I stood up to get a look at her hand. She had eleven points, counting a void in hearts as three of them, with a nice five-card spade suit.

Marylou led, and Dan laid down his hand. He had three aces—spades, hearts, and diamonds—plus the king and jack of hearts and three low spades. This would be an interesting hand to play. I sat back down on the sofa to watch. Sophie relaxed when she saw his hand.

"I'll leave it with you," Dan said. "Marylou, ain't there a john back there by the kitchen?"

Apparently absorbed in the game, Marylou nodded. Dan left the room, and I watched the game for a moment. Sophie seemed to be in good shape, despite Marylou's strong hand. A couple of the finesses Sophie needed worked because Marylou was sitting in the right place, with the high cards on the board.

For a moment, I took my eyes off Sophie and noticed that Marylou's left hand was hanging by her side. Then the hand pointed in the direction of the kitchen. Neither Bootsie nor Sophie appeared to notice anything amiss, and I stared at Marylou's hand. What was going on?

Marylou brought her hand up to play a card. Then, casually, she dropped her left hand again and pointed. Then, feeling like a complete idiot, I realized she wanted me to go into the kitchen.

"Excuse me," I murmured. Glass in hand, I got up from the sofa and headed for the kitchen.

Why did Marylou want me in there? Was she afraid Dan would steal the silver?

As I came nearer to the kitchen, I took care to move as quietly as I could. When I walked into the room, Dan was standing at the table, his back to me.

He appeared to be fiddling with something on the table.

He apparently sensed my presence, or perhaps he heard me breathing, because he tensed slightly. I heard the sound of a zipper in action, and then he turned around. He had a cell phone in his hand, and he slid it into one of his pockets where it produced a noticeable bulge.

"Hey, Emma," he said, and when he moved, I could see his backpack sitting on the table. He picked it up and shoved it onto one of the chairs at the table. "Getting a little bored with just sitting there? Looking for some company, maybe?" He treated me to one of his cocky grins.

"Oh no, I just wanted some water." I brandished my empty glass at him. I walked over to the refrigerator and opened the door. I extracted the water pitcher and refilled my glass. "I think bridge is such a fascinating game, I even like watching other people play." I put the pitcher back and shut the door. "What about you? Don't you love it?" I did my best to sound a little flirtatious, but I was pretty rusty—not that I was ever very good at it in the first place.

With Dan, I quickly realized, it really didn't matter. He was one of those men who was convinced every woman was flirting with him just by breathing.

He moved away from the table toward me. He stuck his hands in his back pockets and swaggered a bit. "Oh, bridge is a pretty good game," he said, coming closer and closer, "but there are some games I like a lot better." He grinned. "And I'm *real* good at 'em."

By now he was a little too close—and too obvious. "I'm sure you do. I mean, I'm sure you are," I said, resisting the urge to step away from him.

"Do you like other games?" Dan asked, leering at me.

I was saved from answering by the sound of Bootsie's voice calling Dan back to the game.

"Later," he said as he stepped past me. He sauntered out of the room, and I watched him go.

Had he been up to something in the kitchen?

He really hadn't had that much time. It probably hadn't been more than a minute after he left the living room that I had followed him in here. He couldn't have done much in that time.

He certainly couldn't have gone to the bathroom. Men were a lot faster at it than women, but not *that* fast.

I walked back into the living room and resumed my seat on the sofa. Dan was dealing, and I eyed him speculatively. He caught me looking and winked at me. I looked away.

"How did you do?" I asked Sophie.

"Made four," she said, turning to face me, "but only because two finesses worked."

"Good for you," I said, and she smiled and turned back to the table.

What had Dan been doing in the kitchen? Maybe my imagination was going into overdrive, and I was trying too hard to put a sinister implication on Dan's visit to the kitchen.

But there was obviously something a little odd about it; otherwise why would Marylou surreptitiously point me to the kitchen?

I would definitely ask her the first chance I had.

I turned my attention back to the action at the table. Dan won the bid at two hearts, and play began. Sophie put down her cards but she stayed at the table to watch. I could tell from her body language she didn't trust Dan not to screw things up.

He appeared to be a pretty fair bridge player, though, I had to give him credit for that. He ended up making three hearts, and Sophie finally relaxed.

Thus far there hadn't been much talk over the cards, and I was a bit surprised. I had expected Marylou to try to get Bootsie talking, but perhaps she was focusing on the game so much she had forgotten the real purpose of tonight's game.

Bootsie was dealing the cards when Marylou spoke.

"I hear you're going to be helping with Janet's funeral arrangements," she said as she collected her cards and organized them in her hand.

"Who told you?" Bootsie's gaze flickered in my direction. "Oh, that's right, Emma was there this morning when Carlene and I talked about it. Yeah, I'm going to help."

"Well, if there's anything I can do, you let me know, okay?" Marylou said.

"Sure," Bootsie replied. She eyed her cards for a moment. "One club."

Sophie passed, and Marylou responded with one no trump.

The bid ended at three no trump, and Marylou played the hand as she talked. Bootsie remained at the table, leaning back in her chair, watching Marylou carefully.

"I still can't get over what happened to Janet," Marylou said. "I know none of us really liked her that much, but who could have hated her enough to do that to her?"

"Might've been Nate," Dan said. He snickered. "If he could remember where his balls were, that is." He laughed uproariously and didn't seem to care much that no one else laughed with him.

"Nate was real mad at Janet," Bootsie said, "but then, who wasn't? Did you hear the latest stunt she pulled? I mean, besides going after that poor old woman about her association dues?"

"No, I don't think I have," Marylou said, peering at her cards and then examining the dummy. "Sophie, have you? Emma?"

"No," Sophie and I said together.

"Well, you know how Amanda and Eric Graham are real big animal lovers, right?" Bootsie leaned forward, propping her elbows on the table.

Marylou and Sophie nodded.

"Everybody knows they've got both dogs and cats at their house, but nobody knew how many. Janet went over there one day last week, and she told me she counted eight cats and seven dogs," Bootsie said. She grimaced. "Can you imagine what that's got to smell like? Pee-yew."

"I didn't realize they had so many pets," Marylou said. "Why should Janet care?"

"Because you need a kennel license if you're going to keep that many animals, and besides, it's against the association bylaws to have that many animals on your property," Bootsie said.

"If they're not bothering anyone, who cares?" I asked. "Had any of their neighbors complained?"

"Yep," Bootsie said. "One of the neighbors who lives right next door called Janet to complain. That's how Janet knew."

"What was Janet planning to do about it?" Sophie asked. "I can't imagine she was going to ignore it, out of the goodness of her heart."

Dan snickered again. Bootsie ignored him.

"Janet was threatening to call the health department and the SPCA. She told the Grahams they were going to have to get rid of most of the animals, or else they'd have to move," Bootsie said.

"How did they take that?" Marylou asked. She had continued playing, carefully and methodically, as the conversation progressed. I was impressed with her ability to concentrate on the game and participate in the conversation at the same time. I don't really like to talk much when I'm trying to make a contract.

"Janet told me Amanda started screaming at her, and she came at her, trying to claw her eyes out," Bootsie said. "Eric managed to grab hold of her before she could hurt Janet, but Janet was a bit shaken up by it, at least when she told me about it. But it also made her real angry, and I figure she was really going to make Amanda and Eric squirm."

"Do you think Amanda was angry enough to poison Janet?" Sophie asked.

Bootsie shrugged. "I don't know. I think Amanda's a little bit crazy. So who knows?"

No one responded to that for the moment, and Marylou finished playing the hand. She had made the contract with a trick to spare.

While Sophie was dealing the next hand, Marylou turned slightly in her chair and said, "Emma, I forgot to ask you. Did you ever get a hold of Paul Hardy?"

"Not yet," I said, puzzled by Marylou's question. What on earth was she talking about?

"I hope you're not planning on letting him handle your finances," Bootsie said in a disparaging tone.

Marylou winked at me before turning back to the table. Sometimes a house has to fall on me before I catch on.

"I was thinking about it," I said brightly. "He seems like a nice guy, and he sure is good-looking. But you don't think he knows what he's doing?"

Bootsie shrugged. "I haven't got any experience with him myself, but according to Janet, he really screwed up with some clients and lost a lot of their money." She looked directly at me. "So you'd better think twice about letting him get his hands on *your* money."

"Thanks for the warning," I said, trying to appear suitably grateful. "I guess I won't call him after all."

The rubber was tied at a game apiece, and Sophie won the bid at five diamonds. As play started, Dan once again got up from his chair and, without comment, headed toward the kitchen.

This time I didn't need any prompting from Marylou to follow him. But I decided to wait a little longer than I had the time before. He might be expecting me to turn up right away, and if I didn't, he would probably relax his guard a bit.

I kept glancing at my watch, and when about three

minutes had passed, I said, "I think I'll have a little bit of that wine. Anybody need anything?"

They all said no, so I headed to the kitchen, once again moving as quietly as I could.

As I neared the kitchen door, I could hear Dan's voice. I tiptoed closer. Peeking around the edge of the door, I could see Dan standing about six feet away, his back toward me.

". . . think you understand me," Dan was saying. After a pause, he continued in a harsh tone, "You ain't got much choice. I got your ass in a sling, and you'd better come up with the money somehow."

Chapter 19

I stood stock-still, hardly daring to breathe. It wouldn't do for Dan to know I was listening to his conversation.

After he uttered his threat, he fell silent for a moment. "I thought so," he said into his cell phone in a tone of grim satisfaction. "I was figuring you'd see it my way."

I was hoping he would say the name of the person at the other end of the conversation, but he didn't. I wanted to yell out in frustration.

"I ain't got time to go into all that now," Dan said. "I'll call *you* when I'm ready to discuss what I want. You got that?" He listened for a moment longer before pulling the phone away from his ear. He punched a button to end the call. "I've got you now, you stupid bastard." He clipped the phone on his belt.

I stepped back a few feet and started humming rather loudly. When I entered the kitchen, Dan was standing near the refrigerator, tucking a handkerchief into his pocket. Hearing me, he turned with a leer on his face.

"Just can't stay away, can you, doll?"

"From the refrigerator, you mean?" I said sweetly. His eyes narrowed. "After all, that's where the chilled wine is, isn't it? And I'm pretty thirsty."

Muttering something under his breath, Dan stomped by me over to the table. He pulled his backpack from the chair where he had placed it. On his way out of the kitchen his boots thudded against the linoleum with such force I was surprised he didn't leave marks on the floor.

I shrugged and opened the refrigerator. Pulling out the wine bottle, I emptied it into my glass. I took a few sips while I stood there and considered what I had overheard.

It didn't take much imagination to understand that Dan was trying to blackmail someone, and it was just as obvious that it must have something to do with Janet's murder. The question was, who?

Bootsie was out, of course, but that still left the rest of our other suspects: Gerald and Nate McGreevey, Shannon and Paul Hardy, and Amanda and Eric Graham.

If only I could get my hands on Dan's cell phone!

Short of luring him into a bedroom, I couldn't think of any other way of obtaining possession of his phone.

I shuddered at the thought of being alone with Dan in a bedroom.

I might as well give up on that idea.

"Emma!"

Sophie was calling me from the living room, and I made haste to return.

When I walked into the room, Marylou said, "We've finished the first rubber, dear. Would you like to take my place for the second one?"

"Sure," I said. I took her place at the table and smiled across it at Bootsie. Thank goodness I wasn't going to have to play with Dan.

To my surprise, Dan, who was standing behind his chair, announced, "Marylou, why don't you take my place? I think I'm going to head on home. You don't mind, do you, babe?" He turned to Bootsie with a big grin.

"Are you sure, honey?" Bootsie asked, obviously taken aback.

"Yeah," he said. "It's been a long day, and I've got

to be up early tomorrow. You stay and have a good time. I'll walk home. It ain't that far." He picked up his backpack from the floor and slung it over his shoulder.

I exchanged glances with Sophie. She was obviously delighted he was leaving.

"I'm glad you were able to play with us," Marylou said, ever the good hostess. She moved forward to show him out, but Bootsie waved her back.

"No, you just sit down, honey," Bootsie said sweetly as she got up from her chair. "I'll walk Dan to the door. Won't be a minute."

As Bootsie and Dan headed for the door, Marylou, Sophie, and I sat at the table and looked at one another.

"What's going on?" Marylou asked softly.

"I'll tell you later," I said. She and Sophie both frowned at me, but there was no way I could tell them anything with Bootsie about to come back at any moment.

When she did return, she appeared pensive. As she took her chair again, Marylou said, "I hope everything is okay. Is Dan feeling unwell?"

"No, just tired," Bootsie said with a brief smile. "He gets up real early every morning to go running." She shook her head. "I don't know how he does it, getting up like that when it's still dark outside. I hate it. I have to wait till the sun's up before I go out."

"It does keep him really fit," Marylou said.

"You got that right, honey," Bootsie said with a roguish grin. "Now, let's play bridge."

Sophie cut the cards for me, and I dealt. We quickly became immersed in the game, because Sophie and Marylou had bid for a grand slam. Sophie, who would be playing the hand, sat forward in her chair, her eyes sparkling. She loved the challenge of playing a hand like this.

I had one jack in my hand, and Bootsie very obviously didn't have much either. The hand went very quickly, and Sophie was triumphant at the end, making the contract of seven hearts with hardly any trouble.

"That was fun," she said as I was cutting the cards for Marylou to deal.

"I'm sure it was," I said wryly, "for you, anyway."

Sophie laughed. "You dealt that hand, Emma, so don't complain."

We all had a good laugh at that, and play continued.

We played two rubbers, one of them rather long, and by the time we finished the second one, Bootsie exclaimed, "Good Lord, look at what time it is. Almost eleven. I'd better be getting home myself."

"Yes, it is getting late," Sophie said, stifling a yawn. "I was so caught up in the game I wasn't paying any attention."

"I enjoyed it, girls," Bootsie said. "Let's do this again soon, okay?" She chuckled loudly. "Maybe next time Emma and I'll win."

"Sounds good to me," I said, laughing ruefully. "I can't have Sophie thinking she's going to beat me every time."

"Don't count on it," Sophie said with a smug expression. "Marylou and I are tough to beat."

Smiling broadly, Marylou escorted Bootsie to the front door, and Sophie and I waited at the table.

"Let's go into the kitchen," Marylou said when she returned. "Much more comfortable in there."

"Don't you want some help cleaning up?" I asked as Sophie and I followed our hostess.

"Heavens, no," Marylou said. "Won't take me five minutes to get everything put away. No, y'all just sit down at the table. Anybody for coffee?"

"Not this late," Sophie said.

"How about some decaf, then?"

Sophie and I both said yes to that, and Marylou set about making it.

While we waited for the coffeemaker to do its work, Marylou joined us at the table.

"Okay, Emma," she said, "spill. Tell us what Dan was up to."

"Of course," I said, "but first, answer a question." Marylou nodded.

"When Dan left the room the first time, why were you giving me the high sign?"

"Oh, that," Marylou said. "I knew something was up, because Dan knows perfectly well that there's a bathroom in the hall, just off the living room. It's much closer than the back bathroom off the kitchen. It's in the utility room, for Pete's sake."

"So he wanted an excuse for going to the kitchen," Sophie said.

"I suppose so," I said slowly. "But why bother with asking about the bathroom? It's perfectly natural to go into the kitchen to refill a glass. Besides, he didn't even get anywhere near the bathroom. He didn't have time."

"That was Dan, trying to be too clever," Marylou said. "He's got no common sense half the time."

"What was he doing in the kitchen?" Sophie asked.

I shrugged. "He was fiddling with his backpack. Very innocuous, actually."

"What about the second time?" Marylou asked. She glanced over at the coffeemaker. "Coffee's ready," she said.

"That was more interesting," I said. I waited until Marylou had served our coffee before continuing. "That time I overheard him having a conversation with someone on his cell phone."

"Well, go on," Sophie said. "You obviously overheard something interesting, or you wouldn't be looking so smug."

I made a face at her. I repeated the gist of what I had heard, and they came to the same conclusion I had.

"Blackmail, obviously," Marylou said. "But who?"

"He never called the other person's name," I said.

Then I was struck by a thought. "But it was probably a man. Yes, it was a man he was talking to, I'm sure."

"Why?" Sophie and Marylou spoke in unison.

"Because, after he ended the call, he said, 'Now I've got you, you stupid bastard.' He wouldn't refer to a woman as a bastard, would he?"

"No, you're right," Sophie said. "He wouldn't. He'd call her a bitch or something worse, knowing him."

"So it was a man," Marylou said. "Gerald or Nate, or Paul or Eric. Could be any one of them."

"Unfortunately I couldn't think of a way of getting my hands on his cell phone, short of seducing him and getting him to take his clothes off. Then I could have checked his phone to see whom he had called." It was hard to keep a straight face while I was saying that, but I managed. The reaction was entertaining.

Sophie nearly spat a mouthful of coffee all over the table, while Marylou merely appeared amused.

"Emma, good grief," Sophie said, "how revolting. Don't make me ill." She shuddered theatrically.

"I know, pretty disgusting thought," I said. "No Mata Hari here, believe you me."

"Perish the thought," Marylou said in a mild tone. "But let's be serious again. Dan was threatening someone. And that must mean he knows something, or at least thinks he does."

"But what *could* he know?" Sophie asked. "Do you think he saw something that night, something the rest of us didn't see?"

"It's possible, I suppose," I said. "But when Janet collapsed, I thought I was the only one close enough to see anything."

"Maybe he saw who put the ground peanuts in the spinach dip," Marylou said.

"Where was he sitting that night?" I said. "Can either of you remember?"

"I can," Sophie said. "He was at table one, and he was sitting with his back to the wall. And that means he would have been facing toward the island where all the food was."

"Maybe he did see something, after all," Marylou said. "But he certainly never let on."

"He wouldn't waste an opportunity like that," Sophie said scornfully. "He's on the make for all he can get. He's probably been bleeding Bootsie dry, and now he thinks he can make a bigger score."

"He's playing with fire," I said. "He's not nearly as smart as he thinks he is. I doubt he'll get away with it."

"You mean . . ." Marylou's voice trailed off.

I nodded, and we all stared grimly at one another.

"Maybe I should call Bootsie," Marylou said, half rising out of her chair.

"What would you say to her?" Sophie asked. "Bootsie, honey, by the way, your lover boy is trying to blackmail the killer, and you'd better stop him before he gets killed?"

Marylou slumped back in her chair. "You're right. She'd probably tell me to go to you-know-where."

"What about talking to Dan?" I said.

"Probably get the same result," Sophie said.

"Maybe so, but at least we ought to try," I said. I looked around for a phone. There was one on the counter. I picked up the receiver. "What's Bootsie's number?"

Marylou called it out, and I punched in the numbers. What would I do if Bootsie answered? How would I explain wanting to talk to Dan?

After three rings, someone answered. "Hello."

It was Dan, thank goodness. I whispered as much to Sophie and Marylou, my hand over the mouthpiece.

"Dan, this is Emma."

"Well, hey there, doll," Dan said, sounding smug. "I knew you'd be calling me at some point. Interested in those games I was talking about, aren't you?"

There was no point in responding to that ridiculous remark, so I didn't.

"Listen, Dan," I said. "I heard what you said on your cell phone tonight, and I know this is none of my business, but you really ought—"

"You're damn right it's none of your business," he said, his voice rough as he interrupted me. "I appreciate your concern, doll, but you let me take care of my business. And you damn well better not be trying to tell Bootsie anything about it, you got that?"

He didn't wait for an answer. He slammed down the phone, and I winced at the sound.

Slowly I hung up the phone and came back to the table. Tersely, I reported Dan's side of the conversation.

"Then I guess there's nothing else we can do," Sophie said. "If you try calling back now, you won't be able to get Bootsie on the phone. He'll unplug it, or he'll find some other way of keeping her away from it." Getting up from her chair, she carried her coffee cup to the sink. "I don't know about you, Emma, but I'm pooped. I can't think about this anymore tonight."

"You're right," I said, sighing. "I don't think there's anything more we can do right now. We should all get to bed. Maybe I can call Bootsie in the morning."

"Maybe," Marylou said, "or I can try."

"Are you sure you don't need help clearing up?" Sophie asked.

"Yes, I'm fine, dear," Marylou said. She yawned, hastily covering her mouth with her hand. "Goodness, I'm tired too. A good night's sleep is what we all need."

Marylou saw us to the front door, giving us each a quick hug before saying a last "good night."

We crossed Marylou's lawn into mine. "Good night, Emma," Sophie said. "Talk to you in the morning." She continued across the grass to her house.

"Good night," I called after her. I unlocked the front door to find Olaf waiting at the foot of the stairs for me. Smiling, I picked him up and carried him up the stairs with me. He was like a faithful little dog, waiting and watching for me to come home. Hilda was already ensconced on the bed, and she blinked sleepily at me when I turned on the light.

I got ready for bed, and I lay in the darkness, both cats purring nearby. My thoughts kept returning to Dan and his blackmail scheme. I had a bad feeling about that, but I didn't think there was anything I could do about it. A couple of times I reached for the phone, but both times I thought better of it. Sophie was right. Dan would make sure Bootsie didn't talk to me tonight.

Finally I drifted off to sleep, only to be troubled by strange dreams.

The phone woke me up, and I gazed blearily at my bedside clock before answering it. It was nearly seven thirty. Amazed that Olaf had let me sleep this late, I reached for the phone.

"Hello," I said, still groggy as I pushed myself up into a sitting position in the bed.

"Emma, you were right," Marylou said, her voice strained. "Dan is dead."

Chapter 20

"Dead," I said blankly. "What do you mean?"

"He was killed in a hit-and-run accident this morning," Marylou said. "While he was out for his morning run."

"Oh, dear Lord," I said. The fog had lifted completely. "How did you hear about it?"

"Bootsie called me," Marylou said. Her voice dropped. "In fact, she's here with me right now, the poor thing." She paused for a breath. "She was so upset when the police came to inform her, they asked her if there was anyone they could call to be with her. She called me."

"Are you still at her house?"

"No, we're at mine," Marylou said. "As soon as the police were finished with her, I brought her over here. Just a few minutes ago. I thought it might be better to get her away from there for a little while."

"Is there anything I can do?" I said, feeling helpless and bewildered. I had predicted this, but that didn't make it any easier to comprehend. Maybe I should just have gone to Bootsie's house last night and insisted on talking to her and Dan.

What I should have done, I realized now, was call Lieutenant Burnes and tell him. But none of us had expected the murderer to act so quickly. I thought we had a little more time to try to get Dan—or at least Bootsie—to see reason.

"Would you mind coming over?" Marylou said. "I hate to ask, but I think I'm going to need help with her. I've never seen her like this."

"I'll be right over as soon as I can get dressed and feed the cats," I said. She thanked me and hung up. I replaced the receiver on its cradle and sat in the bed for a moment, trying to gather the strength to get up.

Dan had paid dearly for his attempt at blackmail, and while I hadn't cared for the man at all, I still felt anger at such a useless death. "Stupid, stupid, stupid," I muttered as I threw back the covers and climbed out of bed.

Olaf watched hopefully while I washed my face, brushed my hair, and then threw on some clothes. "Don't worry," I told him. "I'll feed you first."

Both cats seemed to have picked up on my distress, because Hilda was close on my heels as I ran lightly down the stairs. She usually stays in bed awhile longer.

I checked their water and made sure they both had food in their bowls. I bent to stroke them as they munched on their breakfast. I slipped away while they were eating and went out the front door.

Marylou had obviously been watching for me, because I didn't even have to knock. The front door opened as I came up the walk, and I stepped inside the house.

"Where is she?" I asked, my voice low, and Marylou cocked her head in the direction of the living room. She shut the door, and I walked on ahead.

Bootsie lay supine on the couch, one arm thrown across her eyes. I stopped for a moment to observe her. As I watched, she sobbed loudly, and the sound was so forlorn it made me want to cry along with her. I felt even more guilty now about not having done more to prevent this.

I approached and sank down on my knees near her.

"Bootsie," I said softly, "I'm so very sorry." I touched the arm she had across her face.

Bootsie let her arm fall, and she turned a tear-streaked face to me. Her appearance shocked me. She wore no makeup, and her face was streaked with tears, her skin blotched with red spots. For the first time since I had met her, she looked every year of her age, and more. My heart went out to her.

"Oh, Emma," Bootsie said, her voice hoarse from crying. "How could something like this happen? He was so young."

"I don't know," I said. I did know, but I really didn't think now was the time to discuss it with her. I wasn't heartless enough to tell her Dan had died because he was trying to blackmail someone. I didn't think, not even for a moment, that Dan's death was an accident. There would be time enough later to broach the subject with her.

"Sometimes these things just defy explanation," I said, trying to make my voice as soothing as possible. "It was a horrible, horrible accident. Were there any witnesses?"

Bootsie shook her head. "The police don't think so. Other than the bastard who ran him down."

Marylou appeared behind me, a glass in her hand. "Here, honey, drink this."

Bootsie sat up slowly. "What is it?"

"A little brandy," Marylou said. "It'll do you good." She held out the glass.

Bootsie accepted it with a trembling hand. I thought at first she was going to spill it all over herself, but she managed to drink it down. "Thanks," she said, handing the glass back to Marylou.

"I think I'd like to go to the bathroom now and wash my face," Bootsie said.

"Of course, dear," Marylou said.

I stood up and gave Bootsie my arm to lean on. I escorted her to the bathroom in the hall. She shut the door, and I returned to the living room.

"Poor thing," Marylou said, almost clucking like the proverbial mother hen. "I feel so helpless. Not to mention a little guilty."

"I know what you mean," I said, suddenly shivering. "And especially considering what we were talking about last night."

"Don't dwell on that, Emma. We tried, but the killer acted too quickly," Marylou said. "It won't help either one of us to brood about it. Now come on in the kitchen and have some coffee. You could use something to warm you up."

I made no demur, because I felt a little shaky myself all of a sudden. I think the full import of another sudden death was really starting to sink in.

In the kitchen I accepted a steaming mug of coffee with thanks. "Are you hungry?" Marylou asked.

"No, thanks," I said. "I couldn't eat anything right now."

"I know," Marylou said, sighing. "For once, even I'm not hungry, and I haven't had my breakfast yet. Poor Bootsie."

"Do you think one of us should check on her?" I asked.

"I'll go," Marylou said, rising from her chair.

I waited at the kitchen table for several minutes, and finally Marylou came back, bringing Bootsie with her.

"You just sit down right here," Marylou said, depositing Bootsie in a chair. "I'm going to fix you some coffee, and I want you to drink it."

Bootsie nodded. She had washed her face, and some of the blotches had faded. She still looked old and worn, but some of her distress had receded, at least for the moment.

"There," Marylou said, placing a mug in front of the bereaved woman. "I put in some extra sugar. For shock, you know."

Bootsie nodded again before sipping from her mug. We sat in silence for a few minutes while Bootsie drank her coffee.

"Thank you," she finally said. "Thank you for coming to get me, Marylou. I don't know what I'd have done. I just couldn't stay in that house right then."

Marylou patted her hand. "I was glad to do it, honey. You shouldn't be alone right now. You need friends around you."

"Yes," I said, "and if there's anything I can do for you, please tell me. I'm so sorry about what happened." The words were totally inadequate. I knew them all too well, because so many people had said them to me six months ago.

I was trying hard not to think of a similar scene, after the police had come to tell me that Baxter had been killed. I had been in shock, but I had managed to give the police my brother's name and phone number. He and Luke had arrived soon after, and Sophie only a few minutes after them. They had done their best to comfort me, but what comfort can there be when someone you love is ripped away from you in an instant?

Disturbed by the force of my own memories, I got up from the table and walked over to the sink. I stared blindly out the window into Marylou's backyard. Now was not the time to fall apart. Marylou needed my help, not another grieving person to comfort.

It took me a moment, but I regained my composure. I returned to my seat at the table, and Marylou watched me with compassion. I smiled faintly to show her that I was okay.

"Thank you both," Bootsie said. Her voice was stronger. "I really appreciate it." She turned to Marylou. "But I think I need to be by myself for a little while. Could I go somewhere and lie down?"

"Of course, dear," Marylou said. "You come with me. I have a nice, comfortable guest room, and you can get some rest there."

She escorted Bootsie from the room. "Be right back, Emma," she called over her shoulder.

I sipped at my coffee while I waited for Marylou. I

forced my thoughts away from the events of six months ago and focused instead on what had happened to Dan.

One thing was obvious. I had to tell Lieutenant Burnes about the conversation I had overheard. If I didn't, the police might dismiss Dan's death as an accident. That would be a mistake.

When Marylou returned, I announced, without preamble, "I have to call Lieutenant Burnes."

Marylou nodded as she sat down and picked up her mug of coffee. "Yes, I definitely think you should. He needs to know what you heard last night."

"I'll go home and do it," I said, "but first, what do you think? Do you think Bootsie has any idea that it wasn't an accident?"

Staring down into her coffee, Marylou said slowly, "You know, I think she does. It was pretty strange, I mean when I first got over to her house." She paused as if gathering her thoughts. "It was right after the police left, and I was trying to get her up and out to my car."

"What happened?"

"I had left her alone for a minute or two while I looked for her keys, and when I came back to her, she was mumbling something. I think she was saying, 'It's my fault. I did this,' or something to that effect." She frowned. "As I said, she was mumbling, and I'm not really certain what I heard."

I eyed Marylou doubtfully. "Well, last night she was talking about how he went running before daylight. Maybe she was blaming herself for not talking him out of waiting until after sunrise."

Marylou shrugged. "That could be, I guess, but I don't know. I just don't know."

"We'll have to try to make sense of it later," I said. "In the meantime I should call Lieutenant Burnes." I stood up.

"You can call him from here," Marylou said, getting up from her chair. She walked to the refrigerator and pulled a card loose from the magnet holding it to the door. "Here's his number."

I took the card and went to her phone. For the first time, I noticed that his first name was Frank. Frank Burnes. Why did that sound familiar? Then I remembered. That obnoxious character from *M.A.S.H.*

I banished that thought as I punched in the number and waited. After three rings, a sleepy male voice answered. "Lieutenant Burnes," I said, "this is Emma Diamond. I'm sorry to bother you."

"No, that's okay," he said, sounding instantly alert. "What can I do for you?"

"I have some information I think you need to know," I said, "but I'd rather not discuss it over the phone."

"Would you like me to come to your house?"

"If you wouldn't mind," I said. "This is rather urgent."

"I'll be there in thirty minutes," he said. "Do you need someone there sooner?"

"No," I said, "half an hour will be fine." I said good-bye and hung up the phone.

"He's coming, then?" Marylou asked.

I nodded. "Yes, and I'd better get home and get ready." I glanced down at myself. "I really can't receive him looking like this."

Marylou smiled in a kindly fashion. "Of course not, dear. You go on home, and if I need you for anything, I'll let you know."

As she was escorting me to the front door, she said, "Oh, Emma, I almost forgot about the coffee cake you wanted me to make for you. I can do it this afternoon so it will still be fresh for tonight."

"Thank you," I said, giving her a quick hug. "I had almost forgotten about it. But that would be lovely, if you have time and feel like it."

"I'll be happy to," Marylou said. "Baking is good therapy for me."

"Why don't you come with us tonight?" I said. "I know Jake and Luke would love to meet you."

"Thank you," Marylou said. "But are you sure it's okay? Weren't you planning to play bridge?"

"We are," I said, "but that's okay. We can take turns, like we did last night. Do say you'll come."

"All right," Marylou said, "but you just check with your brother and his partner first. I can always meet them another time."

"I'll check with them," I said. "Call you later."

I hurried back home, letting myself in the front door. I ran up the stairs, debating whether to take a quick shower. I decided against it, electing instead to have a brisk wash at the sink. I brushed my hair again, applied some makeup, then slipped into some slacks and a blouse.

Twenty minutes later, I was downstairs pouring myself a cup of coffee and munching on the remnants of Marylou's coffee cake when I heard the doorbell ring. Pausing only to wipe my hands on a dish towel, I hurried to the front door.

"Lieutenant, thanks for coming," I said, motioning him inside. "I'm sorry for getting you out so early on a Saturday morning, but I wouldn't have if I didn't think it was important." The words came tumbling out. I hadn't realized just how nervous I was.

"Not at all, Mrs. Diamond," he said, smiling. He was dressed in a more casual fashion today, but he still looked official.

"Let's go into the kitchen," I said, leading the way. "How about some coffee?"

"Coffee would be good," he said. "I could use some caffeine."

I gestured for him to sit down, and I poured him a cup of coffee. I also brought him the last slice of Marylou's coffee cake. "Please, have this too. It's delicious. My neighbor made it."

"Thanks, don't mind if I do," he said, breaking off a bit of the slice and popping it into his mouth. He chewed for a moment, then swallowed. "It is delicious."

"She's a wonderful baker. Marylou Lockridge, that is," I said, still feeling a bit jittery.

"Please give her my compliments," Burnes said. "Now, what was it you wanted to tell me? You sounded urgent on the phone."

I took a deep breath to center myself a little. "You won't have heard about this yet," I said, "but this morning, one of my neighbors was killed in a hit-and-run while he was out jogging."

Burnes was instantly on the alert. "Who was it?"

"Dan Connor," I said.

His eyes narrowed for a moment. "He lives with Mrs. Flannigan."

"Yes," I said.

"And you don't think it was just a hit-and-run," Burnes said, his eyes assessing me.

"No, I'm sure it wasn't," I said. "Last night, Marylou Lockridge, Sophie Parker, and I played bridge at Marylou's house. Bootsie and Dan were there too."

"Go on," Burnes said when I hesitated.

"I overheard a conversation Dan was having on his cell phone," I said. I repeated what I had heard. Burnes's eyes never wavered from mine while I talked.

"I see," he said slowly. He pulled a notebook and pen out of his jacket pocket and jotted something down. "So you think he was trying to blackmail someone."

"Yes, I do," I said, "and I think it must have been a man he was talking to. Because he referred to that person as a 'bastard.'"

"You're probably right," Burnes said. "Oh, hello, old fellow." Olaf had appeared from nowhere and hopped into the policeman's lap.

"Olaf," I said, sighing heavily. "You're incorrigible."

Burnes laughed. "It's quite all right, Mrs. Diamond. He's perfectly welcome." He stroked Olaf's head, and Olaf gazed up at him adoringly. "But as much as I'd enjoy sitting here with this little guy in my lap, I think

I had better get to work." He gently dislodged Olaf, who then stalked away, tail in the air, demonstrating his indignation at such treatment.

"I should have called you last night," I said suddenly. "And maybe this wouldn't have happened." I shook my head. "I tried talking to Dan about it, but he wouldn't pay any attention to me." I explained the call I had made to Dan last night.

"I think you did all you reasonably could," Burnes said. "And even if you had called me last night, I don't know that I could have done anything to prevent it myself, short of hauling Mr. Connor downtown and locking him up. The killer acted very quickly to remove the threat, more quickly than I would have expected."

"I suppose you're right," I said.

"Thank you for the coffee and the cake," Burnes said as I walked him to the door. "And thanks for calling me this morning to tell me what you overheard. This could be the break we're looking for."

"I thought you should know," I said. "I don't believe Dan's death was an accident."

"No, I don't think it was," Burnes agreed. "That would be too much of a coincidence, I'm afraid." He smiled. "Thanks again."

"Oh, I almost forgot," I said. "If you need to talk to Bootsie Flannigan, she's next door at Marylou's house."

"Thanks," Burnes said. "I do need to talk to her."

"Good-bye," I said. I watched him for a moment as he headed toward Marylou's house, then shut the door. He really was an attractive man, but I wasn't in the market.

I felt curiously flat after the policeman's departure. I thought about calling Marylou but decided I would wait and let her call me after Lieutenant Burnes was finished next door.

Back in the kitchen, I glanced at the clock and was astonished to see that it was nearly nine thirty. I frowned. Why hadn't I heard from Sophie yet? Normally, she would either have called or put in an appearance by now. What could she be up to?

I had been neglecting my housework the past few days. I still had a couple of boxes of kitchen things that needed unpacking and sorting. I might as well get on with it. Anything to keep me from thinking too much about Dan Connor and what I might have done differently.

The next time I happened to glance at the clock it was approaching noon. I had been so engrossed in my work that I had completely lost track of time.

Remembering that I'd had only a piece of coffee cake for breakfast, I set about making lunch. Sophie deigned to put in an appearance as I was sitting at the table, munching on a sandwich.

"Good morning," she said brightly.

"Or afternoon, as the case may be," I said wryly.

"So it is," Sophie said.

"What have you been up to this morning? You look awfully perky. Not to mention dressed to the nines." I examined her clothes. She was dressed in date clothes.

She dimpled. "Oh, I slept in for once, and then I went out for brunch. I just got back." She slid into a chair and dropped her purse on the table.

"That sounds nice," I said. "And might I ask with whom you had this brunch?" I had a strong feeling I knew the answer.

"Oh, Nate McGreevey," she said in a careless tone. "He called me this morning and invited me, and I said yes."

I bit back the warning I was inclined to offer, about her getting too deeply involved with Nate. It wouldn't do any good, and it would probably lead to one of our occasional fights, when Sophie would accuse me of being overprotective.

"You had a good time, then," I said.

Sophie eyed me suspiciously. "Yes, I did. Nate can be very entertaining."

"I'm glad," I said. "But you obviously haven't heard what happened in the neighborhood this morning."

"No, what?" she said, leaning forward eagerly.

Quickly I told her about Dan's death, and about my conversation with Lieutenant Burnes. She sat back in her chair and stared at me.

"That's horrible," she said finally. "He was a worm, but he didn't deserve that." She frowned. "You tried to talk some sense into him last night, but it didn't do any good."

"No, it didn't," I said, "but it's Bootsie I really feel for now. She's taking this hard."

Sophie nodded. "Maybe she cared more about him than I thought."

"What do you mean?"

She shrugged. "Oh, I always got the impression when I was around them that Bootsie wasn't in love with him. She just liked having a good-looking young stud on a string." She frowned. "The only times I saw her really act like she loved him was when Gerald was anywhere around."

"Interesting," I said. The phone rang, and I got up to answer it. "Hello."

"Emma, it's Marylou," Marylou said, her voice barely above a whisper, "and I'm at Bootsie's house with her and the lieutenant. They don't know I'm calling you."

"What's wrong?" I said, sensing something from Marylou's tone.

"Someone has ransacked Bootsie's house."

Chapter 21

"What is it?" Sophie asked. "What's going on?"

I shook my head at her, and she subsided. "How bad is it?"

"It's a real mess," Marylou said. "Pretty much every room in the house, even the kitchen. Dan's bedroom is the worst. Looks like a tornado's been through it."

"Dan's bedroom?" I said, startled. "He had his own bedroom?"

"Yes," Marylou said. "I was surprised, too, believe me." She paused. "The lieutenant is calling me. Gotta go." The phone clicked off in my ear.

I hung up my phone and turned back to face an impatient Sophie. "That was Marylou, calling from Bootsie's house. Someone has ransacked Bootsie's house."

"Wonder what they were looking for," Sophie said. "Maybe Dan's cell phone?"

"That's a possibility," I said, "but in the long run it really wouldn't matter. If necessary, I'm sure the police could get the records from the service provider to find out whom Dan had called. Who knows what else the killer might have been after?" I frowned. "Marylou said practically the whole house is a mess. But get this. Dan had a separate bedroom."

"You're kidding," Sophie said. "Why would Bootsie and Dan have separate bedrooms? Unless their relationship wasn't exactly what they led everyone to believe."

I nodded. "Exactly. I'm beginning to think the whole thing was a sham. You said as much yourself the other day. When did Dan first turn up with Bootsie?"

Sophie frowned as she considered my question. "About six months ago, I think. And right after that, Bootsie let everybody know Dan had moved in with her."

"Strange," I said. "I wonder if the whole thing with Dan was just part of some scheme."

"Like trying to make Gerald McGreevey jealous?" Sophie asked with a laugh. "I've thought that all along, even though it sounds a little nuts to me."

"To me too," I said, "but if Bootsie is really hung up on Gerald, who knows what she might do?"

"Like kill Janet," Sophie said. "And of course she doesn't have an alibi for Dan's murder either."

"No," I said, thinking about that. "I'm sure the police would have checked out her car and Dan's right away, though. If there was any sign that one of them had been used, the police would be on to her right away."

"Yeah," Sophie said. "And besides, we know it wasn't Bootsie that Dan was threatening."

"So it's pretty unlikely that Bootsie killed Dan," I said. "Besides, she seemed genuinely upset." I remembered something else. "Marylou said, when she first went over to Bootsie's this morning, and right after the police left, that Bootsie was mumbling. And that mumbling sounded like she was blaming herself for Dan's death."

"She's got to be involved in this somehow," Sophie said. "But exactly how?"

"I don't know. There's something really screwy about this whole thing," I said, "obviously. But there's something I can't quite put my finger on." I shook my head. "I don't know. Maybe it will come to me if I leave it alone."

"Good idea," Sophie said. She stood up. "I have some things I need to do this afternoon. If you hear anything else that's interesting, call me. If I leave the house, I'll forward my phone to my cell phone like I always do."

"Sure," I said. "And don't forget about tonight."

"I won't," Sophie said, her hand on the doorknob. "I'm really looking forward to seeing the boys."

"I invited Marylou to come with us," I said, "and that reminds me, I need to let Jake know."

"Sounds fine. See you later." With that she was gone.

Before I forgot again, I went to the phone and punched in my brother's office number. I spoke briefly with the receptionist, and she put me through to Jake's voice mail. I left a message, asking him to call me if there were any problem, but I knew neither he nor Luke would mind my bringing Marylou along tonight.

That chore done, I decided I would work upstairs this afternoon. My closet needed organizing, and I wanted to sort through some of my clothes. I had a large closet in my bedroom, but I didn't want to clutter it up with everything. Both the guest bedrooms upstairs had decent-sized closets, and I wanted to store some of my things in them. I had been putting off this job, but I might as well get to it now.

As I worked on the closets, keeping an eye out for inquisitive felines who could get shut up accidentally, I mulled over the events of the last twenty-four hours.

Bootsie's role in all this puzzled me. If she *was* involved with the killer, had Dan known about it? Had he been a part of the plot all along? Or had he decided to insert himself into it, thinking he could score big?

Those questions prompted another idea. What if Bootsie had nothing to do with it at all? What if Dan had seen something and decided to blackmail the killer, keeping Bootsie in the dark about it all? If their relationship wasn't as intimate as we all thought it was, Dan could well have been acting on his own. Perhaps we were mistaken in putting Bootsie into the equation just because she was known to be carrying a torch for Gerald. Bootsie could be a blind alley altogether.

If Bootsie was using Dan simply as a ploy to make Gerald jealous, that might be enough to make her feel guilty over his death. That could explain the mumbling Marylou had overheard.

The more I thought about it, as I folded and sorted clothes, the more I figured it could be true. It was the simplest explanation, and sometimes the simplest explanation was the true one.

If we could eliminate Bootsie from the suspect list, or at least demote her, where did that leave us? I figured Gerald was still the best suspect, with Nate a close second. Carlene I ranked pretty high because I thought she just might be ruthless enough to murder two people to get what she wanted.

I dismissed Shannon Hardy completely. I didn't think she had the brains to figure out how to go about killing anyone, nor did I think she had the nerve. Her husband might have both the brains and the nerve, but somehow I doubted it. Same thing with the Grahams. They might be really angry at Janet, but I didn't think either one of them had the guts to murder someone.

When I realized I had folded and unfolded the same sweater at least twice, I decided I had better focus more on the task at hand. These endless questions were just that: endless. I didn't feel like I had made any real progress. It was all still so amorphous.

The phone rang about four thirty, and I gratefully left the closets to answer it, after one last, quick check for curious felines.

"Hello," I said, a little breathless from hurrying.

"Emma, it's me," Marylou said.

"Where are you? Are you home yet?"

"Yes, I got here a few minutes ago," she said. "And I brought Bootsie back here with me. She called a cleaning service to come straighten up her house. I didn't think she needed to be by herself tonight." She sighed. "She's lying down in the guest room right now, trying to get a little rest."

"You're right about her needing to be with someone," I said, "after all she's been through. I'm glad she's getting a cleaning service, though I would have been happy to help."

"I know," Marylou said, "and I'm sure she does, too. But she figured it would be a lot easier to have them do it."

"Was anything missing?"

"Dan's cell phone, for one thing," Marylou said. "Bootsie couldn't find it anywhere." She paused. "Or at least she said she couldn't."

"What do you mean?" I asked, puzzled.

"I really couldn't say," Marylou said.

"Has Bootsie come into the room?"

"Yes, exactly," Marylou said. "Bootsie, I'll be with you in just a minute." I heard Bootsie's voice in the background, but I couldn't make out what she was saying.

Marylou spoke into the phone again. "Now, Emma dear, I told you not to worry about the coffee cake. I made it a little earlier today, before we went over to Bootsie's house."

"Good gracious, Marylou," I said, taken aback. "I had completely forgotten about it. But how kind of you."

"Not at all," Marylou said. "Listen, with Bootsie here tonight, I'm afraid I won't be able to go with you to play bridge."

"I hadn't thought of that," I said. "I'm sorry you can't go with us, but you're right, Bootsie shouldn't be on her own." I thought for a moment. "What about you, though? Would you feel better if Sophie and I stayed with you both?"

"No, dear, that's very kind of you," Marylou said, "but Bootsie and I will be just fine. She needs a quiet night, and, frankly, so do I. Don't you worry about us."

"If you're sure," I said.

"I'm sure," Marylou said. "Now, don't forget your coffee cake. I'm sure you want to take it with you tonight." She paused a moment. "I'll bring it over in a few minutes, after I've got Bootsie settled."

"Thanks," I said, and then Marylou hung up.

Marylou was being a bit mysterious, but she obviously had something she wanted to tell me. Something to do with Bootsie and Dan's cell phone—but what?

I was waiting by the front door, watching for Marylou, and the moment she came into view, I opened the door. I practically dragged her in, I was so anxious to hear what she had to say.

"Goodness, Emma," she said, laughing a bit as she handed me a wrapped plate.

"Thank you," I said, taking the coffee cake in one hand and shutting the door with the other. "What were you being so cagey about on the phone? Something to do with Dan's cell phone."

"Oh yes," Marylou said, following me to the kitchen. "Bootsie told the lieutenant she couldn't find it, but, Emma—get this. I saw inside her purse before we left her house, and guess what?"

"What?" I said, setting the plate down on the table and motioning for Marylou to have a seat.

"She had two cell phones in her purse," Marylou said as she sat down.

"Then one of them is probably Dan's," I said.

"Oh yes," Marylou said, nodded emphatically. "Bootsie's is pink, and the other one was a regular-looking cell phone. It was Dan's all right."

"I wonder why she lied to the lieutenant about it,"

I mused. "Do you think we should tell him? This could be really important."

"Well, why don't we see?" Marylou's face split in a huge grin as she stuck a hand in the pocket of her slacks and withdrew a cell phone.

"Oh my goodness," I said, awestruck. "Marylou, tell me you didn't."

"I sure did," she said. "I don't think Bootsie will miss it for a little while, and I'll slip it back into her purse when I go back to the house." She poked a button and turned the phone on.

When the phone was ready, Marylou said, "Go ahead, Emma. Check the last number he called."

I eyed the phone doubtfully. It was a different type from mine, and I wasn't sure I could do it without messing something up. But curiosity got the better of me, and I offered a mute apology to Lieutenant Burnes as I picked up the phone and punched a button.

A menu came up, and I sighed with relief. This was going to be easy, after all. I selected OUTGOING CALLS," and a list came up. I chose the first call and looked at the number. I didn't recognize it, however. But what caught my attention was the time.

"This call was made at nine forty-two last night," I said, frowning.

"That's well after the call you overheard, isn't it?" Marylou said.

I thought back. "It was probably around eight thirty, give or take a few minutes, when Dan made the call I heard. Let's look at the other calls."

I went carefully through the most recent calls, and Dan had made four calls in the time period between 8:37 and 9:42. I got up from the table and retrieved paper and a pen. I made a note of each number, and the time that Dan called it. Then I turned the phone off and gave it back to Marylou.

"Do you recognize any of these numbers?" I said.

"Two of them, the first and third ones, look like numbers in this area."

"Yes," Marylou said. "The eight thirty-seven one is to the McGreevey house, and the third one is to the Grahams. I don't recognize the other two."

"I wonder if they're cell phones, or if they have nothing at all to do with this," I said. "There's one way to find out." I got up to retrieve my phone.

"Emma, do you think that's a good idea?" Marylou asked, sounding alarmed.

"Why not?" I said, and then I realized. "Of course, caller ID. If I call these numbers, my number will come up. Darn." I dropped down into my chair and set the phone on the table.

"But your cell phone," Marylou said. "Your name probably wouldn't come up if you used that, would it?"

I frowned. "I'm not sure. But it might be safer than using my home phone."

"What do you think these other calls mean?" Marylou asked.

"Hard to say," I said, "but my guess is that Dan might have been fishing. You know, calling several people and saying something like 'I know what you did. Now pay up if you don't want me to go to the police.' He may not really have known anything, in that case, or else he knew something but couldn't link it to one person."

"It sounds very complicated," Marylou said, shaking her head.

"Yes, but we'll know more when we know who all the numbers belong to."

"I hate to go," Marylou said, "when it's getting so interesting, but I'd better get back, just in case Bootsie comes looking for her purse."

"Of course," I said, "but you know, we really ought to see that Lieutenant Burnes sees this cell phone. I know it's important."

Marylou grinned. "You just leave that to me. You

work on those numbers, and I'll see that Bootsie turns the phone over to the police."

"Agreed," I said.

"Don't bother seeing me out," Marylou said. "The door will lock behind me, won't it?"

"Yes," I said. I gave her a quick hug. "Be careful."

"I will. Have a good time tonight."

"Thanks, and thanks again for the coffee cake."

With a quick wave, Marylou hurried down the hall, and moments later I heard the front door shut.

My cell phone was in my purse, and the purse was on the counter near the fridge. I dug around until I found the dratted thing. Naturally it was in the bottom. I didn't use it that much, and half the time I forgot it was there.

I waited impatiently for the phone to be ready to use, and when it was, I punched in the first of the two unknown numbers.

Then I panicked slightly, because what would I say if someone answered? I listened to the ringing, and then a voice-mail message came on. "This is Carlene Newberry. I'm unable to take . . . " I didn't hear the rest of it. I ended the call.

I wrote Carlene's name by her number on my list, and then I called the other number. This time a live person answered.

"Hi, this is Nate," he said.

"So terribly sorry," I said in my best British accent, my voice pitched about an octave lower than usual. "Wrong number."

"Whatever," Nate said, obviously indifferent. He ended the call, and I punched my phone off with relief.

I added Nate's name to the list, and then I sat staring at the names and numbers.

Dan had called the McGreevey house first. Had he spoken with Gerald?

He must have, because otherwise he wouldn't have needed to call Nate on his cell phone later.

Carlene was the second call, and the Grahams after her.

One of these five people had killed Dan Connor. The list trembled in my hand.

Chapter 22

During the drive to my brother's house I filled Sophie in on the events of the afternoon.

"Why would Dan make four phone calls? Was he just gambling, do you think?"

"I'm not sure," I said, keeping a watchful eye on a guy in a BMW trying to cut through traffic behind me. The Loop was too crowded for someone to be driving like that. Why did some people get in such a hurry when traffic was heavy? It seemed so pointless.

"Maybe he was just playing a joke on three of the calls," Sophie said. "One of the calls was legit, so to speak, and the other three were jokes." She laughed derisively. "Believe me, that's the kind of humor Dan thought was really funny. So I wouldn't put it past him to have made three of those calls for the sake of annoying people."

"I guess I can see that," I said. Mr. BMW shot around me, crossed two lanes via a small gap in the traffic, and slid into the Westheimer Road exit and disappeared onto the feeder road. I breathed a sigh of relief. "If that's the case, then it leaves us with the question of which call is the true blackmail call."

"The first one, wouldn't you say that seems likely?" Sophie said. "And that was to Gerald, wasn't it?"

"Well, to be accurate, it was to his house, but of course we don't know who answered the phone, him or Nate." We had reached our exit, and I steered the car off the Loop, relieved to be off it. I hated driving on the freeways in Houston.

"But one of the other calls was to Nate's cell phone," Sophie said, an odd note in her voice. "Why would Dan want to talk to him twice?"

"Yes, good point," I said, "and because of that, it seems likely Gerald was on the other end of that first call."

Sophie didn't reply to that, and I glanced over at her. She was staring out the window, her hands twisting in her lap.

"What's wrong?" I asked. "Something is obviously bothering you."

For a long moment she didn't respond, and I thought perhaps she was so lost in thought she hadn't heard me. But then she turned her head slightly toward me. "It's Nate," she admitted. "He's acting a bit strange."

"How so?" I said, forbearing to say that I thought Nate was a bit strange to begin with, in some ways.

"We've been talking a lot since all this happened," she said. "Janet's death hit him a lot harder than I think he expected it would. I mean, he didn't like her, hated her, really, but he's still upset over her death."

"It was pretty awful," I said, "and maybe he's just bothered by the way it happened. Surely he's not mourning her, if he really hated her."

Sophie sighed. "No, I don't think he's in mourning. It's just that . . ." She fell silent for a moment. "I think he's conflicted, because he knows something important, and he knows he ought to tell the police. But he's protecting someone."

"Okay," I said. "That sounds reasonable. Who's he protecting? Gerald would be the most likely person, wouldn't he?"

"Yes," Sophie said, "but I know he's awfully fond of Bootsie, too. She was more like a second mother to him than Janet ever was." She shrugged. "It might be her he's trying to protect."

"What have you said to him?" I had to tread carefully here and not come across as the pushy big sister. I know what I would have said to Nate, but I wasn't sure what Sophie might have done.

"I told him he shouldn't hold back anything," Sophie said. "That it was better for the truth to come out."

"How did he respond to that?"

"He didn't," Sophie said. "He just looked at me with this real sad look on his face, and, well, to be honest, it gave me the weirdest feeling."

"How do you mean?"

"Oh, I don't know," Sophie said. Then she gave a little moan. "Oh yes, I do, Emma. I might as well admit it. He was looking so strange that I thought maybe he was trying in his own strange way to tell me he had done it himself."

When I didn't respond for a moment, Sophie turned to me with an angry look on her face. "Aren't you happy? I know you think I shouldn't get involved with him, and this is why, isn't it? You really think he killed Janet, don't you?"

"No, as a matter of fact, I don't," I said, doing my best to keep my tone level. Now was not the time to respond in an angry manner. "I can't pretend that I'm thrilled to see you get involved with Nate. But I don't know him all that well. I'm willing to give him the benefit of the doubt where you're concerned. Until this is all settled, though, I don't think you should rush into anything."

"I'm not rushing into anything," Sophie said, almost biting the words off. "For heaven's sake, Emma, my divorce isn't final yet, and won't be for another month or so. What kind of idiot do you think I am?"

"I don't think you're an idiot, Sophie," I said, hoping the frost in my voice would cool her down a bit.

"Far from it. I think you're a bright, beautiful, and wonderful person. That's why I always want what's best for you. And if Nate turns out to be that, then I'm fine with that."

Sophie giggled suddenly. "Oh, Emma, I'm sorry. I was acting like a spoiled brat. You're right. I know you don't think I'm stupid." She sobered. "Though I sure act like a stupid, spoiled brat sometimes. I promise I'm not rushing into anything, like I said. I like Nate a lot, but that's all it is at the moment."

"Good," I said. "And let's pray this is all over soon, so we can get on with our lives."

"And here we are," Sophie said, as I turned the car into the driveway of the lovely old Victorian where my brother and his partner had lived for the past four years.

Sophie preceded me up the walk to the front door. She had hardly stepped onto the porch when the door swung open. My brother's partner, Luke Hilton, stood framed in the doorway. At six four, with very broad shoulders, he seemed almost twice the size of petite Sophie as he stepped onto the porch and swooped her into his arms. He swung her around once, then set her down on the porch. She giggled like a little girl and slapped him playfully on the arm.

"Hi, Luke," I said, as he leaned forward to give me a quick peck on the cheek. "You're in fine form this evening."

He laughed as he looked down at Sophie. "I can't help myself, Emma. She's like a little toy, and you know I can't resist playing with toys."

Sophie giggled again. "You're just a big gorilla, and I feel like Fay What's-Her-Name."

Luke grunted like a gorilla, and Sophie responded with peals of laughter.

"As much as I'm enjoying this reenactment of *King Kong*," I said, "I really would like to go inside. It's quite warm out here."

"Yes, ma'am," Luke said. He stood aside and flung out his arm toward the door. "Please come in."

Luke closed the door behind us, and then we followed him down the hall toward the kitchen. Jake would be there, fussing over something on the stove. He's the chef of the family, and he has always loved spending time in the kitchen.

"Hello, Emma," Jake said, his face widening in a smile as I walked into the kitchen. He left what he was doing to give me a big hug. I adored my brother, and he adored me.

He was a couple of inches shorter than Luke, but almost as broad in the shoulders. They both spent time working out on a regular basis, and I admired the results of their dedication to exercise. They were both handsome men, and as they stood beside each other, I enjoyed the picture they made. Jake was dark like me, and Luke was the proverbial blue-eyed blond. Those blue eyes sparkled with mischief—and with love, whenever he looked at my brother.

For a moment I felt a pang of jealousy. I'd had that, up until six months ago. But there was no point in feeling sorry for myself.

Jake picked up on my feelings, however, and he gave me another hug. "How are you doing, Em?" he asked as he went back to the stove. Luke and Sophie had moved several steps away, where Luke was pouring wine for Sophie and me.

"I'm okay," I said, "most of the time."

"Do you think it's been good, your moving to a new house?"

"Yes," I said. "It helps. And at least one of my new neighbors is a dear." Then I realized I had come in empty-handed. "Drat it, I left something in the car. I'll be right back."

"Here's your wine, Emma," Luke said, extending a glass toward me.

"Thanks," I said, pointing to the counter. "Just put it there for me. I'll be right back."

I hurried out to the car to retrieve the coffee cake. I had been so involved in my conversation with Sophie

I had forgotten all about it. I pulled it from the backseat, relocked the car, and went back inside.

When I reached the kitchen, Sophie was regaling Jake and Luke with the tales of our sleuthing. "And here comes Nancy Drew now," Luke said, grinning broadly.

"If you keep that up," I said, mock-severely, "I won't let you have any of this delicious treat I stayed up all night baking for you."

Luke immediately assumed a penitent expression. "My apologies, Miss Drew."

"Now, stop that," I said. "Or I'm going to start calling you Frank Hardy."

Luke shook his head. "No, that wouldn't work. I'd have to be Joe. He was the blond one."

Jake laughed. "So that makes me Frank Hardy, then?" He ran a hand through his dark mop.

Luke batted his eyelashes at him. "I'd rather you were Biff Hooper. Frankly, I always thought Joe and Biff had something going on the side." He laughed. "I know I would have. That Biff was a real hunk."

Sophie was laughing so hard I thought she would start snorting wine through her nose. She set down her wineglass and covered her mouth with her hands.

"Really, this has gone far enough," I said. "Look at poor Bess Marvin there—I mean Sophie—look what you've made her do." That set Sophie to giggling again. I turned to my brother. "Actually, I always thought you would make a good George Fayne."

"I think I'll go with Biff, in that case," my brother said with a haughty sniff. "George was way too butch for me, at least at that age." That got Luke roaring with laughter, and it was at least two minutes before the merriment ceased.

"Come on, let's play a hand or two of bridge," Luke said. "Dinner won't be ready for at least half an hour yet, and maybe we can keep Jake from fussing over the stove."

"Sounds good to me," I said, following Luke into the living room. Sophie and Jake trailed behind.

The card table was already set up, so all we had to do was sit down and start playing. Luke would be my partner, as usual. He and I played well together, and Jake and Sophie seemed to enjoy being partners. As I waited for Jake, sitting to my left, to finish dealing the cards, I glanced around the room.

Jake and Luke had furnished the house themselves, and they had done a beautiful job. They had been collecting the appropriate period furniture for years, and the result was an attractive room that wasn't overly fussy. They had modified some aspects of the typical Victorian style, eschewing covers for table legs and that sort of thing, but the overall impression was pleasantly old-fashioned.

Luke and I won the contract, playing two no trump. On Sophie's lead, Luke put down the dummy and sat back to watch. To my left Jake was fidgeting in his chair, casting glances toward the kitchen.

"Oh, all right," Luke said, sighing, "I'll go check. Just chill, honey. Nothing's going to spoil." As he moved past Jake, he leaned down to brush his lips against Jake's head.

"Make sure the sauce isn't on too high," Jake said. "It needs to be on low heat now."

"I will," Luke said.

"Sorry," Jake said, "I'll be fine once everything is done in the kitchen."

"Don't worry about it," I said absently. I was still examining the board, planning my strategy. I wasn't really paying all that much attention to my brother.

I could count seven tricks easily, between my hand and the dummy, but I would have to work to promote one of the dummy's five clubs into the eighth trick. I thought I had enough transportation back and forth, but I would have to see.

As I played, Sophie rambled on about the murder

investigation. When he returned from the kitchen, Luke was attentive with his questions, and Jake kept fidgeting in his chair. I was starting to get annoyed with him, because he was affecting my concentration. I forbore to say anything, however, because I knew he would settle down once he had finished with his preparations for dinner. He was always like this, and always had been. With something hanging over him, he couldn't rest until it was complete. Once it was done, he would be fine, calm and relaxed.

That's when it hit me. I knew who had put the peanuts in the spinach dip.

Chapter 23

I ended up making two over-tricks, thanks largely to Jake's inattention to the game. Despite Luke's protestations that everything was fine in the kitchen, Jake just couldn't settle down and focus on the game.

For once, however, I was grateful for this normally irritating behavior of my brother's, because his twitchiness while playing had brought back a memory from that fateful night at the McGreeveys' bridge party.

I hadn't recalled it until now, but as that memory surfaced, I realized it provided a behavioral clue to what had happened that night.

During that first hand, when I had been nervously contemplating having to play for a slam, I had been dimly aware of Bootsie, sitting to my right. While that hand lasted, Bootsie had behaved in similar fashion to my brother just now, squirming a bit, and not paying much attention to the game. At the time, I had put her behavior down to disinterest because she could do little to affect the outcome. She had left during the second hand, when she was dummy, ostensibly to go to the bathroom. But she could easily have gone to the island where the food and drink had been.

Once she was back at the table, she was calm, no longer fidgeting in her chair. She focused on the game and played the hand well when she won the contract.

The way I saw it now, Bootsie had been nervous and unable to concentrate, knowing that she was going to mix the ground peanuts into the spinach dip, waiting for her chance to do it without anyone paying particular attention.

Then, once she had done it, Bootsie came back to the table calm, with the evil deed accomplished.

"Emma, it's your turn to deal," Sophie said, poking at me.

"Are you okay?" Jake asked. He shoved toward me the cards he had evidently just cut.

"Sorry," I said. "I was just thinking about something." I picked up the cards and dealt them out. I needed to focus on the game for now. I wanted to spend some more time mulling over my revelation before I shared anything with anyone else.

Luke, the scorekeeper, announced, "Emma and I have a seventy leg. We don't need much for a game, Em, so deal us a good one."

I smiled. Luke was very competitive, just like Sophie, but he didn't let it get too out of hand, thankfully. Since the four of us began playing bridge a few months ago, we had been fairly even when it came to winning. Luke and I had a slight edge, having won the last two times we played, and I knew he would love to stretch the winning streak to three. "I'll do my best," I promised him. "But you know I usually deal myself lousy hands."

And so I had done this time, I saw when I rearranged my cards in order. I had seven points, the ace and king of hearts. "Pass," I said.

Sophie won the contract at three diamonds, and Luke led the queen of hearts. I played low, and when Luke took the trick, he led back another low heart, which I took with my king. There was still a heart on the board, and the ace was my last heart. That meant there were three still out, and I had to hope no one was void. I led my ace, and we took that trick as well.

"Who has lucky number thirteen?" Luke said, his eyebrows arching.

It turned out to be Sophie, and luckily for her, it was the trick she needed to make her contract.

At the end of the hand, Jake suggested we break for dinner. He hurried away to finish up in the kitchen while Luke escorted Sophie and me to the dining room. After he had seated us, he went to the kitchen to help Jake.

Sophie was eyeing me curiously, and I knew she wanted to question me. She knew me too well not to realize that something was distracting me. I shook my head slightly and said, "Later." She nodded.

Jake and Luke came into the dining room then, each bearing two plates. They deposited them with flourishes at each of our places, and then Jake picked up a bottle of wine from the sideboard and filled our glasses.

Over a delicious meal of clay-pot chicken, fresh asparagus with a lovely hollandaise sauce, wild rice, and freshly baked rolls, the four of us had a very enjoyable time. By tacit consent we avoided the subject of murder. Instead, both Jake and Luke took turns telling stories about their respective jobs. Jake was an internal medicine specialist, partner in a very busy clinic, and Luke was the head of a three-lawyer firm. He had worked for one of Houston's leading large firms until three years ago, when he had decided to go out on his own. Two friends had joined him a year after that, and Luke was happier than I had ever seen him.

Dessert was a yummy crème brûlée, and I sighed happily as I spooned the last bit into my mouth. "It's a good thing I don't eat here more often," I said, laying the spoon aside, "or I'd be as big as the side of a house."

"You don't think we have crème brûlée every night, do you?" Jake asked. "My dear sister, I make it only for special occasions."

"Yes," Luke said, making a mournful face, "he only gives me dessert when we have company. Usually I have to go sneak a Snickers bar when he's not looking." He shook his head dolefully.

"You poor baby," Sophie said, "so mistreated." She reached over and playfully slapped the back of Luke's hand. "You're spoiled rotten, and you know it."

Luke grinned. "Guilty as charged, ma'am."

"We spoil each other," Jake said. "I cook, and Luke cleans up, so it works out rather well." He stood up, dropping his napkin on the table. "What say we go back to the bridge table?"

By the time Sophie and I left, we had played six rubbers of bridge, with Sophie and Jake winning four of them. At some point conversation turned to the murders in our neighborhood, and both Jake and Luke expressed their concern over our safety. Sophie and I assured them we would be fine, and I expressed the hope that the police would soon wind things up.

"Do you think the police are handling it well?" Jake asked.

Sophie laughed. "I'm sure Emma does," she said. "She's already got her eye on the handsome lieutenant."

"I do not," I said crossly. "He's a very nice man, and I'll admit he is attractive, but I am not in the least interested in him. It's far too soon."

"I know," Sophie said contritely. "I was just teasing. Don't pay any attention to me."

"What's this lieutenant's name?" Luke asked. "I know a few homicide cops, thanks to a couple of cases I've had in the last three years."

"Burnes," I said. "Do you know him?"

Luke grinned. "If his first name is Frank, I do."

"Yes, that's his name," I said. "What's so funny?"

Luke burst out laughing, and I began to understand.

"He doesn't play for your team, Emma," Jake said, shaking his head at Luke. "In case you haven't guessed by now."

"Well, darn," Sophie said; then she laughed along with Luke.

"The next time I see him," I said, trying hard not to laugh myself, "I'll have to tell him who my beloved brother-in-law is." I paused. "And hope that he doesn't arrest me for consorting with dubious characters."

"Good one, Em," Jake said, chortling.

"Seriously," Luke said once the laughter had died down, "Frank Burnes is very good at what he does. I'm sure he'll solve this thing."

"I'm glad to hear it," I responded. "The sooner the better." I did want the horrible mess sorted out, but if my suspicions were correct, I truly felt sorry for Bootsie Flannigan. I hadn't expected to like a murderer quite so much.

Jake escorted Sophie and me out to my car, while Luke stayed inside to begin cleaning up. He had waved away our offers of help with a smile. "I have to earn my keep, you know."

The drive home went quickly. Traffic was lighter at eleven o'clock, though as usual there were still a lot of cars on the road.

"Are you going to tell me?" Sophie asked.

I didn't answer for a moment, concentrating on merging onto the Loop. "Tell you what?" I finally said once I had the car safely in the lane I needed to be in.

"Whatever it was you figured out while we were playing that first hand tonight," Sophie said. "I saw your face go all funny the way it does when you've sorted something out in your head. So give. What was it?"

"I'm pretty sure I know who put the ground peanuts in the spinach dip," I said. "Bootsie."

"I thought so," Sophie said. "But why are you sure? How did you figure that out?"

I told her how Jake's fidgeting had brought back the memory of Bootsie's similar behavior the night Janet McGreevey died.

"I agree that it seems probable," Sophie said. "But how on earth would you ever prove something like that? Unless you can say you actually saw her put the ground peanuts into the spinach dip, no one is going to take what you've told me as evidence."

"I know that," I said. "And frankly I don't know how the police are going to prove she did it. The more I think about it, though, the more sure I am I'm right."

"I don't doubt you," Sophie said. "I think Bootsie had the motive—if anyone would really consider Gerald McGreevey a strong enough motive for murder." She laughed. "And I guess Bootsie would, if what everyone says is true."

"I know, I don't see it myself," I said. "I mean, what the attraction is with Gerald. But there's no accounting for taste."

Sophie was silent for a moment. I exited from the Loop. Home was only a few minutes away now.

"Say that Bootsie killed Janet," Sophie said. "Do you think she also killed Dan? It would seem logical that there's only one murderer."

"Yes," I said, "that would be the most logical answer. But for some reason, I just can't see Bootsie killing Dan. She was really shaken up by his death, and I don't think she was acting."

"She was pretty cool over Janet's death," Sophie said.

I admitted that she was. "And who knows? Maybe she just felt a lot more guilty over killing Dan than she did Janet. That could be it." I paused. "But still, I'm not sure."

"Well, I'm too tired to worry much about it tonight." Sophie yawned. "Thank goodness we're just about home."

I turned the car down our street, and a minute later I pulled into my driveway.

"Oh no," Sophie said, startling me. "I just thought about something."

"What?" I asked.

Sophie pointed to her right. "What about Marylou? Do you think we ought to tell her?"

"It's okay," I said. "I thought of that. I called her already."

"When?" Sophie asked, puzzled.

"When I was dummy during the hand Luke was playing for a small slam," I said. "I called Marylou and told her I was worried about her having Bootsie in the house with her."

"What did she say?"

"She said she was fine, and Bootsie had taken some sleeping pills, so she'd be out for the night. She wasn't worried, but to be on the safe side, she was going to lock her bedroom door. And though, frankly, I don't think Bootsie would hurt Marylou, I told her to call me the moment anything odd happened, and I would come right over." I opened my door and got out of the car. "Do you want to come in for a minute?"

"No, I'll go on home," Sophie said. "If you and Marylou both think she'll be okay, I guess there's no need for me to worry about it." She waved good-bye as she walked out of the garage. I walked out to watch until she was safely inside her house, then went back in and hit the button to shut the garage door. The garage was connected to the house by a short breezeway, about six feet long.

I let myself into the kitchen only to be greeted by two indignant felines. Hilda chattered at me, telling me exactly what she thought of my negligence. She continued in this vein for the next five minutes or so, allowing me to scratch her head briefly. Olaf twined himself around my legs, and I had to step carefully around him in order to check their food bowls. I replenished their water and dry food, and they munched for a moment.

They followed me upstairs, and I quickly got myself ready for bed. I was tired, but my head was full of questions.

Despite what I had told Sophie, I was a bit nervous

about Marylou being alone in her house with Bootsie.
If what I believed was true, then Bootsie had killed
someone, and maybe two people. Marylou was sharp
enough not to let on to Bootsie that we suspected her,
so I had to believe that Marylou wasn't in any immediate danger. Hopefully the sleeping pill would keep
Bootsie out for the night.

Maybe after a night's rest, things would be clearer,
and I could figure out what was best to do. For one
thing, I had to call Lieutenant Burnes and tell him
what I thought. I had no idea what he would make of
it. Remembering what Luke had told us about the
good lieutenant's preferences, I had to grin, albeit
ruefully.

The cats soon settled down, and I did my best to
empty my mind enough to let me relax. At some point
I drifted off.

The insistent ringing of the phone woke me, and I
fumbled for the receiver. One eye open, I glanced at
my bedside clock. It was 6:37. At least I'd had some
decent sleep.

"Hello," I croaked into the phone.

"It's me," Marylou said into the phone, her voice
low. "I need to see you right away, Emma. I've found
something that I think is important. Are you awake?"

"Of course," I said. Marylou's words had jolted me
awake. "I'll be downstairs in three minutes."

"I'll be there." The phone clicked in my ear.

Chapter 24

I pulled on my bathrobe and ran a brush through my hair to make me look slightly less demented. Pelting downstairs to the front door, I almost tripped over Olaf, who darted in front of me about halfway down. I grabbed the railing and managed to stop myself from going headfirst down the rest of the way.

Olaf sat at the foot of the stairs licking one of his paws. "Oh, I know it's my fault," I told him. "I should be more careful. But you could watch where I'm going." Olaf started licking the other paw.

Stepping past the inattentive cat, I unlocked the front door and opened it about three inches. Peering out, I saw Marylou scurrying across the lawn toward me. She was clutching what looked like a plastic bag to her bosom.

I swung the door open, and she swept in. Quickly closing the door, lest Olaf become curious and dart outside, I turned to regard Marylou. Her face was flushed, and she was breathing a bit heavily.

"Come on in the kitchen," I said, "and I'll make us some coffee." I was burning with curiosity to know what Marylou had in that plastic bag, but I'd be better able to cope with whatever it was if I had some caffeine to bolster me.

I heard a knock on the back door before we were halfway down the hall.

"That'll be Sophie," Marylou said, still huffing a bit. "I called her too."

"Good," I said. I hurried ahead to unlock the back door and admit Sophie.

For once Sophie looked like she had just gotten out of bed. Her hair was slightly flattened on one side, and her bathrobe didn't coordinate with her pajamas.

"You were in a hurry," I said as I shut the door behind her.

She glanced down at herself and made a face. "Marylou sounded so urgent, I just grabbed the first thing I could find." She put a hand up to her hair. "And I know my hair must look like one of the dogs slept on my head."

"You two have a seat," I said, "and let me put some coffee on. It won't take a minute."

Neither of them said a word while I prepared the coffeemaker. When I had finished and approached the table to sit, Marylou thrust the plastic bag, which she had kept tight against her chest, onto the table.

"What is it?" Sophie asked, suppressing a yawn. "Some kind of bomb?" She tittered.

"It might as well be," Marylou said, her voice grim. "Look, but don't touch." She pulled the plastic bag down around the object within it.

What Marylou revealed was a large jar about a third full of peanuts.

"They're peanuts," I said. I shook my head. "Okay, I don't get it. What is so significant about this jar?"

Marylou sighed a bit impatiently. "This morning I woke up early, like I usually do. Bootsie was asleep—and still is, far as I know—so I decided to do a little baking. I was in the mood for making cookies, and so I was looking through the cabinets, trying to find a particular set of cookie cutters that I haven't used in ages. And there it was." She pointed to the jar of peanuts.

"Are you saying that this jar didn't belong in your cabinets?" Sophie asked.

"Exactly," Marylou said. "Someone hid that jar in my cabinet, and I'll bet you that's the jar of peanuts someone used to kill Janet."

"Who do you think hid it in your cabinet?" Sophie asked.

"Dan," I said suddenly. Recalling the odd things Dan had done the night before he was killed, I figured he must have hidden the peanuts the first time he had left the bridge game. He had been zipping up his backpack when I walked into the kitchen, and I was willing to bet he was closing it after having taken the peanuts out of it and hiding the jar in the cabinet.

I explained my reasoning to Marylou and Sophie, and they nodded in agreement.

"Was the jar in that plastic bag?" I asked.

"Yes, it was," Marylou said.

I examined the bag, hooking a finger through one of the handles and lifting it up enough to read the logo printed on it. It had come from a nearby supermarket.

"That was pretty cool of Dan," Sophie said, "to just go into your kitchen and hide this. He had some nerve."

"Ordinarily I would never have noticed it," Marylou said, "because he stuck it on the top shelf, and ordinarily I don't pay much attention to those shelves. They're too hard to reach."

"I guess he figured it would be safer there than it would be at Bootsie's house," I said, "if that's where he got it in the first place."

"Whose fingerprints are on it, do you think?" Sophie asked.

"I don't know," I said. "But I bet this is what the person who ransacked Bootsie's house was looking for."

"Do you think that's the same person who killed Dan?" Marylou asked.

"I bet it is," Sophie said excitedly. "We know it wasn't Bootsie that made a mess of the house, right? She was with Marylou when it happened. The killer knew that Bootsie had gone home with Marylou, and he—or she—sneaked into Bootsie's house to find this jar."

"If Dan got the jar from Bootsie's house," Marylou said, "then I guess it confirms what Emma thinks—that Bootsie killed Janet."

"Yes, I think it does," I said.

"So what do we do now?" Sophie asked.

"First," I said, rising from my chair and going to the counter, "I'm going to pour us all a cup of coffee. We're going to drink a little of it, and then I'm going to call Lieutenant Burnes. He needs to see this jar of peanuts."

"And he needs to see Dan's cell phone," Marylou said. She reached into a pocket of her warm-up pants and deposited the phone on the table beside the jar of peanuts.

"I thought you were going to put it back in Bootsie's purse," I said as I brought the three mugs of coffee to the table. Then I retrieved the cream from the fridge and dug some spoons out of the silverware drawer.

"I did," Marylou said, "and I was going to find some way of dumping everything out of her purse in front of her this morning, and exclaiming over the second cell phone. Then I was going to insist that she call Lieutenant Burnes, and I wasn't going to take no for an answer." She laughed. "But then I found the peanuts. So I just sneaked into her room and helped myself to Dan's phone."

"Bootsie's going to be really pissed when she finds out what we've done," Sophie said. "You don't think she'll do something nasty to retaliate, do you?"

"I don't think she'll be able to," I said, "because I'm sure she's going to be arrested for murder."

For a moment the three of us sat and sipped at our coffee. Marylou and Sophie knew Bootsie far better than I did, and I knew that, as miserable as I felt about having to turn her in to the police, they probably felt worse. How I wished she hadn't done it, but by now I was certain she had.

"Who's the other murderer?" Marylou asked suddenly. "The person who ran over Dan?"

"My money's on Gerald," Sophie said.

I nodded. "I think you're right. I feel sure that the first call Dan made that night at Marylou's is the important one. And I think it was Gerald he was threatening when I overheard him."

"I think you're right, too," Marylou said, "as much as I hate to think it of Gerald. I've always thought he had a really cold, ruthless streak."

"I can't put this off any longer," I said, getting up from the table. I found the card with the policeman's number on it, and I went to the phone.

As I was punching in the number, I heard whispering and then a couple of giggles coming from the table behind me. I rolled my eyes. No doubt Sophie was sharing with Marylou what Luke had told us last night about the handsome lieutenant.

The phone rang three times before someone picked up on the other end. A gruff voice said, "Hello."

That didn't sound like Burnes, and for a moment I was afraid I had punched in a wrong number. "Could I speak to Lieutenant Burnes, please?"

"Just a minute," the voice grunted at me. I caught a word or two as the phone was being passed over, and I had the impression that Burnes was complaining that the other man had answered the phone.

"Burnes here," he said into the phone. "How can I help you?"

"Lieutenant, this is Emma Diamond," I said, "and once again, I apologize for calling you so early in the morning. But we've found something I think you should see right away."

"What is it?" Burnes asked.

"The jar of peanuts that were probably used to kill Janet McGreevey," I said.

"Where did you find them?" Burnes asked. "No,

don't answer that. Just hang on, and I'll be there as quickly as I can. You haven't actually touched the jar, have you?"

I assured him that the jar had been handled carefully—at least since we had found it. With that, he hung up the phone, and I returned to my seat at the kitchen table.

Marylou and Sophie were staring at me with the silliest overly solemn expressions on their faces.

"Oh, good grief," I said, "the two of you look like you've been constipated for three months. Stop it."

They burst out laughing, and I joined in. "If Luke hadn't told us last night," I said, smiling, "then I certainly would have figured it out this morning."

"What do you mean?" Sophie asked.

"Another man answered the phone, didn't he?" Marylou looked smug.

"Exactly," I said. "And now that we know the lieutenant is beyond the reach of you two yentas, maybe you'll leave me alone." I smiled to show them that I was teasing.

"Now, what about Bootsie?" I asked after the laughter had ceased. "Do you think we should go check on her?"

"No," Marylou said. "I think she'll be out for a while yet. Those were some pretty powerful sleeping pills she took last night. Besides, I left her a note to tell her where I'd be." She grinned. "I just didn't tell her what I'd be doing, or what we'd be talking about."

"Good," Sophie said. "I don't look forward to facing her again."

"I know what you mean," Marylou said.

"I don't know about you two," I said, "but I'm getting hungry. While we wait for the lieutenant to arrive, why don't I fix us a little something to nibble on?"

"A piece or two of toast would be good," Sophie said.

"Marylou?" I asked as I got up from my chair. "What about you?"

"Toast is fine with me," Marylou said. "I don't usually eat much for breakfast anyway."

"Toast it is," I said. I had a large toaster, one that would toast six slices of bread at once. Baxter loved toast in the morning, and he had had this toaster when we got married.

"Sophie, will you get the jelly out of the fridge?" I asked as I popped slices of wheat bread into the toaster. "All I have is wheat bread. I hope that's okay."

"Fine," Marylou said. She joined Sophie at the fridge. "What kind of jelly do you have? Oh, good, I love apricot jam."

"And grape jelly for me," Sophie said.

"I keep it just for you," I said, laughing. "Get out the apple for me, will you?"

I had just finished my second piece of toast when I realized that I was still wearing my bathrobe, as was Sophie. "Good grief," I said, jumping up. "Burnes will be here any minute, and we're still in our bathrobes."

Sophie muttered an impolite word under her breath. She was out of her chair like a shot and out the back door before I had taken three steps.

"Marylou, I'll be back down in three minutes," I said. "Will you let the lieutenant in if he arrives before I get back?"

"Sure," Marylou said. "Go get changed."

I was back downstairs, dressed in slacks and a shirt, with three minutes to spare, when the policeman rang my doorbell. I ushered him in as I apologized again for getting him out of bed so early.

"It's okay," he said, though he had a funny look on his face, as if he were debating whether to say something about the person who had answered the phone.

"By the way," I said in a casual tone before he could say anything more, "I think you're acquainted with my brother-in-law, Luke Hilton. I saw him last night, and he mentioned he knows you."

Burnes relaxed, smiling at me. "Yes, I do know Luke. And I think I've met your brother a time or two, as well. He's a doctor, isn't he?"

"Yes," I said, "an internal medicine specialist. Now, please come on through to the kitchen. The others are waiting there for you."

"Thank you," he said, as I escorted him to the kitchen. Sophie was back, neatly attired in a colorful cotton skirt and blouse, looking like she was attending a garden party.

"Good morning, Mrs. Lockridge, Mrs. Parker," Burnes said. He immediately focused on the jar of peanuts on the table. He approached it softly, nodding to acknowledge the greetings from Marylou and Sophie. For the moment he said nothing about the cell phone lying on the table.

"So tell me about finding this," Burnes said, pointing to the jar.

I motioned him to a chair, and he sat down as Marylou began to recount her story.

Burnes hadn't been in the chair three minutes before Olaf appeared and hopped into his lap. With one hand absently stroking the happy cat's head, Burnes listened intently to Marylou.

"Thank you, Mrs. Lockridge," he said when Marylou was done. "This could be the break we've been looking for. I'll need you to come downtown and make a formal statement, if you don't mind."

"Be glad to," Marylou said.

"Good," Burnes said. "I'll call you later and arrange a time. I'll go and get an evidence bag in a moment. But was there anything else you wanted to tell me?" He looked from Marylou to Sophie to me with a polite, questioning expression. "Something about that cell phone, perhaps?"

"Oh my, yes," Marylou said, and now she told Burnes about finding the phone in Bootsie's purse.

She didn't tell him we had looked for the calls Dan had made that night, however.

"Thanks again," Burnes said when Marylou had finished. "It seems like I'm going to owe you three quite a lot when this case is over. You've been a big help. Now, is there anything else before I go?"

"Yes, there is," I said. "Sophie and I played bridge last night with my brother and Luke, and while we were playing, something came back to me. Something about the night Janet McGreevey was poisoned."

"What was that?"

I shifted slightly in my chair, aware of the lieutenant's intent, unwavering gaze. It sounded rather foolish in the light of day, but I was sure it was important. I explained my theory about Bootsie's behavior the night of the murder.

"I see," Burnes said when I had finished. "That's very interesting." He thought a moment. "Where is Mrs. Flannigan right now? Is she at home?"

"No, she's right next door," Marylou said. "She spent the night in my guest room, and she's probably still there, sound asleep."

"Good," Burnes said. "I'll need to talk to her as soon as she's awake. In the meantime, I'm sure I don't have to ask you ladies not to talk about any of this with anyone else, right?"

We gave him our assurances, and he went out to his car to retrieve the evidence bags. When he came back we watched as he carefully sealed the plastic bag and jar of peanuts in one bag and the cell phone in another. He wrote something on each one, then thanked us again.

"Would you like us to call you as soon as Bootsie is up?" Marylou asked. "Or you're welcome to wait at my house until she's up, if you want to."

"Thanks, but I think I'll run these downtown first." He indicated the two bags. "I'd appreciate it, though, if you'd call me the minute she's up, but don't let on to her that I want to talk to her," Burnes said. "Mrs.

Diamond has my number. Or if necessary, call the emergency number and have the dispatcher send over a squad car."

"We won't tell her," I said. "Would you like me to see you out?"

"Thanks, but I know the way by now," Burnes said, smiling. "I'll be back shortly."

We watched him leave, and I felt suddenly deflated. What I had been expecting, I wasn't certain, but I hadn't anticipated this feeling of business unfinished. We had been busy little detective bees, and now things were out of our hands. That was proper, of course, because the police were the proper ones to handle the case from this point on.

Still, I felt let down. Looking at my two friends, I could see they felt the same way.

"How about some more toast?" I asked. "Or more coffee?"

"More coffee," Marylou said. "I need something to perk me up a little."

"Me too," Sophie said.

I was refilling their cups when the front doorbell rang. "I'll just go see who it is. Maybe the lieutenant forgot something." I gave Sophie the coffeepot and headed for the door.

I had barely opened it when Bootsie Flanningan pushed her way in. Her hair was tousled, and she looked about ninety years old. But she was angry, judging by the fire in her eyes.

"What the hell is going on? Who's been going through my purse?"

Chapter 25

"Where's Marylou?" Bootsie demanded when I didn't respond to her other questions. She pushed past me. "I bet she's here. I want to know why she's been going through my purse."

I caught at Bootsie's arm, but she jerked away from me. "Marylou, where the hell are you?" By this time she was bellowing like a maddened bull.

"Keep your voice down," I said sharply. Hilda and Olaf would be terrified by the shouting, and I didn't want them upset.

Bootsie glared at me as she stomped on toward the kitchen, but at least she had stopped yelling.

"Hello, Bootsie," Marylou said, a bright smile on her face, as I trailed the irate woman into the kitchen. "Did you sleep well, dear?"

"Cut the crap, Marylou," Bootsie said. "I want to know what the hell is going on. Since when do you go through your guests' belongings?"

"Since I know they're hiding things from the police that they shouldn't be hiding," Marylou said very sweetly. Then her expression turned fierce. "Why don't you shut the hell up, Bootsie dear, and sit down?"

Those last two words were uttered with considerable force, so much so that even Sophie and I almost jumped. Marylou sounded like a drill instructor, but it had the desired effect. Bootsie didn't say another word. She sat down in the chair Marylou indicated.

"That's better," Marylou said in a normal tone. "Now, dear, I know you're upset, but the time has come to start telling the truth. Would you like some coffee?"

Bootsie nodded. She hadn't taken her eyes off Marylou, but her hands were busily twisting themselves into and out of knots in her lap.

I poured out the last bit of coffee in the pot and gave it to Bootsie. I figured I should be calling Lieutenant Burnes right about now, but I was afraid to do anything to break the spell that Marylou seemed to have cast. I decided it wouldn't hurt to wait a few minutes to make that call. The lieutenant had said he would be coming back anyway. I slid into my chair and waited for Marylou to make the next move. I cast a quick glance at Sophie, and she was staring at Marylou with a look of admiration and a little awe.

"I'll confess, Bootsie," Marylou said. She folded her hands across her chest and regarded Bootsie like the Buddha at his most benign. "I did find Dan's cell phone in your purse."

"What did you do with it?" Bootsie asked. "Where is it now?"

"The police have it," Marylou said, "which is what should have happened in the first place. Why were you pretending you didn't know where it was?"

Bootsie had paled at the news the police were in possession of the cell phone. "I don't know, I guess I just wasn't thinking," she said, almost stumbling over the words. "I've been so upset I couldn't think straight."

"You'll have to come up with a better answer than that," Marylou said, still gentle, "if you expect the police to believe you, don't you think?"

"But it's the truth," Bootsie protested.

Marylou shook her head. "No, it isn't."

Bootsie stared at her for a moment, and then her

eyes shifted to mine. I kept my face expressionless, and after another moment, she turned to look at Sophie. Sophie just shrugged.

Marylou caught my eye and moved her head the tiniest fraction in my direction. By that I took it to mean she wanted me to do the talking for a bit. I thought quickly.

"Bootsie," I said, keeping my voice neutral, "were you driving the car that hit and killed Dan?"

"No," Bootsie said, "no, it wasn't me." She started crying, the tears flowing down her face. She made no move to wipe her eyes or to hide her face, just sat there crying quietly.

"Then don't you think the person who killed him should be caught and made to pay for what he did?"

She cried a little harder, and I felt so sorry for her then, I almost got up from my chair and went to hold her. She was such a pathetic figure. I risked a glance at Sophie, and I could see the tears welling in her eyes. She looked away from me.

"Bootsie," I said, "you can't shield him any longer. The police now have evidence that can link him to Janet's murder, and I'll bet it won't be long before they find the car he used to kill Dan with."

"I don't know what you're talking about," Bootsie said.

"Now, Bootsie dear, don't lie to us," Marylou said, sounding very stern again. "We know you're lying, and there's no point. It's time for you to tell the truth."

"What kind of evidence, then?" Bootsie's voice was hoarse with emotion.

"Marylou found the jar of peanuts where Dan had hidden them in her cabinets the other night," I said, watching her face carefully for a reaction.

Bootsie's eyes widened in shock. "Dan had it? Dan. What the hell was he doing with it?" She stared at me as if willing me to explain.

"I don't know," I said. "But I'm sure he put it

there. The other night, when we were playing bridge at Marylou's, I walked into the kitchen twice. Both times I found him acting oddly. The first time was when I think he had just hidden the jar of peanuts in the cabinet."

"So Dan had it all this time," Bootsie said, shaking her head in wonderment. "I thought I was going crazy because I couldn't find it." She looked at me again. "What was he going to do with it?"

"Blackmail someone," I said. She shook her head at me as if in protest, and I nodded. "Yes, blackmail. The second time I walked in on him, he was talking on his cell phone, and he was threatening someone."

Bootsie didn't respond. Her gaze had turned inward, and she no longer saw me.

"Do you know who he was talking to?" I asked. When she didn't appear to have heard me, I repeated my question, but in a louder, firmer tone. This time she heard me.

"No, how could I?" she said. I knew she was lying, though. Her gaze skittered away from mine.

"The number he dialed was the McGreevey house," Marylou said. "We think he was talking to Gerald."

Bootsie shook her head slightly.

"Yes," I said, "it had to be Gerald. And Gerald drove the car that killed Dan, Bootsie. You know that, and you've known it all along."

She just kept shaking her head.

"Why are you protecting him?" Sophie asked, her voice sharp. "Don't be stupid, Bootsie. They're going to arrest you for murder. Don't you think he should pay for what he's done? Dan didn't deserve to die that way, did he? Did he?"

"Stop it," Bootsie shouted. "Stop it. Dan's death is my fault. It's all my fault. I killed him, too." She sat there, trembling, staring into space.

"Were you driving the car that killed him?" Marylou asked. "Were you?"

Bootsie shook her head. "I might as well have been," she said softly, after a moment.

"Why is it your fault?" Sophie asked. "Dan tried to blackmail Gerald, and Gerald killed him. That's not your fault."

"Dan never would have been involved in any of this if it weren't for me," Bootsie said. She wiped her face with the sleeve of her robe.

"How did he get involved?" I asked.

Bootsie sighed. She looked down at the table. "I met him at a bar one night. We really seemed to hit it off, and he didn't act like the age difference bothered him. So we started dating. I know what people said behind my back." Her voice turned bitter. "And they were right. I found out soon enough that he was after money. He thought I had money, and he wanted to live off me. I should have kicked him out."

"Why didn't you?" Marylou asked.

"Because I fell in love with him," Bootsie said. I turned away from the naked misery in her face. "Isn't that the stupidest, most pathetic thing you've ever heard? I fell in love with a cheap hustler. And he worked me for everything he could. And I let him do it."

For a long moment, none of us responded. I don't think any of us knew quite what to say.

Marylou cleared her throat. "How could you afford to keep him hanging around? You told me you don't make a lot of money at your job." Then, with a sharp intake of breath, she said, "Oh, good Lord. That's what she meant."

"What are you talking about?" I asked.

"Janet," Marylou said. "The afternoon before the bridge party, I had a chat with her about some homeowners' association business. We were talking about Mrs. Anderson, you remember, the elderly woman who was behind on her dues?"

I nodded, vaguely remembering the conversation in

my own house the day Janet McGreevey had come over with her brownies.

Bootsie wasn't saying anything. She sat there, her eyes closed, as if she weren't a part of the conversation.

"Well, Janet said something about the books, something about needing to check something because of a discrepancy she had noticed. She said she was going to have to talk to Bootsie about it, because Bootsie was responsible for it, she felt sure. Then Janet changed the subject, and we talked about something else. I had almost forgotten it."

Sophie, Marylou, and I exchanged glances. We were all thinking the same thing.

"Were you embezzling money from the homeowners' association, Bootsie?" I asked. "Was that how you could afford to keep buying things for Dan?"

For a moment, I didn't think she was going to answer. Finally, though, she lifted her head and looked at me. "Yes, I did. Janet had found out about it and was going to cause a big stink."

"Did Janet threaten you?" Sophie asked.

Bootsie shook her head.

"Then how did you know she knew?" Marylou asked.

Bootsie sighed deeply. "Gerald came to me, as a friend, he said. He told me he had overheard Janet talking about it to a lawyer. She was planning to ambush me at the next meeting. She was going to see that I was arrested and put in jail."

"Why was Gerald telling you this? Because he was your friend?" I asked.

"Yes," Bootsie said. "He felt sorry for me, he said, and he wanted to warn me." She laughed bitterly. "He told me he would lend me the money to pay it all back, if only he could. He didn't have it, though. Janet controlled the money, and there was no way he could get that kind of money from her without arousing suspicion."

"When did this conversation take place?" Marylou asked.

"The day Janet died," Bootsie said.

"Where did it take place?" I asked, as a sudden thought occurred to me.

"At my house," Bootsie said. "It was early afternoon, and I was in the kitchen, working on something. He dropped by, said he needed to talk to me."

"Was Dan there?" Sophie asked.

"I thought he was in his room," Bootsie said, "playing around with his computer."

"But he may have overheard some of your conversation with Gerald," I said.

Bootsie nodded.

"What exactly did Gerald say to you?" Marylou asked.

"He told me what Janet planned to do, and then he said he wished he could help me, like I told you," Bootsie said. "And then . . ." Her voice trailed off.

"And then?" I prompted her.

"I had been snacking on some peanuts," Bootsie said. "I had practically a brand-new jar open on the table where I was working. Gerald laughed and picked up the jar. He said, 'This could be the answer to all your problems, and mine.' Then he set the jar down and just looked at me. I was shocked at first, but then I realized he was serious. I never would have thought about doing it, but he gave me the idea."

"And that was the jar that Dan had taken and hidden away," I said.

"Yes," Bootsie said. "I ground up a lot of the peanuts and put them in a plastic bag to take with me that night." She sighed. "I wasn't sure I would go through with it, but Janet took me aside right after Dan and I got there that night. She said she wanted to talk to me about something to do with the homeowners' association books. That was when I decided to go through with it."

"You did it during that second hand at our table,

didn't you?" I asked. "When you were dummy. You
had been fidgeting before that, but when you came
back to the table, you were calm. No more fidgeting."

Bootsie nodded. "Once I had done it, I felt calm.
It was done, and there was nothing I could about it.
I put it out of my mind then. Until . . ." Suddenly she
choked up, and the tears started flowing again. She
buried her head in her arms, against the table.

I eased out of my chair and went to the phone. I
hit the REDIAL button as I walked out of the room
into the hallway. Lieutenant Burnes answered on the
second ring.

"This is Emma Diamond," I said. "Bootsie Flannigan is up now, and she's just confessed to the three
of us. Are you on your way back yet?"

Burnes muttered something that sounded suspiciously like a curse, then said, "Yes, I am. I'll be there
in about five minutes."

I ended the call and was about to head back into
the kitchen, when the doorbell rang.

Frowning, I wondered who on earth it could be.
Then my whole body went cold. What would I do if
it were Gerald McGreevey?

Chapter 26

That thought stopped me dead in my tracks. Then I realized all I had to do was not open the door, if it really was Gerald. I didn't think Gerald would try to break the door down. Plus I could always yell through the door that the police were on the way. I didn't need to be afraid of him.

I went to the peephole and peered through it.

Carlene Newberry stood on the doorstep, and she looked upset. While I was staring at her, she punched the doorbell again.

I couldn't see anyone with her, so I stepped back from the peephole and opened the door.

"Good morning, Carlene," I said.

She stepped inside before I could invite her in. "Is Bootsie Flannigan here by any chance? I went next door to Marylou's, but no one answered there." She was tense, her hands clenched at her sides. I pushed the door shut.

"Yes, she and Marylou are both here," I said, eyeing her with caution. "And so is Sophie Parker. Do you need to see Bootsie about something?"

"Where is she?" Carlene demanded. "I need to talk to her right now."

"Come with me," I said, turning down the hall toward the kitchen.

Carlene almost stepped on my heels in her impatience. As I reached the door of the kitchen I stepped nimbly to one side, and she practically ran into the room.

Spotting Bootsie sitting at the table, Carlene drew up short. Hands on hips, she addressed a startled Bootsie. "Do you know what that bastard has done?"

Nobody asked what bastard she was talking about. I figured we all knew whom she meant.

"What?" Bootsie asked, her voice trembling.

Carlene uttered a few obscenities that cast grave doubts on the chastity of Gerald McGreevey's mother, and then she said, "I'll tell you what that bastard did. He used *my* car to run over your boyfriend, that's what he did. And then he had the nerve to lie about it."

"Calm down, Carlene," I said, "you're going to burst a blood vessel or have a stroke if you don't ease up a little." I laid a hand on her arm, but she shook me off.

"I don't need to calm down," Carlene said, almost snarling at me. "What I need is to get my hands on that bastard's balls. I swear I'm going to rip them off."

"Sit down, Carlene," Marylou commanded, using her drill instructor voice, and a startled Carlene did just that. "Now, take a few deep breaths, and tell us, calmly, about Gerald using your car."

"All right," Carlene said after a moment. "I'm calm. But I'm still going to get that jackass if it's the last thing I do." She paused. "I went out to the garage this morning for something I had left in my Volvo. That's the car I usually drive to work," she explained, looking at me, and I nodded.

"I got to looking at the Jag," she continued, "and I noticed something odd about the right front headlight. When I looked closer, I saw that it was slightly cracked. I knew it hadn't been that way the last time I had driven it, which was over the weekend."

"You only drive it on the weekends?" I asked.

"Most of the time," Carlene said. "I almost never

drive it to work, and I knew the headlight didn't have a crack in it when I had driven it last weekend." She paused for another deep breath because she was beginning to get really angry again. "Anyway, I checked inside, and I could tell that someone had adjusted the driver's seat. It wasn't in its usual position."

"So someone else had driven it," Sophie said. "Obviously. But how do you know it was Gerald? How would he have gotten the keys to the car?"

For the first time since her tirade had begun, Carlene faltered. She had a strange look on her face. Then she sighed. "Well, hell, I might as well admit it. Gerald spent the night with me that night. He obviously got up that morning while I was still asleep, swiped my keys, and then used the Jag without my knowledge, or my permission. The son of a bitch used it to kill Dan."

Then, as if exhausted by her admission, Carlene sank back in her chair and dropped her head. She was crying quietly.

"Oh my," Marylou said. She looked at Sophie and me as if to say, "What do we do now?"

"Lieutenant Burnes will be here any minute now," I said. "Carlene, Bootsie, you both have to talk to him and tell him everything you know."

Carlene lifted her head and looked at Bootsie. "Bootsie, was it you?"

"You mean did I poison Janet?" Bootsie said flatly. She nodded. "I did. Gerald told me what Janet was planning to do to me, and I panicked, I guess. I think I went a little crazy."

"What was Janet planning to do?" Carlene asked, puzzled.

Bootsie explained Janet's intention to confront her about the embezzlement.

"Embezzlement?" Carlene asked, shaking her head. "I had no idea. I wondered where you were getting all that money, but I never thought you were embezzling." She shook her head again. "But Gerald was lying to you."

"What the hell do you mean?" Bootsie asked, her voice harsh. "How was he lying to me?"

Again Carlene looked a bit shifty, and I guessed that Gerald must have told her during pillow talk. "Because he told me what Janet was planning to do. And it had nothing to do with you. I don't think she even knew you were embezzling."

"What was Janet planning to do, then?" I asked.

"She was going to start proceedings against that old woman who is so far behind on her dues," Carlene said. "Gerald said he tried to talk Janet out of it, but she was adamant. And she was going to talk to Bootsie about it, to make sure Bootsie would support her."

Bootsie and Carlene stared at each other. They had both been used by Gerald, and in Bootsie's case, cruelly manipulated. To put it in bridge terms, Gerald had finessed Bootsie into murdering his wife for him.

I hoped he would rot in hell for what he had done.

"What about a lawyer?" Sophie asked. "Don't you think Bootsie should have a lawyer with her when she talks to the police?"

"That's a good idea," Marylou said. "Bootsie, do you have a lawyer you can call?"

"No, I don't," Bootsie said. "I don't care, though, I just want to get this over with."

I looked at Carlene. She shrugged.

Once more the doorbell rang, and I went to answer it. I checked before opening the door, just to be sure, but thankfully it was Lieutenant Burnes. With him were a couple of patrol officers. "Thank goodness you're here," I told him, as I motioned him and the other officers inside. "You know the way to the kitchen."

I stood back and let the lieutenant lead the way, the other two men trailing behind him. I brought up the rear.

The moment Burnes entered the kitchen, Bootsie and Carlene both started talking to him, going ninety miles a minute, waving their arms and hands about, and it sounded like utter chaos.

Burnes froze for a moment, then spoke loudly over the noise. "Please, ladies, one at a time. Mrs. Flannigan, I'd like to talk to you in private. Mrs. Diamond?" He turned to me.

"How about the living room?" I suggested, and he nodded.

"Please come with me, Mrs. Flannigan," Burnes said, and he escorted her from the room. As he was leaving, he motioned for one of the patrolmen to come with him. The other one stayed behind.

Carlene went up to him. "Officer, I need to report something."

"Ma'am?" he asked, startled. "What is it?"

While Marylou, Sophie, and I sat at the table, Carlene told her story to the patrolman. He pulled out a notebook and started jotting things down. When she had finished, he asked her to have a seat. "The lieutenant will need to hear this. I'll be right back."

When he had left the room, Marylou said, "What do you think will happen next?"

"For one thing," Carlene said, in a voice dripping with hatred, "they damn sure better go and arrest Gerald's sorry ass."

"What could they charge him with?" I asked. "Bootsie's already admitted to poisoning Janet, and unless they can find physical evidence in your car to link him to the hit-and-run, it's only your word and Bootsie's against his."

"You leave that to me," Carlene said. "I know several people in the D.A.'s office. One way or another, Gerald is going to pay for what he's done."

"Hell hath no fury," Sophie muttered. Carlene shot her a nasty glance, but Sophie smiled.

The patrolman returned then to resume his watch. After informing Carlene that Lieutenant Burnes would speak with her once he had finished with Mrs.

Flannigan, he didn't say another word. He stood watching us, his face expressionless.

The four of us sat there for a moment, staring at one another. How long was all this going to take?

"Get out the cards, Emma," Marylou said. "We might as well play a little bridge. Who knows how long we'll have to wait?"

I stared at her for a moment, figuring she was kidding, but I quickly realized she wasn't. "What the heck?" I said. "Might as well." I retrieved the cards from the drawer where I kept them, along with a score pad and pencil. I handed Marylou the cards, and she began to shuffle them. Carlene was sitting across from me, and Sophie across from Marylou.

Sophie cut the cards, and Carlene dealt.

We managed three hands before Carlene was summoned to speak with Lieutenant Burnes. Sophie, Marylou, and I played three-handed for a few minutes before putting the cards down. We were all wondering what was going on in the living room.

Lieutenant Burnes appeared a few minutes later. "I'm taking Mrs. Flannigan and Ms. Newberry downtown," he said. "I'll be back later on to talk to the three of you. In the meantime, please don't talk about what you've heard."

We all nodded. "Lieutenant," I said as he turned to leave. He turned back.

"Yes, Mrs. Diamond?" he asked politely, but I could tell he was impatient to be gone. I was probably overstepping my bounds, but I had to ask.

"What about Gerald McGreevey?" I asked.

Burnes stared at me for a moment, as if debating whether to answer my question.

"He's on his way downtown now," Burnes said. "Now, I really have to go. I'll be back later." He left, and the patrolman who had been in the room with us left with him.

"Poor Bootsie," Marylou said. "I hope they don't take her downtown in her bathrobe."

"Surely they'll let her change her clothes first," I said.

"I'm sure they will," Sophie said. She got up from her chair and left the room. She returned soon to report that she had just seen Bootsie, dressed in outdoor clothes, being escorted from Marylou's house to a waiting squad car by a female patrol officer.

"That's that, then," Marylou said.

"I really wish Bootsie had asked for a lawyer," I said. "She really should have some legal support."

"Right now I don't think she really cares about anything," Marylou said sadly. "Once she realized just how badly Gerald had manipulated and deceived her, I don't think she cares whether she lives or dies."

"Do you think Gerald will get away with it?" Sophie asked.

"If Carlene has anything to say about it," Marylou said, "he won't. I've never seen her so angry."

"He screwed up badly by trying to implicate her," I said. "The man has to be the most colossally arrogant person I've ever met, to think he can push women around like pieces on a chess board."

"Or play them like cards in a bridge game," Sophie said. "He sure tricked Bootsie into doing something really stupid."

"He didn't have the guts to kill Janet himself, or just divorce her," Marylou said.

"No, he was evidently too greedy," I said. "He wanted to be rid of Janet, but he wanted to keep her money."

"Maybe he won't get it now," Sophie said, "if he's convicted, that is. I wonder who will, then?"

"Probably her sister," Marylou said.

"I hate to think of him not getting convicted," Sophie said. "Surely there's got to be some way to find him guilty. Maybe as an accessory?"

"I don't know," Marylou said. "We'd have to talk to a lawyer about that."

I had been mulling over something. "Sophie, why don't you call Nate? If he didn't accompany his father downtown, I'm sure he must be pretty upset right now."

"Oh my goodness," Sophie said. "You're right. Poor Nate! I will call him." She got up and went to the phone. After punching in the number, she waited, her body tense, for an answer.

"Nate, it's me," she said. "How are you? We heard about what happened."

She listened for a moment, looking at Marylou and me. I gestured to her.

"Look, sweetie," Sophie said, "I'm here at Emma's with her and Marylou. Why don't you come over here? You shouldn't be alone at a time like this." She paused. "No, really, it's okay. Yes, come on over right now." She listened for a moment longer, then hung up the phone.

"He's coming over right now," Sophie said. "He sounded really upset." She shook her head as she resumed her seat at the table.

"I'd better make some more coffee," I said. "I don't know about you two, but I could certainly use more caffeine." Marylou and Sophie nodded.

The doorbell rang a few minutes later, and Sophie went to answer it. The coffee would be done in another minute or two, and I was checking the refrigerator to see if I had anything I could offer as snacks.

Then I realized I had never fed the cats this morning, and I guiltily checked their bowls. They were both nearly empty. I put food in them, wondering where Olaf and Hilda were. Probably hiding, because all the people coming in and out of the house would have unnerved them. They would both turn up as soon as things were quieter. Olaf would be looking for food pretty soon.

Nate and Sophie entered the kitchen. Sophie had

her arm around Nate, and he leaned gratefully into her. He had obviously been crying. His face was still red and puffy.

"Nate, I'm so sorry," Marylou said. She got up to give him a hug, and he hugged her back, clinging to her for a moment. "Here, honey," she said, "you come and sit down. Emma's just made some fresh coffee, and I think it would do you good."

"Yes, thanks," Nate said. "It was horrible."

"What do you take in your coffee?" I asked.

"Black is fine," Nate said. I poured a cup and set it in front of him. "Thanks," he muttered, wrapping his hands around the cup before taking a sip.

"What happened?" Marylou asked softly.

"Dad was packing a suitcase," Nate said. "I asked him where he was going, and he said something had suddenly come up, and he had to go out of town." He paused. "And then the police showed up."

None of us said anything, and in a moment Nate continued. "I guess he was trying to get away before the police caught up with him." He shook his head.

"What did he say to the police?" I asked.

Nate shook his head again, as if in wonderment. "He tried to bluff his way through. He said he had an important meeting in Denver, and that he would be back tomorrow. Surely they weren't going to stop him from going."

"He didn't really think they would let him go, did he?" Marylou asked.

"He's a high-and-mighty lawyer," Nate said bitterly. "He's used to getting his way. At least, most of the time."

"He didn't get his way with Janet, though," Sophie said.

"No, he didn't." Nate shrugged. "She had the money. He'd been gambling again, and he was desperate. He needed money from her to pay off his gambling debts." He stared down into his coffee. "I sneaked a look at some of his bank records on the computer. As near as I can figure, he owed more than a quarter of a million."

"Jeez Louise," I said, shocked. "No wonder he told Bootsie he couldn't help her pay back the money she had embezzled."

Sophie and Marylou glared at me, and I cursed myself. I had promised Lieutenant Burnes not to say anything, and I had broken my word.

Fortunately for me, Nate apparently hadn't registered what I said.

"A quarter of a million," Nate said. "How could somebody gamble that much money away? I just don't understand it. He must have been crazy."

"Or arrogant," I said softly.

Nate heard me that time. "Yes, he's arrogant. He always thinks he can do what he wants, and nobody will stop him."

"This time someone has to," I said. "Nate, look at me."

Puzzled, Nate met my gaze.

"Nate, where were you that night when Janet collapsed? You weren't in the kitchen or in the living room with us, were you?"

"No, I wasn't," Nate said, stiffening. "I was in the den, just off the kitchen."

"But you came into the kitchen when you heard the commotion, didn't you?"

Nate stared at me like a deer in the headlights. "Yes," he said softly.

"You saw what your father did, didn't you?" I was gently persistent. I had a dim memory of having glimpsed Nate in the doorway after Janet collapsed, and now I was working on that.

"What do you mean?" Nate gripped the coffee cup so hard I thought it might shatter from the force.

"When your father was searching for Janet's epinephrine," I said. "Or pretending to search."

Nate stared at me, and I met his gaze without flinching.

Finally his gaze dropped. "Yes, I saw him," he said, his voice dull. "I saw him." He breathed deeply for a moment, as if to steady himself. "Janet had her Epi-pen with her. He found it, and he palmed it, pretending she didn't have it with her."

"That's when you went to get the other one," I said. Nate nodded.

"Why didn't you say something?" Sophie asked, an angry edge in her voice.

Nate wouldn't look at her. "I couldn't. Dad was staring at me. He . . . I'd never seen him look like that." He expelled a shaky breath. "So I just ran as fast as I could to get the other one. But it was too late."

"What are you going to do about what you saw?" I asked. Sophie started to say something, but I shook my head at her. She huffed and crossed her arms across her chest. Marylou didn't say a word.

Nate set the cup on the table. His hands trembled so badly I thought he might drop the cup.

When he spoke, he looked at Sophie. "I guess I'll have to tell the police what I saw."

Sophie smiled a little and nodded. She reached across the table and grasped his hand. He held on to it like a lifeline, and Sophie covered his hand with her free hand.

We all sat there, not speaking, for a little while.

Then I got up and handed Nate the phone. I gave him Lieutenant Burnes's card. He punched in the number, and then he grasped Sophie's hand again while he waited for an answer.

Emma Diamond's Bridge Tips

In *On the Slam* Emma has been playing bridge for only a few months. Like her creator, she had long resisted learning to play, because she thought bridge was a game that only very stuffy socialites like her parents played. (Note from the author: Emma's parents are the stuffy ones; mine were anything but!) Once Emma's brother, Jake Brett, finally prevails upon her to learn, she discovers that she actually enjoys the game.

Emma is lucky in that she has two very enthusiastic players, Jake and his partner Luke Hilton, to teach her. For anyone interested in learning more about the game, there are numerous resources. A quick search on the Internet will reveal numerous sites devoted to bridge, and you can even play bridge online these days. Both Bicycle and Hoyle market computer bridge games that are helpful to the novice and the more experienced bridge player. Many community centers offer bridge classes, and experienced bridge teachers are available, too.

There are numerous bridge books available, and here are a few that Emma (and I) have found useful:

- Silberstang, Edwin. *Handbook of Winning Bridge (2nd ed.).* Cooper Station, NY: Cardoza Publishing, 2003.

- Grant, Audrey. *Bidding* (ACBL Bridge Series). Memphis: American Contract Bridge League, 1990.
- Grant, Audrey. *Play of the Hand* (ACBL Bridge Series). Memphis: American Contract Bridge League, 1999.

The American Contract Bridge League, headquartered in Memphis, Tennessee, was founded in 1937. As an organization it offers many resources to bridge players, novice and experienced alike. They also publish a monthly magazine, the *ACBL Bridge Bulletin*, which features columns by bridge experts covering every aspect of play. Their Web site, www.ACBL.org, offers many of the same things, in addition to free educational software for learning the game and opportunities to play bridge online.

One of the first concepts aspiring bridge players must learn is the *finesse,* because making the contract often depends on the success of a finesse. *Finesse* is a word familiar to most readers, and in the context of bridge, the meaning isn't really that different. But here is a proper "bridge" definition of a finesse:

An attempt to win a trick card that is lower than one held by the opponents in the same suit. (From Silberstang's *Handbook of Winning Bridge,* p. 172) Here's a typical example of how a finesse works: Having won the contract, I am playing the hand. I hold the jack and queen of spades in my hand, and the ace is on the board, part of the dummy's hand. I know that one of my opponents has the king, but I'm not sure which one of them does. To see whether my left-hand opponent has it, I lead the queen from my hand. If my left-hand opponent does hold the king, more than likely she will play it, and I will be able to take the trick with the ace on the board. If the king doesn't drop at this point, it means my right-hand opponent probably has it, and there's no way I can finesse it and win the trick.

Another term that might not be familiar to non-bridge players is the *slam* of this book's title. A *small slam* is contract to take twelve tricks, and a *grand slam* is a contract to take all thirteen tricks. Emma and Carlene play for a grand slam in their first game at Janet McGreevey's house. As any bridge player will tell you, contracting for a slam can be exciting, and often difficult as well, but the success of such a bid depends to a large extent on how the partners communicate in getting to the right contract. This is a case where bridge conventions can be very useful, and Emma and Carlene make use of two conventions in bidding their grand slam.

The first convention they use is the *Stayman*. When Emma bids one no-trump, Carlene responds with two clubs. This signals to Emma that she should name her best four-card major suit (either hearts or spades). Emma then bids two spades, to tell Carlene that spades is her best major suit.

When Carlene comes back with the bid for no-trump, she is invoking the *Blackwood* convention. (This also means that she is happy with Emma's spades; otherwise she would have responded differently.) This was invented by Easley Blackwood of Indianapolis in the 1930s as a means for players on their way to a slam to communicate effectively about the strengths of their respective hands. Carlene's four no-trump bid is designed to ask Emma how many aces she holds. Emma would respond with five clubs if she has no aces or if she has all of them, five diamonds if she has one, five hearts if she has two, and five spades if she has three.

After Emma responds appropriately, Carlene can also, if she needs further information, ask Emma how many kinds she holds. A bid of five no-trump from Carlene will elicit the desired response. Emma would respond according to the guidelines for aces. In the game in this book, Emma's response to Carlene's four no-trump bid is five hearts, telling Carlene that she holds two aces. With that information, Carlene looks at her own hand and bids seven spades, a grand-slam contract. Go back and take a look at the game in chapter three, and you'll see how this works, and how Emma makes the contract.

Read on for a preview of the next
Bridge Club Mystery

THE UNKINDEST CUT

Coming from Signet in April 2008

I stared at my hand. Was it strong enough for the course of action I was attempting?

There was only one way to find out. I hesitated a moment longer, then clicked on the button to bid six hearts.

I half expected my computer opponent to double, and when that didn't happen, I grinned. I had been playing this computer bridge game for a little more than six months now, and I had yet to understand all its vagaries of bidding.

Olaf stretched and yawned in my lap, his claws kneading the side of my thigh. Thank goodness I clipped his nails yesterday, or else I would have had little spots of blood all over my sweat pants by the time he was through. I rubbed his head, and his purring hit overdrive.

Hilda, my other cat, contemplated me sleepily from her napping spot on the desk by my computer. I had long ago given up trying to dissuade the two cats from climbing all over me and my computer when I was trying to work—or to play bridge, which happened a lot more frequently than work these days. We had settled on a compromise—Olaf in my lap, Hilda on a comfy pad on the desk where she could keep an eye on Olaf and me.

I focused my attention on the computer, which had

now made the opening lead. Once it had done that, my dummy partner's hand was revealed. I quickly counted the points in it, and then I grinned again. With my eighteen high-card points and dummy's thirteen, we had enough for a slam.

Before playing out of dummy's hand to continue the first round, I made some quick calculations. I could easily make six hearts, but only if the king of spades was held by my left-hand opponent.

I began to play the game, clicking away with my right hand while the left continued rubbing Olaf's head. I had just finessed the spade king from my left-hand opponent, assuring me victory, when a voice called from downstairs.

"Emma! Where are you?"

"Up in my office," I yelled back. "Come on up." Then I grimaced as Olaf dug his claws into my leg as he prepared to jump to the floor. Even clipped, those claws were still sharp enough to penetrate the skin when ten pounds of cat decided to use my leg as a launching pad.

I quickly finished the game, and as I shut down the computer, my next-door neighbor and best friend, Sophie Parker, appeared in the doorway. "Morning, Emma," she said. "Did you win?" She tilted her head toward the computer.

"Morning, and yes, I did," I said, examining her from head to toe. I marveled as always at the fact that she almost never appeared anything other than immaculately turned out. Ruefully, I glanced down at my own ratty old sweatpants and faded Rice T-shirt. My hair was probably sticking up in spikes, not to mention the hated cowlick with which I fought an endless battle.

Sophie's blond head shone, her hair neatly pulled back into a sleek ponytail. Her sweats, made of an iridescent multicolored silk material, probably cost more than the most expensive dress in my closet. Then there were the running shoes—shoes that were never used for running, of course. Sophie was elegantly thin, and though she reputedly spent time on a treadmill every day, I had yet to see this fabled machine.

"What is it, Emma?" Sophie asked, smiling.

I shook my head. "Nothing. I'm wondering, yet again, how you always look like you just stepped out of the Neiman Marcus catalog."

She giggled at that. "You do say the sweetest things. But I guess that's what best friends are for."

I couldn't help smiling back at her. We had been best friends for a long time, ever since she was four and I was twelve. We had grown up next door to each other, and both of us had parents who were flaky in vastly different ways. Sophie and I, and my younger brother, Jake, had looked out for one another, especially since the so-called adults in our lives were too busy with other things to pay much attention to their children.

"Don't you get tired of sitting at that computer?" Sophie asked. "I swear, you're playing bridge on it every time I come over lately."

"It passes the time," I said, "and it does help me with my bridge game."

"You are playing very well these days," Sophie said, "so I suppose the computer does help." Olaf twined himself around her legs, and she reached down and scratched his head. Sophie had two dogs, Boston terriers, and Olaf loved rubbing himself on her legs. No doubt it drove Mavis and Martha crazy when their mommy came home smelling of cat, and that's exactly what Olaf intended, I was sure. On the few occasions when my cats and Sophie's dogs had shared the same space, they had not been happy about it.

"Thank you," I replied. Sophie played very well, too, though I didn't think she worked at it the way I did. Some people are naturally good at many things without a lot of effort, and Sophie was one of those people. If I didn't love her so much, I could have cheerfully killed her on many occasions.

I glanced at my watch. It was a few minutes past eight thirty. "How about some coffee?" I said as I led the way downstairs.

"Sounds good," Sophie replied. "And do you have any of that yummy coffee cake left?" She sighed. "I really shouldn't have any, but it's so wonderful, I simply can't resist."

I laughed as she followed me into the kitchen. "Yes, I do have some left. I keep telling Marylou she doesn't have to bring coffee cake all the time, but she never listens to me."

"Thank goodness," Sophie said as she helped herself to coffee from the pot on the counter. "I like being spoiled."

I retrieved some dessert plates from the cabinet and cut generous slices of coffee cake for each of us. Then I poured myself some coffee and sat down at the table across from Sophie.

"Have you talked to Marylou this morning?" Sophie asked as she pinched a piece of coffee cake and popped it into her mouth.

"No," I said, "but now that her friend is visiting, I'm sure she's busy with her."

Marylou Lockridge, a widow in her midsixties, was my neighbor on the other side. In the past few months, since I had moved into this house, Sophie and I had grown very close to Marylou. We shared coffee every morning, usually in my kitchen since my house was between theirs, and this morning it felt distinctly odd not to have Marylou's motherly presence at the table with us.

"At least we'll see her at lunch today," Sophie said. "I wonder what her friend is like."

Marylou had invited us both to lunch at her house. She wanted us to meet her friend, about whom she had told us next to nothing.

"I'm curious, too," I admitted. "I wonder why Marylou hasn't said much about her."

"Maybe she simply hasn't thought about it, not realizing that we're both dying of curiosity," Sophie said. She ate the last morsel of her coffee cake, then gazed longingly at the remaining piece on the counter.

"Go for it," I said, trying not to laugh. "With your metabolism, you'll burn it off very quickly."

"I suppose," Sophie said, her tone indicating that she actually doubted it. I just rolled my eyes. The girl had the metabolism of a hyperactive chipmunk, and she could eat anything and not gain more than an ounce or two. She got up from her chair and put the last piece of coffee cake on her plate.

I, on the other hand, had only to look at chocolate, and I immediately put on two pounds—despite the fact that I went for an extended walk along the nearby bayou at least five times a week. *Make that four,* I amended silently, remembering that I had decided to skip my walk this morning in favor of computer bridge.

Sophie broke the piece in two and put half of it on my plate. I sighed. At this rate I would never lose the ten pounds I really ought to shed. Marylou's coffee cake, like everything she baked, was heavenly and completely irresistible.

"Did Marylou tell you she had a surprise for us?"

I frowned at Sophie. "No, I don't remember her saying anything about a surprise. Did she tell you what it is?"

Sophie shrugged. "I don't think she actually said 'surprise,' come to think of it." She thought for a moment before continuing. "I think maybe what she really said was she had something she wanted to ask us, and she sounded kind of excited."

"And that's all she said to you?"

"Yeah," Sophie said. She finished her last bite of coffee cake.

"Then I guess we'll just have to wait until lunch to find out," I said. "She said twelve thirty, didn't she?"

Sophie nodded before sipping from her coffee.

"Then I have plenty of time to do some cleaning

before I have to clean myself up," I said. "My hair is really beginning to get out of control. I should make an appointment to have it cut."

Sophie eyed me critically. "Yes, Emma, you could use a good cut. I wish you'd let me make an appointment for you with my hairdresser."

Considering that Sophie usually spent about a hundred and fifty dollars when she had her hair done, I wasn't certain I really wanted an introduction to her stylist. It wasn't the amount, because I could afford it. My late husband, Baxter Diamond, had left me handsomely provided for, but something in me rebelled at spending that much money on my hair.

Easily interpreting my lack of response to her offer, Sophie laughed. "I guess I should know better by now. But one of these days I'm going to kidnap you and take you myself. You ought to let yourself be pampered sometimes, Emma."

"If I want pampering," I said, "I can think of many ways to pamper myself other than by spending too much money on my head."

"Like your expensive wardrobe?" Sophie arched an eyebrow.

"Ha ha," I said. "You might like to wear the gross national product of Uruguay on your back, but I prefer to pamper myself in other ways. Mostly books."

Sophie shook her head. "You and your first editions."

And Baxter's, I added silently. I kept adding to the collection of first-edition mysteries that had been Baxter's pride and joy. For a moment the tears threatened to come, and I turned my head slightly away from Sophie to get myself under control.

"Honey, I'm sorry," Sophie said. "I really am a cat sometimes, and you know I didn't mean anything by what I said."

"I know," I said, reaching across the table to accept the hand she proffered. I returned her quick squeeze of affection, then withdrew my hand and sat back in my chair. "It just hits me sometimes."

"It hasn't even been a year yet," Sophie said, her voice soft. "It takes time."

I nodded. Time—day after day, night after night, without my beloved husband. Most of the time I did okay, but every once in a while the pain hit me so hard that I couldn't do anything except curl up into a tight little ball on the bed and cry myself into exhaustion. Olaf would scrunch up beside me, watching me anxiously, occasionally licking my hand, while Hilda would rub her head against mine. Without them, and without Sophie and my brother and his partner, I think I would have gone completely mad.

"How do you think we should dress for lunch next door?" I said.

Sophie shrugged. "I don't think we need to be too formal. I mean, good gracious, it's just lunch at Marylou's."

"Yes," I said, "but she's inviting us to meet her friend, so I think we should make an effort for her sake."

Sophie leveled one of her looks at me, and I almost turned red. It wasn't Sophie that Marylou would worry about. I held up a hand. "Okay, message received. I know you'll be dressed appropriately. But what should I wear? I'm sure you have a suggestion or two."

Sophie smiled. "One of these days I'm going to take you shopping, honey, and we're going to update that wardrobe of yours. But for today, I think you should wear that lilac sheath with your pearls. It's understated, not too dressy, and it's a lovely color on you."

"Thank you," I said. Most of the time I preferred to run around in casual clothes, but I did like to look nice when the occasion demanded. I simply had never spent as much time on my appearance as Sophie did. But then I wasn't beautiful, like she was. People often mistook her for a model.

"I suppose I should go home and let you get busy with your cleaning," Sophie said. She rose from her chair. "I'll see you at Marylou's." She waved a hand at me as she exited through the back door.

I spent the next two hours cleaning. First I did the bathrooms; then I vacuumed my bedroom and most of the upstairs, and I ended with some dusting. By the time I finished, I was hot, bedraggled, and dusty. A cool shower soon revived me, and I had enough time to dress and do my makeup so that I didn't have to rush.

At twenty-eight minutes past twelve, I walked out my front door, taking care to lock it after reassuring myself that I had put my keys in my purse. Sophie answered the door for Marylou, informing me that our hostess was in the kitchen. "Her friend hasn't come down yet," Sophie said, shutting the door behind me.

I followed her into the living room, and Sophie put out a hand to restrain me when I would have continued toward the kitchen.

"What is it?" I said.

Sophie glanced in the direction of the kitchen, and when she answered me, she had lowered her voice to little more than a whisper. "Marylou told me that her friend can come across as a bit strange, but she wants us to know that she's really a nice person, once you get to know her."

Looking askance at Sophie, I was about to reply when someone spoke from behind us in very angry tones.

"He deserves to die, and if it doesn't happen soon, I may take care of it myself."

About the Author

Honor Hartman is the pseudonym for a mystery author who has lived in Houston, Texas, for more than twenty-five years, has two cats and thousands of books, and plays bridge as often as possible.

Deadly Greetings

A Card-Making Mystery

by Elizabeth Bright

Getting customers into Custom Card Creations is hard enough. Now Jennifer is getting plenty of unwanted visitors—like a ghost in her new apartment, a pushy downstairs neighbor, her ex-fiance, and a drunken deputy. Then one of her most beloved card club members, Maggie, is killed in an accident—or was it? When Jennifer receives a card written by the victim before she died, referring to someone trying to murder her, she must investigate before she loses another good customer to more grim tidings.

"Elizabeth Bright shines in this crafty new series."
—Nancy Martin, author of the
Blackbird Sisters mysteries

0-451-21877-9

**Available wherever books are sold or at
penguin.com**